D1084287

THE EYE

THE MYSTERIOUS PRESS · NEW YORK

EYE

BILL PRONZINI AND
JOHN LUTZ

Design by Holly Johnson at the Angelica Design Group, Ltd.

Jacket illustration copyright © 1983 by David Tamura.

Library of Congress Cataloge Number: 83-63042
    ISBN: 0-89296-075-2

FIRST EDITION

PART 1

**FRIDAY
SEPTEMBER 20**

3 A.M.
MARTIN SIMMONS

At eight o'clock that evening, Simmons didn't know Jennifer Crane existed. Five hours later he was making love to her. It was funny the way things worked out sometimes. He had been to the East Side singles bar, Dino's, half a dozen times without making a score; tonight he'd gone there without much hope—Thursdays were only fair action nights—and nothing much happened in the first hour. He'd had a couple of drinks, he was bored and thinking he might as well go home, and bang, Jennifer walked in and sat down next to him at the bar.

She was young and attractive and she had a good body; he liked what he saw. But it hadn't seemed at first that she was particularly interested in him. She'd let him buy her a brace of vodka gimlets, she'd talked openly enough; still, he had

the impression she was looking for somebody else. Not a Mr.
Goodbar; she wasn't the type. Maybe somebody she knew,
maybe somebody she wanted to know instead of him. So
when he'd suggested that they go to his apartment he had
more or less expected a polite rejection. Only she'd surprised
him by saying, very quiet and matter-of-fact, "Why don't we
go to my place instead? I've got to be up early in the
morning."

Her place turned out to be a brownstone on West Ninety-
eighth between West End Avenue and Riverside Drive.
There was something about the address that struck a chord
in Simmons' memory — something in the papers recently, a
couple of street shootings. But he hadn't paid much attention
to the news stories. New York was full of crime: muggings,
burglaries, stabbings, shootings. Everyday occurances in
every neighborhood. He didn't let himself think about it. It
was an odds game; you could live a lifetime without violence
touching you or anyone you knew. He'd never had any
trouble himself, so what was the sense in worrying? You
could turn yourself into a bundle of neuroses if you fretted
about the goddamn crime rate in Manhattan.

Jennifer's apartment was large, tastefully decorated, with
a lot of framed magazine illustrations on the walls. He
supposed they were Jennifer's work — she'd told him she was
a freelance magazine illustrator — but he hadn't had a chance
to look closely at them. Two minutes after she locked the
door behind them, they were in a clinch and she had her
tongue halfway down his throat. And two minutes after that,
they were naked in her bed, humping like cats in a
barnyard. New York women knew what they wanted, all
right. Which was still a source of wonder to Simmons; that
wasn't the way it was out in Kansas City. He'd been in
Manhattan for almost two years now and still its women
amazed him.

She came at least three times, mewling and scratching,
before he had his own orgasm. Like several of the women

4

he'd known in Manhattan, she cooled off fast as soon as all the passion was spent. No cuddling, no postcoital kissing or caressing. She rolled him off her, pulled up the covers, fluffed her pillow, and reached for the obligatory cigarette from her pack on the nightstand.

"Not bad for the first time," she said in a satisfied way. "Not bad at all."

Simmons didn't say anything. He had a vague feeling of being used, a feeling he'd had before. He'd tried to make himself believe it would be different with Jennifer, that underneath her reserved exterior she was more dependent, more vulnerable than the rest. Not that he was looking for anything permanent; he was only looking to get laid. But still, it would be nice to meet a woman who would take off her mask in bed, show him some human qualities other than lust.

Masks, he thought, that's the thing. Everyone wore them in this insane city, himself included. It was one big masquerade ball — maskers balling each other blindly in the dark.

Jennifer lit her cigarette and then offered him one; he took it. She seemed to want to talk, but not about anything personal or meaningful, not as though she wanted him to know her better, not as though she felt any closeness to him. Just Manhattan bed talk. One stranger making polite conversation with another. Simmons tried to steer her into discussing her magazine illustrating, but even though she complied briefly, it was in glancing generalities that told him nothing about how she felt, who she was beneath the mask.

He did some talking about himself, the presentation he was working on at the agency, his theory that the real creative talent of the culture, with the arts dead or at least pushed to the borders, was in advertising and public relations. Only the same thing happened: It came out in generalities. He couldn't bring himself to lower his mask any more than she had been able to lower hers. Rules of the game. He'd only been playing it two years, but already he'd been playing it too long.

They each smoked another cigarette, lingeringly. Then Jennifer rolled toward him, began to fondle him, and he felt himself responding; that was part of the game, too. So he made love to her again—a more relaxed coupling this time. She only came once that he could tell, shuddering, with her nails biting into his hips, and then she seemed to lose interest. Even though she kept on moving, using her hands and her body to bring him to his own climax, he sensed the detachment in her, the withdrawal into her own private world. He tried to make himself hold back for a while, as a kind of punishment, but she was good, she knew all the little tricks, and she made him come within two minutes. Just like a whore, he thought as he slid away from her. Just like a damned whore.

Another cigarette each. No talk this time, though; they had both run out of things to say. The evening was wearing down. He knew what was going to happen next, and he was almost relieved when she switched on the bedside lamp, glanced at her digital clock-radio, and then gave him the Look. He'd seen the Look before; he knew it and he knew what it meant.

"It's almost three o'clock," she said.

"Getting late."

"Yes. And I have to be up fairly early. It's been nice, Marty...very nice. But I think you'd better go."

"No chance of my spending the night?"

"I'd rather you didn't. Maybe another time."

"Sure," Simmons said. "No problem."

"You can get a cab on West End Avenue."

"Sure," he said again.

He climbed out of bed and began to dress. A certain moody cynicism took hold of him. He was thirty years old, he was getting laid regularly, and yet the swinging singles scene no longer had the appeal that it had five years ago when he was getting nothing much in Kansas City and hoping to make it to New York. Nothing wrong with casual sex, even with a masked stranger; but it was demeaning, somehow, to have the woman you'd just been intimate with throw you out as if you were an electrician or a plumber: service rendered. Women were changing these days, the traditional roles and mores had shifted — he understood that and accepted it. And enjoyed its advantages. Still, it bothered him that Jennifer had been in complete control all along, that he'd penetrated her body without being able to touch her soul.

While he finished dressing she got up and slipped into a nightgown that had been folded on a nearby chair. She did it quickly, so that he only had a glimpse of her breasts, the dark triangle of her pubic hair. He smiled without humor. She wasn't being demure; she was being impersonal. Let him have her body, let him screw her twice, but she didn't want him to see her naked. She would never let any man see her naked, he thought, at least not in the truly intimate sense. No matter who she was with, the mask she wore would always be in place.

He ran a comb through his hair, looking at her. In the lamplight, with her auburn hair tousled and most of her makeup rubbed off, she looked younger than the thirty-one she'd told him she was. She looked about nineteen — and hard, not soft. Cold and finely chiseled, like something fashioned from white marble.

He said, "I'll give you a call tomorrow," just to see how she would respond.

"Tomorrow is now today," she pointed out.

"Okay, I'll give you a call today. Tonight."

"I'm going to be busy tonight."

"So I'll call you tomorrow after all."

"Well. . . if you like."

Which meant she was willing to screw him again. It had been pretty good, she was satisfied, an encore performance

7

was all right with her. Maybe two or three. But then it would be over, and she would throw him out for good. Well, maybe he'd call her and maybe he wouldn't. It all depended on how he felt tomorrow, how horny he was, whether or not he felt like playing stud for her again. It never hurt to keep your options open. He could use her the same way she wanted to use him.

She gave him her phone number and he wrote it down in his address book. Then he went over to kiss her. Her lips were cool and stiff; she gave him nothing, not even a promise. He let his hand wander to the softness of her breast, under the thin nightgown, but she caught his wrist and pulled it away. Her smile was as impersonal as her lips, her eyes.

"We don't want to start again, do we," she said.

"No," Simmons said. "No, we don't."

She ushered him to the front door, let him kiss her again, briefly, and eased him out into the hallway, saying, "It *was* nice, Marty, I'm glad we met. Call me. Good night." Then the door closed between them and he heard the rattling of the chain and the Fox lock as she slid them into place.

He rode the elevator downstairs, went out through the empty lobby to the street, all the while thinking that he'd changed too, accommodated himself to the New York life-style with more ease then he'd ever believed possible. Sometimes, such as right now, he didn't much like the new Marty Simmons; but at the same time, he had never felt more alive. New York did that to you: It created a paradox. The life-style, while frivolous, was also highly charged; the relationships were self-contained and yet they were also intense. That was life in Manhattan in the 1980's—intense but superficial. Glitter, excitement, one big endless masquerade ball.

It was still warm outside, muggy; he could smell the faint, unpleasant odor of the nearby river. The street and sidewalks were deserted. Clouds roiled overhead, hiding the moon, and the night seemed darker than it should have been, even with the streetlamps. Hushed, too. The only sounds were the whispery passage of a car on West End Avenue, the distant tired shouts of some late revelers, the just audible pulse of the city as it drifted toward sleep.

Simmons started toward West End, walking rapidly, his footfalls making hollow clicks in the stillness. This was the one really bad aspect of the singles game, going home on these dark streets in the middle of the night. He wasn't afraid, but he still didn't like being out this late. It unnerved him a little. He hoped he wouldn't have any trouble finding a cab. Just the thought of having to walk all the way to his apartment at Seventy-third and Columbus made him nervous.

The black mouth of an alley loomed ahead. Simmons glanced into it as he passed; there was nothing to see except the vague, huddled shapes of a pair of garbage cans. He shoved his hands into his jacket pockets, started to walk faster.

Something made a scraping sound behind him.

A coldness brushed Simmons' neck; he looked over his shoulder. A man was coming out of the alley, walking toward him. Instinctively, feeling a cut of fear, he veered toward the street. His city reflexes were already well-developed; you *moved* at the unexpected and you moved fast.

But he didn't move fast enough.

The man was only a few steps away, and when Simmons heard him say in a sharp voice, "Stop right there," he looked back again. And that was when he saw the gun outlined in the man's hand.

No, he thought, *Jesus no!* He wanted to run but the gun was pointed at him, he could see the cruel black eye of it glaring in the spill of light from a streetlamp. He froze. The man came toward him purposefully — a big man wearing a dark windbreaker, holding the gun steady in his hand.

Stay calm, Simmons told himself. *People get mugged all the time, it's no big deal, it's just an odds game and this time you lost.* "I don't have much money," he managed as the man reached him. "Just thirty or forty dollars, that's all —"

"I don't want your money, sinner," the man said.

And Simmons understood then. He understood and he couldn't believe it, things like this didn't happen, it couldn't happen to *him,* he had just gotten laid, he was only thirty years old, he had never done anything to anybody, it wasn't fair. "No," he said aloud, "oh God no, no . . ."

They were his last words, his last perceptions.

He never heard the crack of the gun and he never felt the bullet that slashed through his temple and took away his life.

8 A.M. — E.L. OXMAN

As soon as Oxman walked into the Twenty-fourth Precinct he knew there was trouble.

He could see it in the face of Sergeant Drake, behind the high muster desk, and in the faces of the uniformed patrolmen hanging around waiting for their tour to start. It was in the air, too; you got so you could smell it after a while. He went past the desk, past the sign that said *All Visitors Must Stop Here and State Their Business,* past the other sign that said *Detective Division* and had an arrow pointing upstairs, and climbed to the second floor. Nothing much seemed to be going on in the squadroom when he entered; the other detectives, some coming on duty as he was, some going off, were engaged in normal activities, and there were no visitors and nobody in the holding cell. But one look at his partner, Art Tobin, and Lieutenant Smiley Manders conversing at Tobin's desk was all Oxman needed for confirmation. There was trouble, all right. Big trouble.

He hung up his hat and coat, and signed himself in on the roster board. He needed a cup of coffee; Beth hadn't bothered to make any this morning and he hadn't had time to do it himself, but Manders was already gesturing at him.

10

"Over here, Ox." Oxman reluctantly bypassed the table with the coffee on it.

"What's up?"

"Another street killing on West Ninety-eighth early this morning," Manders told him. He was tall and thin, with a long jowly face and a perpetual frown. The detectives under his command called him Lieutenant Smiley, though never to his face. "That makes three in two weeks. It looks like we've got a psycho on our hands."

"Who got it this time?"

"Man named Simmons, Martin Simmons."

"He live on the block like the other two?"

"No. He was an advertising copywriter, lived on West Seventy-third. We don't know yet what he was doing on Ninety-eighth."

"When did it happen?"

"Sometime between two and three A.M.," Manders said. "Richard Corales, the super at twelve-seventy-six, found him at six o'clock, just inside the alley adjacent to his building."

"Any chance it was a straight mugging?"

"None. The victim had thirty-eight bucks in his wallet and a fancy watch on his wrist."

"Who took the squeal?"

"Gaines and Holroyd. They haven't turned up much."

"No witnesses, no leads," Oxman said sourly.

Manders nodded. "Same as in the other two cases. So far, nobody even owns up to hearing the shot."

"Anything from Ballistics yet?"

"Too early. But you can bet the bullet will match the ones used in the previous homicides."

Tobin said, "It's got to be a random thing, Elliot Leroy. A psycho with a gun."

Oxman glanced at his partner. Tobin was twelve years his senior, just turned fifty-four—one of the first blacks taken on the force in the postwar period when there was a halfhearted

11

attempt to include the minorities. He was a complex and private man; Oxman had worked with him eight years now, but he still didn't know him well, still didn't understand what made Artie run. A good cop, though. Efficient, intuitive, disciplined. He also had a dry sense of humor and a penchant for needling people in a mild fashion, as if that was his way of paying back the white majority for past injustices. Like calling Oxman by his given names. He knew Oxman hated the names his parents had saddled him with, that he preferred to be addressed as Ox or E.L. But Tobin never missed an opportunity to call him Elliot Leroy.

"Why would a psycho start killing people on one particular city block?" Oxman asked him.

Tobin shrugged. "Do psychos need reasons?"

"Yes. They don't have to be rational reasons, but a psycho always has some sort of purpose. You know that, Artie."

"Maybe he lives on the block and hates his neighbors."

"Then why kill an outsider like Simmons?"

"Could be Simmons used to live on the block," Tobin said, "or had a connection with one or both previous victims."

"That's an angle you'll want to check out," Manders said. "You're handling the other two shootings, you get this one too. It's your baby; deliver it."

Oxman asked, "Are Gaines and Holroyd still over on Ninety-eighth?"

"Yeah. But they're due back any minute. Wait until they get here so they can brief you; then I want you on the case full time. You know how the damn media is. They'll turn this into a scare circus, sure as hell."

Manders clumped away and disappeared inside his office. When the door closed behind him Tobin said, " 'It's your baby; deliver it.' Smiley's in rare form this morning."

"He's always in rare form."

"So what do you think, Elliot Leroy?"

"I think I'm going to get a cup of coffee," Oxman said.

12

"Then I think we ought to go over what we've got on the previous shootings."

Tobin sighed. "I just love psycho cases."

Oxman poured his coffee, laced it with milk and sugar, and took it to his desk. Tobin came over with the reports they had written on the first two West Ninety-eighth Street homicides. Methodically, while they waited for Gaines and Holroyd, they went over the material that Oxman already knew by heart, looking for some sort of common denominator.

First victim: Charles Unger. Retired grocer, Caucasian, age sixty-five, widower, native of Manhattan, resident of apartment building at 1250 West Ninety-eighth. Found near the mouth of an alley between 1250 and 1252 by a passing patrol car, at eight A.M., September 7. Shot once in the chest at close range with a .32 caliber weapon. No witnesses, nothing in the way of evidence on the scene. Neighbors and relatives of the deceased stated that he was well-liked, had no apparent enemies. Robbery ruled out as a motive; Unger's wallet, containing fourteen dollars and three major credit cards, untouched in his pocket.

Second victim: Peter Cheng. Import-export dealer, Chinese, age forty-three, unmarried, native of Hong Kong (no relatives in New York metropolitan area), resident of apartment building at 1279 West Ninety-eighth. Found in a doorway on Riverside Drive, just around the corner from Ninety-eighth, by the driver of a newspaper delivery truck at six forty-five A.M., September 15. Shot once between the eyes at close range with the same .32 caliber weapon. No witnesses, nothing in the way of evidence on the scene. Friends and business associates of the deceased stated that he was a hard-nosed businessman but had no apparent enemies. Suggestion that Cheng was a homosexual, but no verification. Check into his business dealings negative; his import-export firm was respectable and moderately

13

profitable. No apparent connection with Charles Unger, no indication that the two men even knew each other.

Zero. No common denominator except for the fact that the two victims lived on the same block of West Ninety-eighth Street.

And now, with victim number three, that commonality no longer existed: Simmons hadn't lived on West Ninety-eighth or anywhere else in the neighborhood. The only evident factor linking the three homicides was that the victims had all died on that same city block.

Tobin said the same thing Oxman was thinking: "There's just nothing here, Elliot Leroy. A retired grocer, a Chinese import-export dealer. Throw in Simmons and it makes even less sense."

"Unless Gaines and Holroyd have turned up a connection. Or we do."

"Want to bet that won't happen?"

"No. But there's got to be some reason for the killings, some reason why even a madman would start blowing people away on one particular block."

"Yeah," Tobin agreed dryly.

"We'll find it. And we'd better do it fast, because if it is a psycho he'll go after number four sooner or later."

"Motive isn't the only thing we'd better find fast."

"You mean the psycho himself?"

"I mean," Tobin said, "it's our baby. We'd better find a way to deliver it."

THE COLLIER TAPES

He didn't live on the block.

Martin Simmons did not live on the block!

I should have been more careful. But what was Simmons doing there? He should not have been there at that time of night. Closed community, very stable for the West Side, not many late visitors. How was I to know when I saw him come out of the building that he was a stranger, an interloper? Martin Simmons, 112 West Seventy-third Street, advertising copywriter—it was all there on the radio this morning. How was I to know? But I should have been more careful. Jennifer Crane, the harlot who lives in 1276, has brought home men before; she picks them up in singles bars and brings them to her apartment. The Eye has seen her stepping out of taxis with half a dozen different men. Martin Simmons was probably one of her conquests. Of course: That explains what he was doing on the block at three A.M.

Poor Martin. My apologies and regrets, and I promise for your sake that I will not make the same mistake again with someone else. I will be much more circumspect, I will not make any more random choices. If I began to act indiscriminately, if I do not limit myself to residents of my little universe, if I bring down my wrath upon visitors, guests, passersby, then I will have fallen from grace and descended to the level of psychopathology. That must not happen.

Lewis B. Collier, former adjunct Associate Professor of English, Keeper of the Eye, Lord and Conscience of West Ninety-eighth Street, is not a psychopath.

I am *not* a psychopath.

I am a deeply and righteously angered Avenger; I am the Angel of Death. Be sure your sin will find you out. And the wages of sin is death. Order, structure, motive, discipline. I will be justified unto the grave and vindicated in the Hereafter.

A half hour has passed since I began dictating this entry. I spent those thirty minutes on the balcony with the Eye.

God's Eye.

Have I discussed the Eye in any detail? No, I don't believe I have. It is a powerful six-inch reflecting telescope, a much-refined version of the type first constructed by Sir Isaac Newton in 1668. It weighs approximately fifty pounds. It has several eyepieces, including a high-magnification six millimeter piece which I had specially ground some months ago by an expert who works for the local astronomy clubs. The polished concave mirror at the Eye's base, which gathers light and forms the image, has also been specially ground.

I purchased the Eye a year ago, when I imagined myself interested in astronomy. Contemplation of the heavens, however, did not amuse me as much as I had anticipated. It was only when I realized that it could be used to observe *people,* stars in a different and far more flawed firmament, that I began to appreciate its true worth. Now it has become the Eye of God, through which I can follow the petty, sometimes sinful lives of the inhabitants of the West Ninety-eighth Street block, two miles away across the Hudson River.

Think of it! Here I am, in my twentieth floor apartment in the Crestview Towers, in Cliffside Park on the New Jersey palisades, and yet with a twist of the Eye's delicate rack-and-pinion controls I can bring those inhabitants of Manhattan into such sharp focus that I am able to see the color of their eyes, the smallest blemishes on their skin. I can assume their lives more intimately than they: walk with them, live with them, observe and weigh their value and their sins. They are of my universe, and I, high above them, am both their conscience and their avenging deity. As they sow, so shall they reap. The judgment is the Eye's, not mine.

I am an avenging deity, yes, but I am not without compassion. It grieves me to have had to mete out punishment to Charles Unger and Peter Cheng. That I was the angel of their deaths only deepens my sadness, makes more wrenching my sense of loss. They are my children. I do not enjoy plucking the life from their bodies; I wish it could be otherwise. I mourn for their sins. But vengeance is mine, sayeth the deity. The judgment is the Eye's, but the vengeance is mine.

16

T.S. Eliot was quite right: The spirit killeth. But the letter giveth life.

This is why I am so upset over Martin Simmons. He did not live in my universe, I had no right to exact punishment on him for his sins. I *must* be more careful. I am not a psychopath, I am just a deity. Only mine must reap what they have sown.

And there will be others who must pay the wages of sin. Sin is rife in my little universe. It must be expunged, the wicked must be destroyed.

I shall return to the Eye now. It is the noon hour and many of the children are out: the dog-walkers, the grocery shoppers, the artists and writers and musicians coming out for their first breath of the hot late-summer air. The police are there too, have been since poor Simmons was found, and I find their antics amusing. They do not know that the Eye is upon them. They do not know that the Angel of Death observes their every movement. No one on the block will ever know.

The Eye and I will soon decide which of the sinners will be punished next. Perhaps the evil one from 1272. But there are several evil ones in 1276; perhaps one of them instead. Or perhaps another on the block. The Eye will judge. And the risk does not matter; there are too many and they must all be destroyed before they contaminate the rest.

God's Eye remains open. And my vengeance shall be swift and merciless.

12:30 P.M. — WALLY SINGER

Singer said, "You're a stupid woman, the stupidest woman I've ever known. I don't know why the hell I ever married you."

"Don't you?" Marian asked. She was in one of her calm periods — reasonable, icy-voiced, talking to him as if he were a child. He hated her when she was like this; he preferred

17

her angry and yelling, or better yet, off sulking somewhere. "It was because of the ten thousand dollars my father gave me to pursue an art career, remember?"

"Bullshit."

"I don't think so. You married me for my money."

"That goddamn ten thousand was gone years ago."

"Yes," Marian said. "Because *you* went through most of it. All those painting lessons — what a waste."

"Are you going to start that again?"

"Why shouldn't I? It's the truth. You have no talent, Wally, none at all. You simply won't admit it to yourself. How many paintings have you sold in fifteen years? Exactly three, for a grand total of seven hundred dollars."

"I've had bad luck — "

"You've had good luck. Somebody as talentless as you should never have sold *any* paintings."

"You think you've got talent? Those sculptures of yours are crap. Who buys them except cheap specialty stores? There's not a gallery in the city that would touch them."

"You're forgetting the Morton Gallery, aren't you?"

"That was six years ago. And a fluke, just a fluke."

"A five thousand dollar fluke."

Singer didn't like to be reminded of her one big score; it set his teeth on edge every time she brought it up. "So some stupid Texas oilman who wouldn't know art from a cow turd walks in and sees a piece of crap and plunks down five grand for it. So what?"

"*Windblown* was not a piece of crap."

"*Windblown.* Jesus Christ, what a name for that graceless monstrosity."

"You're jealous, that's all."

"Jealous? Of what? How many other pieces of crap did you sell at that showing? How many pieces of crap have you sold since for more than nickels and dimes?"

"Those nickels and dimes have kept us eating," Marian said. "They've paid the rent, they've given us a home — "

"You call this a home? Look at this place, it's a fucking pigsty." He waved a hand at the cluttered apartment: tools, hunks of metal, pieces of glass, blocks of plastic and wood, dozens of small abstracts that she'd started and then abandoned. At least he kept his corner of it, under the skylight, halfway swept and tidy. "Why don't you clean up after yourself once in a while?"

"Why don't you do it, if it bothers you so much? Better yet, why don't you go out and get a job?"

"Here it comes," Singer said. "The same old tune."

"You haven't contributed one cent to this household in years. All you do is sit around and swill beer and ruin perfectly good canvases. I don't know why I put up with you."

"So don't put up with me. Throw me out; the lease on this pigsty is in your name."

"You'd starve."

"Maybe I would and maybe I wouldn't. There are places I could go."

"Oh, no doubt. Right across the street, for instance?"

"What the hell is that supposed to mean?"

"You know what it means, Wally dear."

He wanted to hit her. His hand actually twitched. The urge came on him more and more often lately, but he had never quite worked up enough courage to do it. One of these days, he would. They'd have this argument again, the same damned argument over and over, and she would provoke him once too often and he would slap her chubby face until it glowed. She damned sure deserved it.

A small wiry man with a spade beard and graying black hair that he still wore long and tied into a ponytail, he stalked away from her, over to one of the windows in the west wall. The view from the window was pretty good: Riverside Park, the West Side Highway, the wide expanse of the river, the apartment buildings on the Jersey shore. Sometimes, when the sun hit them right, all the windows in those high rises looked as though they were on fire. He'd tried to paint that scene once, to capture the burning aspect in oils, but it hadn't come out right. Like most of his paintings, he thought bitterly. Something always failed between the eye and the hand, and they just wouldn't come out the way he envisioned them.

Nice view, nice roomy apartment on the top floor, complete with skylight. They couldn't have afforded to live here if the building wasn't rent-controlled. If he did leave Marian, where would he go that was half as comfortable, half as conducive to artistic expression? Not across the street, that was for sure; not with Cindy's ex-husband always hanging around. *Face it, Singer,* he told himself, not for the first time, *you're not going anywhere. Like it or not, you're stuck here with Marian.*

After a time he turned from the window. Marian had put on a lightweight summer jacket and was brushing her dishwater-blond hair. A jacket in this weather! It was stifling in here even with the air conditioner on. The jacket was belted and she looked fat and dumpy in it. She'd put on at least twenty pounds since their marriage, and if she put on any more he wouldn't be able to get near her in bed. The doughy feel of her body was enough of a turn off as it was.

He said, "Where do you think you're going?"

"Out shopping. You won't do it; somebody has to."

"Go ahead, then. Stay out all day for all I care."

"You'd like that, wouldn't you?"

"Ah, the hell with it. Bring back some beer; we're almost out."

"Buy your own beer. I'm not your slave."

She picked up her purse, went out without looking at him. He crossed over and locked the door after her, and then stood there for a minute or so, to make sure Marian hadn't forgotten something and would come back. Then he moved back to where the telephone was.

Cindy answered on the second ring. "I've been waiting

and waiting for you to call," she said. "I've been half-frantic all morning."

"Why? What's the matter?"

"Wally, don't you *know?* There was another street shooting last night. Right outside your building."

Singer felt a ripple of coldness on his back. "Jesus. Who was it this time?"

"I don't know. A stranger, somebody named Simmons. Didn't you hear all the commotion this morning?"

"No," he said. The apartment was in the rear of the building, away from Ninety-eighth, and both he and Marian were heavy sleepers. He had a vague memory of sirens, but he never paid any attention to sirens. Not in Manhattan. Nobody had called, either; they didn't have any friends in the building or on the block. "Have the police found out anything?"

"I don't know that either. Wally, I'm frightened. That's three murders in two weeks, all right here on this block."

"Just take it easy," he said, as much to himself as to Cindy.

"It must be a maniac. What if he lives here? What if he lives in my building? Or yours?"

"Calm down, will you? You're making it worse than it is."

"Can you come over? God, I need to see you. I don't like being here alone."

"All right. But I can't stay long."

"Hurry, Wally. Please hurry."

Singer put down the receiver. Another shooting. Three in two weeks. Maybe there *was* a maniac in the neighborhood; who else would go around killing people at random on this particular block? Jesus!

He hurried across to the door. The hell with Marian; if she came back and he wasn't here, let her think what she wanted. She seemed to know about Cindy anyway, or at least suspected, and it couldn't matter much or she would have sent him packing already. Stupid woman. Goddamn cow. He unlocked the door, pulled it open.

A man was standing there, tall and lean, with sandy hair and a sandy mustache, wearing a jacket and a tie in spite of the weather. Singer jumped when he saw him, startled; then he recognized the man. A small uneasy knot formed in his stomach.

"I'm sure you remember me, Mr. Singer," the sandy guy said. "Detective Oxman, Twenty-fourth Precinct. I'd like to talk to you again, if you don't mind."

1:15 P.M. — MARCO POLLO

With his horn case tucked under one arm, Marco walked into the Green Light Tavern at 109th and Broadway and scanned the place. A few noon-hour drinkers and a couple of kids from Columbia University scattered along the bar. Big Ollie behind the plank, slicing lemons and limes into wedges. And Freddie in his favorite booth, in back near the juke box.

Marco licked his lips, feeling relieved. He hadn't been sure Freddie would show. Things were tight on the street these days, lots of heat, big cleanup campaign going on.

He went up to the bar, got a draft from Big Ollie, and took it to Freddie's booth. Freddie was playing solitaire, cheating like always. He had a new set of threads: fancy black coat, ruffled shirt, designer slacks, a big gold chain around his neck. The crunch wasn't hurting him much. He was a cat, Freddie was; he landed on his feet no matter what.

"What's happening, baby?" Freddie said as Marco slid in across from him, laid his black horn case down on the table. "You look a little wired."

"Yeah, well, another dude got wasted on my block last night. Number three. Looks like a psycho, man, and that spooks me."

"Bad news," Freddie said. "It's a twitch bin out there, you know what I mean? More crazies on the loose every day."

"Yeah."

"But you can't let it get to you. Make *yourself* crazy if you do, you know what I mean?"

"Yeah."

"So how was it over in Brooklyn?"

"Not bad. Last night was the wrap-up. Tomorrow we play Jazz Heaven, down in the Village. Two-week gig."

"Nice. You oughta be rolling in it these days."

"Doing okay," Marco said. He took a sip from his draft, then leaned forward and lowered his voice. "You bring the shit?"

"You bring the dead presidents?"

"Hey, man, you know I always pay."

"Sure you do," Freddie said. "That's why I like you. I'm going to the john, take a leak. You know what I mean?"

Freddie slid out of the booth and ambled through the door into the men's can. Marco lit a Salem, wishing it was a joint instead; he felt spooked, all right. Up half the night, blowing over in Brooklyn, come home, cops all over the street, guy lying there dead on the sidewalk with a blanket over him. Christ, who wouldn't be spooked? Freddie was right about it being a twitch bin out there. As soon as he could afford it, he'd get the hell out of the city, find a pad on Long Island or over in Jersey. Or maybe head south for New Orleans, if he could talk Leon and the other guys into a change of scenery.

He jabbed out his cigarette after two drags, eased a look around the room. Nobody was paying any attention to him. He picked up his horn case, walked across to the can and went inside. Freddie was in one of the stalls, with the stuff arranged on the greasy top of the toilet tank. Marco locked the door, moved over to lean against the edge of the stall.

"Half-ounce of coke, one kilo of Mexican grass," Freddie said. "Good shit, you won't be disappointed."

"Looks sweet, man."

"Like candy. You want a taste?"

"No. Bad vibes in here. I'll wait until I get home."

Marco had the cash in the pocket of his Levi's; he slid it out, slipped off his gold money clip, and handed over the bills. Freddie thumbed through them, quick and easy, like a teller in a bank. Then he nodded and grinned.

"Twelve hundred," he said. "Right. It's all yours, baby."

Marco opened his horn case. The case was empty; he'd left the trumpet back in his pad on West Ninety-eighth. He put the bags of coke and grass into the velvet-lined depression inside, closed the case and flipped the catches. Nothing like a horn case for carrying shit on the streets. Leon had taught him that, among other things.

"You go out first," Freddie said. "I want to comb my hair."

"Sure. Thanks, Freddie."

"Any time. Listen, maybe I'll drop down to Jazz Heaven tomorrow night, catch your gig."

"Do that, man. We're blowing sweet and pretty these days."

"Nothing like those high notes to mellow you out," Freddie said. "You know what I mean?"

There were only five drinkers left in the bar when Marco came out of the can. Big Ollie gave him a two-fingered salute as he made for the door; none of the other dudes looked at him. Clean buy. All right.

Marco went down Broadway to West End Avenue, down West End to Ninety-eighth. He started walking faster. Sunshine, good air, plenty of people around, but he still felt spooked. He needed a snort of coke to lift him up, set him free of the jangles.

Nothing much was happening on the block. Couple of old ladies sitting on the stoop of the corner brownstone, chattering about the murder last night; no sign of the pigs. Marco cut across the street, went into 1276, took the elevator up to the second floor.

When he stepped out, a middle-aged black dude was coming down the hallway. Marco didn't know him; no black dudes in the building. Cop? Visitor? Or—Christ—a crazy with a piece in his pocket? For all he knew, it was a black cat from Harlem who was wasting people on the block.

Marco eased on past the guy, stopped in front of his door. The black dude stopped too, and was looking at him. Marco dragged out his keys, sweating a little now. Just as he shoved the right key into the lock, the guy came toward him.

"Marco Pollosetti?"

"Yeah?" He had a tight grip on the horn case; if the guy tried anything, he'd get the case shoved down his frigging throat.

"Detective Tobin, Twenty-fourth Precinct," the dude said, and hauled out his shield to prove it.

Marco didn't know whether to feel relieved or even more spooked. Here he was with twelve hundred bucks worth of coke and grass in his hand, eyeball to eyeball with a cop. That much shit meant a possession charge; they could even nail him for dealing if they felt like it.

He licked his lips, tried to make himself look friendly and cooperative. "What can I do for you, officer?"

"Like to ask you a few questions about the homicide last night."

"The shooting, yeah. Hell of a thing. But I don't know nothin' about it; I was over in Brooklyn when the guy got blown away, didn't get home until about three."

"You didn't notice anything on the street when you came in?"

"Not a thing. But I wasn't looking."

The pig had hard eyes; he kept looking at Marco as if trying to see inside his skull. "Mind if we talk inside?"

Marco tried to remember if there was anything in the pad he didn't want the pig to see. No, it was cool; the only shit he had was in the horn case. And the pig wasn't a narc. "Sure," he said, "no problem. Only like I said, I don't know nothing about what happened."

He keyed open the door, led the way inside. The pig took in the black-painted walls, the blow-up covers of the two

25

albums the combo had cut, the rock and jazz posters, the funky lamps and decorations, the rabbit-fur coverings on the furniture. His mouth twitched into a half-smile that didn't reach his eyes.

"Nice place," he said, but he didn't mean it. It was wise-ass cop sarcasm. "You a musician, Mr. Pollosetti?"

"Yeah. Leon Davis combo, maybe you heard of us."

"I'm afraid not. Jazz doesn't do much for me."

"Soul music's your bag, right?"

"Classical music," the pig said in his wise-ass way. "Brahms, Mozart, Khachaturian."

"Good people," Marco said, thinking: Fuck you, man.

The pig nodded at his horn case, which suddenly seemed ten pounds heavier. "Trumpet?"

"Right, trumpet." The jangles were like cymbals clanging away inside Marco. What if the pig wanted him to open the case so he could take a look at the horn? "That's what I blow. That's what I was doing over in Brooklyn last night—blowing with the combo."

"You have a gig this morning too?"

"No. Not until tomorrow night. Why?"

"You came in with the horn. Or do you always carry it around with you?"

"Oh. No, I needed a new mouthpiece; I took it over to a place on Fifth to have it fitted."

The pig kept on looking at him. Then he said, "Suppose we sit down and talk."

"About the shootings, you mean?"

"That's what I'm here for."

Marco felt a relieved giggle slide up into his throat; stifled it. It was going to be okay. The pig hadn't tumbled, hadn't made a connection. Close call. He'd been sweating bricks there for a minute.

"Sure," he said. "Sure thing."

He went over to the bar cabinet and laid the horn case down on its top. When he came back the pig was sitting on one of the chairs, legs crossed, notebook open on his knee. Marco sat down facing him. The jangles were gone now; he felt a little high with the release of tension, as if he'd taken a few tokes off a good joint. It was a kind of kick sitting here talking to a cop with all that shit safe and sound a few feet away. A sweet little joke. Leon would bust a gut when he told him; Leon had a terrific sense of humor.

"Ask away," Marco said to the pig, chuckling inside, thinking of Leon's reaction. "Anything you want to know."

1:45 P.M. — MICHELE BUTLER

As always on Friday afternoons, Bloomingdale's was jammed with shoppers. In most sections of the store, harried salespeople were faced with long lines and short tempers; they were too busy to pay much attention to individuals who seemed more interested in browsing than buying.

Michele had been standing at the Fine Watches and Jewelry counter for the past five minutes, pretending to be just another browser. She felt very nervous, much more nervous than she had at the audition this morning. She had given a good reading — the play was an off-Broadway revival of Elmer Rice's *Street Scene* and she'd read for the role of Anna Maurrant — but she hadn't got the part. It should have gone to her, she had delivered her lines more professionally than the woman the director finally picked; she had broken down and cried in the dressing room afterward. No part. No other prospects, either. And that was why she had come here to Bloomingdale's.

The heavyset woman on her left kept studying a velvet-lined tray full of twenty-four-carat gold rings, all of them with expensive jeweled settings. The saleswoman behind the counter was trying not to look impatient; her attention was on the heavyset woman. Michele feigned interest in a modest cameo locket, but what she was really looking at was the pigeon's-blood ruby ring in the nearest corner of the tray.

27

The ruby had been cut cabochon—in convex form and not
faceted—and in its deep purplish-red depths she could see a
six-rayed star. It was a valuable stone. It made her palms
moist just to look at it.

Other customers milled about in the area, some of them
beginning to besiege the saleswoman with demands for
attention. Finally, in self-defense, the saleswoman let some
of her impatience show through.

"Madam," she said, "will you please make up your mind?
I have other people waiting."

"That is precisely what I'm trying to do," the heavyset
woman said in a snappish voice. "I am not an impulse
buyer."

"That's for sure," an irritable-looking man on her left said.
"You're a selfish buyer, lady. A counter hog."

The woman glared at him. "Why don't you mind your
own business?"

"Why don't you go fall down the elevator shaft?"

An indignant squawking sound came out of the woman;
she turned her glare on the saleswoman. "I won't stand for
this!" she said. "He has no right to talk to me that way!"

"I'm sorry, madam—"

"Well, you ought to be!"

"Oh, lady, shut up," the irritable-looking man said.

"How dare you!"

None of them was looking at Michele or at the tray. And
none of them saw her pluck the ring out, palm it, turn from
the counter, and drop the ring into her purse as she started
away.

Without looking back, she hurried through the crowded
aisles toward the Lexington Avenue exit. Her heart
stammered; there was a fluttery feeling in her legs, as if they
might give out at any second. But no one tried to stop her.
After what seemed like an hour her legs carried her out
through the doors, into the stream of pedestrian traffic on the
sidewalk.

At Forty-ninth Street she stopped and leaned against the wall of a building to catch her breath and collect herself. She could almost feel the presence of the ring in her purse, as though it were generating palpable heat. Hot ring. Stolen ring—

Thief.

The word echoed in her mind: an accusation, a brand. But it was not new to her. She had called herself that and worse the first time she'd been forced to shoplift a piece of expensive jewelry, each of the other two times as well. She accepted it now. She was a thief.

But it wasn't her fault; she was not immoral, she was not compulsive, she only did it as a means of survival. She had been *driven* to theft—by life in the city, by a hundred broken promises, by insensitive producers and nasty-minded directors who cared more about raw sex than raw talent; by her unfulfilled dreams.

I'm not guilty, she thought. *I'm a thief but I'm not guilty.*

The pace of her heart gradually slowed; she no longer felt quite so nervous or shaky. It was over. And perhaps she wouldn't have to do it again, perhaps this was the last time. Perhaps at the next audition she would be given a part she deserved. She didn't believe it, and yet it was a small hope to cling to, because hope, like dreams, dies hard.

She walked to Forty-second, turned west and made her way crosstown past the porno movie theaters and the lurid sex shops and the cruising prostitutes of both sexes, until she came to Eighth Avenue. There were several pawnshops in the area; she was careful not to pick one she had gone to before. She settled on a place near Forty-first, steeled herself and went inside.

A fat man with funny eyes was peering into a glass case full of knives while the proprietor looked on. Michele pretended to examine a shelf lined with small appliances until the fat man made a purchase and hurried out. Then she crossed over to where the proprietor stood.

He was a middle-aged man, gray-haired, bored-looking; but he had shrewd moneylender's eyes. He said, "Yes, miss?"

"I'd like to pawn a ring."

"Yes?"

She took the ruby ring out of her purse, laid it on the counter cushion in front of him. "My boyfriend gave me this two months ago," she said, "before we broke up. It's very expensive and I haven't worn it much. I just don't want to keep it any longer; it reminds me of David. And I'm afraid I need the money."

The pawnbroker picked up the ring, fitted a jeweler's loupe to one eye, and studied the ruby. "Nice stone," he said in a noncommittal way.

"Yes, it is."

"I can let you have, oh, three hundred for it."

"Three hundred? But it must be worth five times that!"

"Not to me. Why don't you try to sell it?"

"I don't have time. I really do need money; I have to pay my rent . . ."

He was appraising her, now, with shrewd eyes. *He knows,* she thought. *He's seen thieves before, he's probably seen a hundred or a thousand in here. He's a thief himself. We're all thieves.*

"Three hundred," the pawnbroker said again.

"Can't you let me have at least five hundred?"

"Not much turnover on an item like this. But you seem like a nice lady. Tell you what I'll do: three twenty-five, just for you."

"But I need more than that —"

"You could try one of the other shops," he said. "You won't find a better deal, though. Not for a ring like this."

His meaning was clear: Take it somewhere else and she would run the risk of another pawnbroker realizing it was stolen and calling the police. "All right," she said bitterly. "Three twenty-five."

"Done."

He came up with a soiled register book for her to sign. She

made up a name and address—Kathryn Newcombe, 411 Houston Street—and he nodded and gave her a pawn ticket. Then he opened his safe, carefully counted out three hundred and twenty-five dollars. When he handed the money to her he smiled, and one of his eyelids twitched in what might have been a wink.

"Come back any time," he said.

Outside, away from him, Michele started back toward Forty-second Street. Three hundred and twenty-five dollars. Coupled with what she had left at her apartment, it was enough to pay next month's rent and the grocery and utility bills. Which meant that unless a job turned up on or off Broadway, she would have to visit Saks or Bergdorf's or one of the other big department stores in four weeks. It had been three *months* since the time before today, five months before that; but then she had been getting a part here, a part there, all turkeys that folded after a few performances. She hadn't had a part in almost three months now. Nothing but an endless series of headshakes, propositions, sorrys.

Well, at least she hadn't succumbed to any of the propositions. Nor would she. She was not promiscuous; she believed sex was an act of love and she had been taught not to cheapen it. She may have become a thief, but at least she had that much of her dignity to hang onto.

Where to now? she asked herself. She didn't want to take the subway home to West Ninety-eighth; the apartment was cheerless and barren and she spent enough time in it as it was, waiting for the phone to ring. And there was that shooting last night, the third one now, all right there on her block. She was strong, you had to be strong to survive in Manhattan, in the theater, and she didn't frighten easily. But those shootings frightened her. There was something inexpressibly evil in an act of senseless violence. And when it happened, kept on happening, where you lived, you could almost feel the evil like something cold and poisonous in the air.

There was only one thing to do, she decided, only one place for her to go, the place she always went when she was alone and unhappy, the place of escape, the place of dreams. She walked up to Broadway and entered one of the movie houses to watch the images of people whose dreams had come true.

3:25 P.M. — RICHARD CORALES

Across the table in his basement apartment, Corales watched Willie Lorsec study the fan of cards in his hand. *A queen,* he thought. *Come on, Willie, I need a queen. Discard a queen, Willie. A nice smiling queen of hearts.*

They had been playing for twenty minutes now, ever since Willie stopped by with his junk bag to see if any new throwaways had turned up, and Corales had won nine straight hands. He had never in his life won nine straight hands; it made him feel warm inside, powerful, like one of those Las Vegas gamblers. He wanted it to be ten straight. Nine straight was good but ten straight was something special, ten straight was a major-league winning streak. He'd really have something to brag about if only Willie would discard a pretty little queen of hearts.

Come on, Willie, he thought. *Queen me!*

But Willie was still studying his hand. His big, lined face was scrunched up in concentration—not on the cards, though, Corales could sense that. Willie had something else on his mind today. Usually he played fast and easy; usually he won, too. Which was another reason why Corales wanted to win ten straight from him. They only played for pennies and he'd never lost more than a quarter at a sitting, but he was tired of losing. He wanted to come away the big winner for a change. He wanted to show Willie that he could be smart too, at least when it came to playing gin rummy.

Corales didn't understand why somebody as smart as Willie would become a junk collector and dealer and live in a rooming house and play gin rummy all the time with somebody like himself. Willie could have been anything in the world, lived over in one of those fancy buildings on the East Side with a doorman and everything, traveled in Europe and places like that. But no. He was happy being a junkman, he'd told Corales just after he moved into the neighborhood. He made pretty good money at it; all sorts of fascinating and salable things turned up in junk piles and trash cans, he said. Besides, he'd traveled before and didn't like it much. Worked at a variety of jobs and didn't like those much either. He was doing what he liked to do and it made him happy. That was what counted, wasn't it?

Corales supposed it was. But he still didn't understand it. *He* wasn't happy; he'd have given anything to be something other than a building superintendent on West Ninety-eighth Street. Something special. Only he wasn't special. And he wasn't very smart; that was what people said and he believed them. He wasn't much of anything except a thirty-seven-year-old, half-Puerto Rican building super. Not that he minded being half Puerto Rican. He was proud of that, proud of his father for having come over from the Island in the forties and worked his way into a good job in the construction business, proud of his mother for having put up with all the racial crap heaped on her for marrying a Puerto Rican. No, that wasn't why he was unhappy. He was unhappy because he wasn't anything special like his father and mother.

But he wasn't unhappy right now. Right now he *was* something special because he'd won those nine straight hands, and maybe it would be ten straight if only Willie would discard a sweet red queen.

Queen, Willie, he thought. Couldn't wishing hard enough sometimes make things happen? *Queen, queen, queen!*

And Willie took a card out of his hand and laid it down on the pile, and it was the queen of hearts.

Corales let out a delighted whoop, snatched up the queen,

put it with the other three queens in his hand, discarded, and laid the fan down on the table triumphantly. "Gin!" he said. "That's ten straight, Willie! I won ten straight hands!"

Willie smiled at him. "Good for you. Dame Fortune is in your corner today."

"Ten straight," Corales repeated. "Wow!"

"Quite a winning streak, Richard."

"Yeah. Now I'm going for eleven."

"My deal, isn't it?"

"Your deal, Willie."

Willie shuffled the cards, dealt out a new hand. When Corales picked up his cards he saw happily that he already had three treys, two tens, and a possible four-card diamond run. All he needed was another ten and the six of diamonds — just two cards. Two cards and he'd have won *eleven* straight, by God.

The face-up card was a king. No help. Willie didn't want it either, so Corales drew the top card from the face-down pile. Jack of clubs. No help. He discarded it.

Willie was studying his hand again. He said, "Have the police been to see you again, Richard?"

"What?"

"The police. About the murder last night."

"Yeah, they were here. Three times now."

"Why three times?"

"I don't know. Who knows with cops?"

"You don't like the police much, do you."

"No. They used to hassle us when I was a kid."

"Why?"

"Mixed family, I guess. Anything went wrong in my neighborhood, they always came around to out house first. Damn cops."

Willie discarded a deuce. No help. Corales drew a card, and it was the ten of spades. The excitement in him grew; now he needed only one card for eleven straight. The six of diamonds. Just the six of diamonds.

"Who do you think is responsible?" Willie asked.

"Responsible for what?"

"The shootings."

"I don't want to talk about that," Corales said.

"Why not? Everyone is talking about it."

"I know. That's why I don't want to. Too much talk."

"Aren't you frightened, Richard?"

"Why should I be? Nobody'd want to shoot me."

"The police seem to think the victims are picked at random," Willie said. "That means it could happen to anyone. You, me — anyone."

"I don't want to talk about it," Corales said.

"Perhaps you're right. There's no sense in worrying, is there? Life goes on. We just have to be careful on the street."

"Yeah."

Corales watched Willie draw a card. *Six of diamonds,* he thought. *Come on, Willie, give me the six of diamonds.*

Willie discarded a nine. Corales drew a seven of clubs. No help. He discarded it. *Six of diamonds, Willie,* he thought. *Just give me a pretty little six of diamonds.*

Draw. Discard: king. No help. Corales drew a five of hearts, threw it down.

Six of diamonds, Willie, six of diamonds!

Willie picked up the king. And discarded the six of diamonds.

Corales let out another whoop, grabbed the six, and shouted, "Gin! Eleven straight!"

"Very good," Willie said. "You *are* lucky today." He paused, and a thoughtful look came into his eyes. "Much luckier than poor Martin Simmons."

"Who?"

"The man who was shot last night."

"I don't care about him," Corales said. "I told you, I don't want to talk about that. I'm going for *twelve* straight now."

"All right." Willie sighed, leaned back in his chair. "It's your deal, I believe."

"Eleven straight," Corales said as he picked up the cards and began to shuffle them. He couldn't keep from grinning. "Wow!"

He really was something special today. He really and truly was.

4:10 P.M. — JENNIFER CRANE

She had just returned home and was about to mix a much needed vodka gimlet for herself, when the doorbell rang. The peephole in the door showed her a rather attractive, fortyish man with sandy hair and mustache, dressed in a rumpled suit; she knew instantly that he must be another policeman. Two detectives had already talked to her that morning, before she left for the *Vogue* offices, because they had found her name and number in Marty Simmons' address book. But she'd expected another visit sooner or later. Whatever else you could say about the police, they were thorough.

"Detective Oxman, Twenty-fourth Precinct," he told her when she opened the door on its chain. He held up his badge in its leather case. "I'd like to ask you a few questions, Miss Crane."

She took the chain off and pulled the door open. "Come in, please."

He entered and stood looking at her as she reset the locks. There was something more than the usual frank but impersonal policeman's appraisal in his eyes, she thought as she faced him. Approval, attraction, veiled desire. She had seen that look in the eyes of hundreds of men. It had been in the eyes of Marty Simmons last night at Dino's.

But she refused to think about Marty Simmons. She had spent the entire day not thinking about him, and she wasn't going to start again now. She would answer Detective Oxman's questions, willingly, but she didn't have to think about Marty to do that. She wasn't going to go through what she had this morning, when the other detectives had caught her unprepared: the momentary loss of control, the stirrings of guilt.

No. She was in command of herself again; she intended to stay that way. Detective Oxman was just another man, and she knew how to deal with men — especially men who found her attractive.

"You're staring," she said.

He blinked. "Was I? I'm sorry."

"Don't be. Would you like a drink? Scotch, bourbon, whatever?"

"Thanks, no."

"I was about to make myself something. Do you mind?"

"Not at all."

She smiled. "Sit down, if you like."

He sat on the cream-colored sofa. Jennifer went into the kitchen, got ice cubes out of the fridge, carried them back into the living room, and mixed a gimlet. She took it to the small beige chair opposite Oxman, sat down, crossed her legs. They were good legs, and she was wearing a light summer dress; his gaze strayed to them, then lifted abruptly, a little self-consciously, to her face.

"I stopped by a couple of times earlier," he said. "You've been out all day."

"Yes. I had meetings with the art director and some other people at *Vogue* magazine. I'm a freelance illustrator."

He nodded, glancing over at the chrome-framed illustrations hanging on one wall. "Your work?"

"Yes."

Another nod. He opened a notebook, consulted it for a moment. "According to what you told Detectives Gaines and Holroyd this morning, you only met Martin Simmons last night. Is that correct?"

"Yes."

"Where did you meet him?"

"A place called Dino's on the East Side."

"That's a singles bar, isn't it?"

"Yes."

"Do you go there often?"

"Not very. Every few weeks."

"Did Simmons pick you up or was it the other way around?"

Jennifer raised an eyebrow. "Pick up, Detective Oxman? Your terminology is outdated. We met, we talked, we agreed to leave together. That's all."

He seemed uncomfortable, vaguely annoyed. A moralist? she wondered. Or just old-fashioned?

"Did you come straight here from Dino's?"

"Yes. And we went straight to bed after we got here. That was your next question, wasn't it?"

"I'm not interested in your sex life, Miss Crane," he said flatly. "I'm only interested in finding out who shot Martin Simmons. What time did he leave?"

"Around three. He wanted to stay the night, but I told him no."

"Why? For any particular reason?"

"I like to sleep alone."

"What was his reaction when you asked him to leave?"

"He had no reaction. He just said he'd call me, I gave him my number, and he left."

"Wasn't he worried about being out on the street at that late hour?"

"He didn't seem to be."

"Miss Crane," Oxman said, "doesn't it bother you that you were the last person other than his killer to see Martin Simmons alive? Doesn't it bother you that a man you were intimate with has been murdered?"

"Of course it bothers me."

"You don't seem bothered."

"Would you prefer it if I'd sat here all day crying? I hardly knew the man."

"You went to bed with him."

"Are you sitting in judgment of me, Detective Oxman?"

"No," he said.

"It sounds as if you are."

"I told you, Miss Crane, I'm just trying to do my job."

She gave him a long speculative look. For some reason that she couldn't quite grasp, he interested her in a detached sort of way. Of all the men she had known intimately, none of them had been a police officer; maybe that was it. "Oxman," she said. "The name suggests a plodder. But I suspect you're something more than that."

"Plodding is part of every policeman's job," he told her. "I'm a cog in the mills of justice that grind exceedingly fine."

"The mills of the gods do that," she corrected.

"Sometimes there isn't any difference."

She shrugged. "No, I suppose not."

He looked at her legs again, caught himself, and shifted his gaze to his notebook. "Do you own a firearm, Miss Crane?"

"Why do you ask that? Am I a suspect?"

"Everyone who had any contact with Martin Simmons, and the opportunity to kill him, is a suspect."

"I see. No, I don't own a firearm. I don't like guns."

"Neither do I — in the wrong hands. Did you know either of the other two victims? Charles Unger and Peter Cheng?"

"No."

"Not even to speak to on the street?"

"No."

"All right. Is there anything else you can tell me that might be of help?"

"I'm afraid not."

Oxman let out a breath, closed his notebook, and stood up.

"Is that all, then?" Jennifer asked.

"For now, yes. We'll want you to make a statement at the precinct house."

"When? Tonight?"

"Tomorrow will do. Give some thought to the time you spent with Martin Simmons; maybe you can remember something you can't think of right now. Make notes if that will help jog your memory."

Jennifer nodded, then stood to show him out. He was looking at the nearest of the framed examples of her work, a romantic illustration of a man and a woman embracing on a cliff overlooking an angry sea, another of a young girl sitting at a bay window and gazing out beyond a flower box exploding with geraniums. She knew both illustrations were slickly commercial, but she also knew both displayed a sure cleanness of line and an undeniable sensitivity.

"Good," he said, nodding at the illustrations.

"Schmaltzy," Jennifer replied. An honest self-appraisal.

"Good nevertheless. There's nothing wrong in using your talent to make a living."

"True enough." She smoothed her dress over her thighs, watching him as she did so. He noticed the gesture; there wasn't much that he wouldn't notice, she thought. About a woman he found attractive, or about anything else.

At the door she asked, "How about tomorrow night after work?"

The question seemed to startle him. "What?"

"For my statement," she said. "Or I can make it during the day, if that would be better."

"Any time that's convenient," he said.

Jennifer opened the chain lock, then the door. "What's your first name?" she asked then. "Or were you Detective Oxman even as a child?"

His mouth quirked wryly. "E.L.," he said.

"Just initials? Or do they stand for something?"

"Elliot Leroy." He said the names as if he were challenging her to laugh, like a defensive little boy.

She decided not to comment. Perfectly serious, she asked, "Should I ask for you at the precinct house?"

"That won't be necessary. Thanks for your help, Miss Crane."

"Not at all. Will you be talking to me again?"

"I'll be talking to you again," he said.

He went out and down the hall without looking back at her. She waited until he had reached the elevator before she closed the door.

E.L. Oxman, she thought as she reset the chain lock and the dead-bolt Fox lock. *Yes, an interesting man.* In spite of herself, and in the same superficial way, she found him as attractive as he found her.

Jennifer kept him in her mind while she finished her vodka gimlet and then made another. Thinking about Oxman was better than thinking about Marty Simmons. Much, much better.

9:30 P.M. — BENNY HILLER

The alarm clock on the table next to Hiller's bed jangled loudly, and the shrill sound yanked him toward wakefulness. His left arm snaked out; he slapped the glowing button on top of the clock and the jangling stopped.

He sat up immediately, licked his lips, and ran his tongue around the inside of his mouth to rid it of the cottony taste of sleep. The apartment was silent except for the occasional hushed sounds of traffic filtering in from West Ninety-eighth Street three stories below. Darkness had fallen; only the faintest bars of light showed around the edges of the pulled shade on the window across the room. It was time to get dressed for work.

Hiller swiveled on the mattress and stood up, nude, as he always slept. He bent and switched on the green-shaded lamp by the bed and then padded barefoot toward the bathroom. He was a medium-tall, lithe man with stringy, muscular limbs and a sculptured stomach. There was a

41

compact economy of motion about him; he was a man of agility and endurance, though his sharply creased features and graying hair revealed that he was past forty. There was both a feral cunning and a youthful eagerness in his face, in his clear blue eyes. Astronauts and trapeze artists had that look. So did born commandos.

So did professional burglars.

After a quick cold shower, he toweled himself dry and dressed unhurriedly but with efficient ritualism, as if each move had been planned and practiced. He slipped into a navy blue shirt and dark slacks, then sat on the edge of the bed and put on black socks and dark blue Nike jogging shoes.

From the top shelf of the closet he pulled a small, almost flat nylon packet—a Totes carry-all bag that folded into a package that would take up little room in a traveler's suitcase, yet was spacious and sturdy enough to stuff with bulky souvenirs on the return trip. He slipped the folded Totes bag inside his shirt and worked it around so he could insert it beneath his belt in the small of his back. It was hardly noticeable there.

Hiller buttoned his shirt, then got his toolbox from under the bed. He wasn't going to go through any doors tonight, so he wouldn't need the picks and tension bars, the set of punches and driftpins, the cold chisel, the pick gun, or any of his other burglary tools. All he took from the box were a Swiss army knife with various attachments ranging from a screwdriver to a can opener, and a small penlight. These he put into his pants pockets.

He left the apartment, locking the door carefully behind him—he didn't want to be burglarized while he was out, he thought with a grin—and walked down to the street. Usually he worked at a much later hour, but he'd cased this job thoroughly, as he did all of his scores, and it called for an early hit. The target was a woman who ran a minor-league call-girl operation and dealt a little dope on the side; she was always out in the early evenings, never came home until after eleven.

Hiller preferred working nights himself, despite the fact that if you got busted on a B and E charge, the penalty was stiffer — a possible Burglary Two — for an after-dark hit than it was for a daylight hit. In the long run, he felt it was safer to work at night, although a lot of other professionals thought otherwise.

He took a cab to West End Avenue and Seventy-second Street and then walked to Central Park West and Sixty-ninth where the woman's apartment was located. It wasn't as ritzy as Park Avenue, or even Fifth, but it was classy; women and drugs were lucrative professions, even on a small scale. She'd have plenty of cash around, and he'd know where to look for it. And she could hardly report its disappearance to the law. This was shaping up to be one of his easiest and safest jobs.

Hiller moved slowly along the sidewalk until he reached the narrow gangway alongside the building he planned to enter. There were plenty of people on the street, so he didn't bother trying to disguise his actions. He simply turned in as if he knew some sort of shortcut and had every reason in the world to be there.

But he didn't cut all the way through; he stopped beneath the window he'd earmarked for his entry. The gangway was deeply shadowed, and someone on the sidewalk would have to pause and look closely to see Hiller in his dark clothing.

He took his time moving a large metal trash can, so as not to make any noise, and then stood on its lid so he could reach the window. Inside he could see a dark kitchen, white stove and refrigerator like pale tombstones. The window was over a sink; he made a mental note of the cannisters on the counter so he wouldn't kick them over when he crawled inside. There was an iron lattice over the window, but it was fastened to the frame with small screws. Hiller used the screwdriver on his Swiss army knife to loosen the screws on one side of the latticework, then bent the rusty iron back and out of the way.

The window was locked. Switching to the large blade of the knife, he worked on the old, brittle putty holding in the glass until he'd loosened the corner of the long center pane near the lock. He slipped the point of the knife blade beneath the glass and pried back. With almost no sound, a neat square of glass popped out into his hand, allowing him easy accesss to the lock. He inserted the handle of the knife through the opening in the pane and flipped the catch.

He was inside within half a minute, dropping nimbly from the sink, his soft-soled jogging shoes noiseless on the kitchen floor. He knew the layout of the apartment because one of the woman's dope customers had described it to him: a long living room along the front, the rear section divided between bathroom and small bedroom. The first thing he did was to stand for a moment and let his eyes get accustomed to the dimness; then he flashed the narrow yellow beam of the penlight around briefly, to orient himself; and then he made his way to the bedroom.

Surprise, surprise. Two people were sleeping in there.

Even before he reached the open bedroom door, he heard the regular breathing of the two. He tensed, cursed wordlessly — but those were his only reactions. He'd worked before with his victims on the premises, a time or two by choice. He could tell when someone was about to wake up, because he had learned to monitor their breathing; he was an expert on the sounds of sleep. So the woman had dragged somebody home with her tonight. So what? It was too bad, but it didn't change things much at all.

A streetlamp outside provided faint illumination in the room, so when Hiller looked in he could see that it was a man the woman had in bed with her. The window air conditioner was on, and the bedroom was cool. The man had the white sheet tucked up under his chin; the woman lay sprawled on her back with one slender, pale leg exposed. The room contained the stale, unmistakable scent of frenzied sexual coupling.

44

For a moment Hiller experienced a sensation of power. He knew their secrets, these two, and if he wanted to he could have the woman; they both would be easy enough to deal with while they slept. He could shove the man into a closet, spend the rest of the long night with the woman. Just knowing that was all he really needed. The woman was no prize anyway; the guy in her bed was either hard up or a junkie who hadn't had the price of a fix. Or maybe just a guy who liked his women ugly.

Hiller slipped into the bedroom, shielding the penlight beam with his hand. He went to the dresser and silently checked the drawers, all the time with an ear cocked to the rhythmic deep sleep breathing of the couple in bed. He found a diamond ring that might be worth a few hundred dollars, and some earrings and a necklace that might or might not be paste.

In the closet he found an expensive mink stole; he had been in the business long enough that he could appraise furs by feel. He draped the stole around his own shoulders and returned to the dresser, checking to see if anything was taped to the backs of the drawers. Nothing. He checked behind the drapes to see if an envelope was pinned there below window level. Nothing. And the jumbled shoe boxes on the closet shelf contained only shoes.

The woman made a sighing sound.

Hiller froze — a still, displaced shadow.

She rolled onto her side and nuzzled the man's shoulder. He continued to breathe in a regular nasal rasp through his nose. The woman's softer breathing evened out.

Hiller's heartbeat slowed; the momentary fright left him, and the feeling of secret power returned. It wasn't uncommon for burglars to piss or shit in the homes of their victims, to show their disdain and the power they'd held. Hiller didn't need that; just knowing was enough...just knowing.

He went to the nightstand by the bed. It yielded nothing

THE EYE

except the man's wristwatch — considerate of him not to risk scratching the woman. On the way back to the door, he removed the man's wallet from his pants laid out neatly on a chair and slipped it into his own hip pocket. He would check its contents later. The man was wearing a gold wedding ring, but the hell with that. It would be much too risky to try to work it off his finger.

Hiller didn't want to search the kitchen unless he had to; it was easier to make an accidental noise in the kitchen than in any other room. He went to the living room instead. In there, beneath some cellophane-wrapped mints in a candy dish, he found several small plastic containers of white powder. But he left the cocaine alone — if that was what it was. He didn't mess with hard drugs, not selling, not buying, not using. He needed all his wits all the time.

It took him less than five minutes to find the rubber-banded wad of bills hidden inside the hollow base of a lamp. How fucking original! Grinning, he slipped the bills into his pants pocket.

Almost finished now. He moved into the kitchen, over near the window. Then he unzipped and unfolded the Totes bag, began stuffing the mink stole and assorted smaller items inside.

Not five feet away, on the other side of the wall, a toilet flushed. The abrupt sound was like a watery explosion.

Hiller held his breath, poked the rest of the stole into the bag and worked the smooth nylon zipper that he'd lubricated with soap. He was steady. He'd had close calls before — plenty of them.

As he straightened, holding the bag by its strap, the floor creaked behind him. Hiller spun around. The man standing naked in the living room doorway was broad-shouldered, thick through the chest, strong-looking. Hiller didn't know why he hadn't gone back to bed after using the bathroom; hungry, maybe, or thirsty. Who could tell? That was the risk of the job: people's unpredictability.

46

He didn't panic; he never panicked in a tight situation. He used his brain instead, his intelligence. Running for the window was a dangerous move; he had no way of knowing how the big man would react. And there was no way to make the front door. Let the big guy make the first move, then. Hiller kept his tensed body still, his eyes on the other man—waiting, calculating distances and angles.

It was another ten seconds before the big man moved. He picked up a wine bottle from the top of the refrigerator, but he didn't come forward with it. Hiller saw the glint of his gold wedding ring, thought he knew what the guy was thinking: Here he was with a woman not his wife, and if he got mixed up in police business everyone would find out and maybe he'd be in deep shit.

"It's your lucky night, fuckhead," the man said. He didn't sound the slightest bit afraid. It crossed Hiller's mind that, Christ, he might be an off-duty cop.

Hiller dropped the Totes bag full of loot. He wanted his hands free. "Lucky how?"

"I ain't between you and the window," the man told him.

Hiller received the message with a surge of relief. He spun on his heel, jumped onto the sink, knocking over the cannisters, and was out the window like a spooked cat. He vaulted off the lid of the trash can and hit the gangway pavement running.

He stopped running when he came out on Sixty-ninth, because he didn't want to attract attention; but he walked fast, and he kept looking back over his shoulder. Nobody was chasing him. But that didn't stop him from sweating; his shirt was sodden and already plastered to his skin. He rolled up his sleeves and unfastened the top button of the shirt.

Near the park, an elderly couple emerged from the door of a restaurant and walked toward him, the old guy holding on to the woman's elbow as if he were guiding her through a mine field. Neither of them glanced at him as they passed, and he felt better.

A Checker cab turned the corner, its roof light glowing. On impulse, Hiller stepped into the street and hailed it. He told the driver to take him to West Ninety-sixth and Amsterdam. He could walk home from there after making sure he wasn't being followed.

As he settled back in the rear seat and the cab accelerated, he felt the pressure of the stolen wallet against his right buttock. His hand moved to the roll of bills in his side pocket. He felt like laughing out loud. The big son of a bitch would be sorry he'd let him go, and even sorrier when the woman found out the money was missing from the lamp. Probably there'd be one hell of a fight.

Well, screw both of them; they were lucky he had only had stealing in mind. What if the big bastard had walked in on somebody with a gun? Fat lot of good a wine bottle would have done him then. And the woman still had her mink and jewelry. Sure, they were both lucky; not as lucky as Benny Hiller, but lucky enough.

Hiller began to feel some of the euphoria he felt after every job. Luck was a thing some people emerged from the womb with, and he'd been born with his own plus someone else's share. By Christ, he could go on forever without getting nailed by the law. Forever!

He rested his head against the seatback, smiling. One side of him knew he was taking on more and more risk lately, almost as if he were challenging the laws of man and the laws of chance. Another side of him, the side Hiller listened to, thought that was bullshit. The last thing he wanted was to get caught, to spend years in a goddamn cage. The challenge was there, maybe, but it was all calculated so that the odds were heavily in his favor. And he had the luck, didn't he? He had the luck.

When the driver dropped him off on West Ninety-sixth, Hiller tipped him a five. Why not? Share the wealth. There was no need to worry about the cabbie remembering him as a fare, because the cops would never get on to tonight's

caper; the woman and her big bastard boyfriend would
never report it.

Hiller walked home grinning, breathing night air sweet as
nectar.

10:35 P.M. — E.L. OXMAN

Oxman was exhausted. He'd spent most of the day and part
of the evening interviewing residents of the twelve hundred
block of West Ninety-eighth. Nearly everybody who lived on
that block had been covered, either by him or Artie Tobin or
Gaines and Holroyd, and none of them knew a damned
thing about Martin Simmons' murder, or were willing to
admit it if they did.

Slumped in his desk chair at the Twenty-fourth, Oxman
sipped coffee from the squadroom pot; even doctored with
milk and sugar, it tasted bitter, gritty. He was wired enough
already, but he needed the coffee to pump him up and get
him through the last few minutes of paperwork before he
could go home.

He looked around at the stifling, disorganized clutter of
the squadroom. Two months ago he'd again been passed
over for promotion, which not only would have meant a
much-needed increase in salary but a potential transfer to a
better precinct than the Twenty-fourth. He remembered, a
little bitterly, what Jennifer Crane had said about his name
suggesting he was a plodder. He knew he gave others that
impression. Maybe Jennifer Crane was one of the few who
sensed something deeper in him than the bent of a creature
of routine. The Department conceded that he was
relentless — his record made that evident — but they made the
mistake of interpreting relentlessness as lack of imagination.
He was a good cop, damn it. He deserved that promotion.

His gaze shifted to the three yellow file folders before him
on the desk. The Peter Cheng, Charles Unger, and Martin
Simmons files, containing the scant information regarding

their murders. The Ballistics report on the Simmons homicide was also there; he picked it up again and glanced over it. The weapon they were after was a .32 caliber Harrington & Richardson automatic, rifled with a six-groove left-twist spiral. Pitch, ten and a half inches; groove depth, ten-thousandths of an inch; groove width, forty-two thousandths...

He slapped the report down, rubbed at his tired eyes. Elsewhere in the squadroom, there were the sounds of night-shift activity: one of the detectives joking with a patrolman while he booked a suspect; another detective talking to someone on the phone; one of two black men in the holding cell complaining, "It ain't fair, man! It ain't mothafuckin' *fair!*" Someone outside in the corridor let out a loud horselaugh. Somebody else shouted for Adams in Clerical. And all of this was backgrounded by the distant, monotonous voice of the dispatcher directing patrol cars about the miles of Manhattan streets in a blank-verse litany of violence. The sounds of Oxman's world. They stayed with a cop forever, echoing in the recesses of the brain as long as the mind functioned. There was no genuine retirement from his job, not ever.

He picked up one of the case folders from his overflowing In basket — just one of several other cases he was supposed to be dealing with. The world didn't stop for anyone or anything; life lurched on, and so did death.

Oxman realized he was getting maudlin. He took another sip of the bad coffee, opened the folder. He was shuffling through it when Tobin came in.

Tobin crossed the room to Oxman's desk and cocked a hip against one corner of it. He looked as tired as E.L. felt. His gray pinstripe suit was wrinkled and his shirt was partly untucked beneath his vest. He was developing quite a paunch, Oxman noticed.

"How's it going, Elliot Leroy?"

"You know, you're putting on weight around the middle,"

Oxman said. Hell, he could play it mean too. Nobody liked pounding the bricks till past ten at night when you were supposed to be on the dayshift. Sometimes Tobin seemed to think he was the only one who suffered. Artie was one efficient cop, but he'd been hired at the wrong time and he still carried traces of a persecution complex from the time when he *had* been persecuted because of his race.

Tobin gazed at him out of his flat brown eyes with the crescent of white showing beneath each pupil. "I guess it's the good life," he said, straight-faced.

Oxman grinned wearily. "Yeah."

"Anything new?"

"Not over on Ninety eighth. How about you?"

"Same thing. What did Gaines and Holroyd turn up on Martin Simmons?"

"Not much," Oxman said. "He was an advertising copywriter for Flick and Flick on Madison Avenue. Lived alone, didn't have many close friends, or so it would seem. They say at the agency that he was a bit of a swinger, liked to frequent the singles bars. Been in Manhattan a little less than two years, originally from Kansas City."

"Kansas City," Tobin repeated.

"Sure. Home of the Royals, the Chiefs, and the Kings."

"Uh-huh. Did Simmons ever live on West Ninety-eighth?"

"No. The apartment on Seventy-third is the only one he's had since he came to the city."

"Any acquaintances on Ninety-eighth?"

"Just Jennifer Crane, evidently."

"You talk to the Crane woman?"

"I talked to her."

"I don't suppose she could be the perp?"

"Doubtful. Can you see a woman giving somebody her phone number, then following him outside and shooting him near her building?"

"Don't rule it out," Tobin said.

"I don't. I just can't see it happening."

51

"Maybe this Jennifer Crane brought Peter Cheng and Charles Unger home too, zapped them after they balled her."

"Sure, the black widow murderess. Good news copy."

Tobin ran spread fingers through his thinning, wiry hair. "Okay, so how do you see her?"

Oxman shrugged. "Like thousands of other New York career women, doing her job, humping on the treadmill." Oddly, he regretted the words as he spoke them. He did sense some difference in Jennifer Crane, though nothing he could frame in words for Tobin.

"Well," Tobin said, "you've got better insight with these white chicks than I do."

Oxman let that go; the hell with Artie and his subtle baiting.

The frosted glass door to the lieutenant's office opened and Manders came out. Oxman thought, as he had many times before, that Lieutenant Smiley resembled a starving basset hound. But he was a basset hound with stamina; Oxman had seen him work twenty-four-hour days without any noticeable effect, and right now he appeared as fresh as if he'd just reported for work.

When he saw Oxman and Tobin his lean, sad features gave in to gravity and he frowned. "So you two are still here," he said. He was a good one for stating the obvious.

"Wrapping up some paperwork," Oxman said, motioning with his head toward his In basket.

"The hell with that stuff. I'll have Davidson do it in the morning. You concentrate on the Ninety-eighth Street thing. The goddamn media is already onto the idea that we might have a random serial killer on our hands."

"It could be they're right."

"Yeah." Manders lit a cigarette, held it at arm's length and stared at it through a haze of smoke as if it, too, was part of a plot to make his life difficult. "I'm going to put somebody in undercover tomorrow. See if anything turns up that way."

"Good idea," Tobin said.

"There's a vacant apartment at twelve-forty. I've already talked to the building super; he'll let the undercover man use it."

"You know who it'll be yet?"

"Not yet. I'll let you know in the morning."

"He'll work with us, though, right?"

"Right," Manders said. He drew deeply on his cigarette; ashes dropped onto his shirtfront and clung there. "Why don't you two go home? I'd rather have you here fresh in the morning than sitting around late tonight hashing things over."

That suggestion was fine with Oxman. He stood and replaced the West Ninety-eighth Street files in the cabinet; then he shrugged into his suit coat. Tobin was standing also, carefully tucking his shirt in around his burgeoning gut.

"Anything comes up during the night," Manders told them, "I'll get you on the phone."

"Thanks," Tobin said. "I feel so much better knowing that."

Oxman said good night to Tobin in the squadroom and left the precinct house alone, down the thirteen concrete steps to the street. As he walked to his car, he glanced about him at the darkened apartment and office buildings nearby; the night concealed the disrepair of the old brick structures. The warm air seemed clean and oddly comforting. His footfalls gave off a resonant, larger-than-life sound that seemed to fly back at him from all directions.

Like most New Yorkers, his feelings about his city were paradoxical. He was a native; he'd been born in Brooklyn, and he'd lived there near Prospect Park until his mother's death from cancer when he was nine. Then he'd been sent away to Chicago to be raised by an aunt who had treated him decently enough but always in a brisk and impersonal fashion that was the antithesis of his mother's natural effusiveness and warmth. He remembered most his mother's

THE EYE

rich laugh, her head thrown back, her long dark hair swaying with her mirth. She had been healthy-looking, vital, right up to the final days. His mind, but not his heart, had finally forgiven her for leaving him and his father alone.

At eighteen, after his graduation from high school, he had returned to live with his father, who had managed a chain of dry-cleaning establishments in Queens. He and his father had never been close, and he had resented the decision to ship him off to Chicago after his mother's death, although he understood that it was grief that had made the old man do it. But after his return they had spent time together, and grown to know each other; they had remained close until his father's death seven years ago. They had exchanged letters regularly during Oxman's hitch in the Army in Europe, then during his brief stay at the University of Michigan.

With both the Army and his fling as a student among younger and more serious scholars behind him, he had returned again to New York. Always he seemed drawn back to the city. From its majestic towers to its miserable tramps in the Bowery, it was part of him, and he of it. Though he had never been able to articulate the fact, he had known it even in his early twenties. In a way, it was the reason why he had married Beth—a native New Yorker like himself—four months after meeting her at a party in the Village. And it was what had compelled him to join the New York City Police Department that same year.

He'd been a good cop from the beginning. Stable. Steady. Marked by superiors as a methodical and conscientious officer whose career would be useful and rewarding, if never meteoric. He had never questioned an order, never questioned the law. He had always understood the law, at least that aspect of it that made being a cop difficult sometimes, that a cop had to accept and learn to work around.

Then, four years ago, he had been injured in the line of duty, struck by a getaway car driven by a frightened armed

54

robber who was out on parole at the time he tried to heist a luggage shop on West Forty-fourth. Oxman had seen his face through the windshield; the felon had realized that, had stopped the car and reversed it, deliberately swerving to run him down. Oxman had leapt out of the way, but not soon enough to avoid a broken pelvis. He'd still managed to draw his revolver and fire several shots at the car, blowing a tire; the holdup man had been caught and charged with attempted murder as well as armed robbery. But plea bargaining had gotten him off with a seven-year sentence, and he had been paroled after two years and three months and was still free as far as Oxman knew. Oxman had spent weeks in a hospital bed and almost a year as an outpatient. He still limped a bit in cold weather.

Maybe that incident was what had made him begin to wonder about the law, about his life. It was about that time that the worm of doubt had started to bore into his mind. It was easy enough to accept the law's faults if you looked at them objectively; but this was something else. This was personal. And the assailant, protected by the law, had gotten off with nothing more than a slap on the wrist.

From that time on, he had fallen into the habit of looking at things through the eyes of the victim, or through the eyes of the horrified bystander. A cop shouldn't do that. A cop *couldn't* do that and keep on being a good cop.

Or, hell, maybe he could; Oxman just didn't know anymore. He didn't know anything anymore, he thought as he unlocked and opened his car door. Maybe the city had finally begun to wear him down. Or maybe his marriage had, because it had stopped being a good marriage a long time ago. A combination of things, probably, burdens accumulated by time and growing heavier by the year.

I'm getting old, he thought. *Old and tired.*

When he arrived at his house in Queens he saw that the windows were dark. It was eleven thirty; Beth would no doubt be in bed asleep. He let himself in, moving as quietly as the burglars he had sought over the years. He made his way through the dark living room to the kitchen, switched on the overhead light. There were dirty dishes in the sink. Water from the faucet dripped steadily into one of the dishes with a rhythmic *plink, plink, plink.*

He gave the faucet handle a twist and the dripping stopped. He got a glass down from the cupboard, poured some milk, drank it in three long gulps. Then he set the glass in the sink along with the other dishes, turned off the light, and went into the bedroom.

Beth was lying on her side: mound of hip, fan of tousled blond hair splayed over her pillow. The portable TV she used as a nightlight was tuned soundlessly to the *Tonight Show.* While he removed his clothes he thought about waking her, but only fleetingly. He knew that if he did, the result would be rejection and dissatisfaction along with guilt that he couldn't pity her for her sexually debilitating headaches that puzzled even the best of doctors.

As he placed his holstered service revolver on the dresser, he saw Beth's vials of pills on the table by the bed and wondered how many of them were placebos. More than one doctor had suggested that her headaches were a mental as well as physical affliction and might have to do with impending menopause. But no psychiatry for Beth, oh no. Twice she was to begin psychoanalysis and each time she had stomped out on the first visit.

One of the psychiatrists had confided to Oxman that she might in some way enjoy suffering, as if that idea might be a revelation for him. But it wasn't. Everyday he saw unconscious motives compel people to destroy their own and others' lives.

Stepping into his pajama bottoms, he glanced at Johnny Carson moving in his curiously marionettelike way before his studio audience. If it hadn't been for Beth, Oxman would have turned up the volume; he just wasn't ready for sleep yet. As it was, he switched off the TV just as Ed McMahon appeared cradling a box of dog food, beaming down at a scottie eagerly lapping the product from a bowl. He was careful not to disturb Beth as he crawled into bed. He lay curled on his side, facing away from her, toward the deeper darkness of the wall. His eyes were wide open. The homicides on West Ninety-eighth Street were still heavy on his mind, but they weren't the only things that were keeping him awake. In spite of himself, he couldn't seem to stop thinking about Jennifer Crane.

THE COLLIER TAPES

Slip of darkness, blackest patch of night, shadow in smooth motion among shadows—how futile! The Eye has observed the evil ones come and go, seen them through the windows of their apartments. Though they don't know it, they live only on my whim. I must confess that I enjoy that. Any time I choose I can cancel all their debts and favors owed, put an end to their petty lives and send them into the depths of hell. Heed the Book of Common Prayer, evil ones: "Man that is born of woman hath but a short time to live, and is full of misery."

Only a matter of time. Only a matter of my choosing.

My first choice was Charles Unger. Have I explained about him? Not in enough detail, perhaps, and he is important. Because he was the first, and because it was through him that I realized my destiny and achieved my apotheosis.

The Eye had closely observed him, along with all the others in my universe. A cantankerous old man, red of nose and gray of hair, a prodigious consumer of alcohol. But it was not drink that led to his death, except indirectly; it was rudeness. For he was rude to me, and that is a form of blasphemy.

I was walking one afternoon in the midst of that which is

mine, having parked my car some distance from West Ninety-eighth, as I generally do. I felt my power that day as I walked among my children, felt it surging through me like an electrical current. And Charles Unger, whom I considered to be without sin at that time, rudely shoved me aside so he could cross an intersection before the traffic light changed. A cab screamed to a stop quite near me. Furious, I protested. But Unger was drunk; he became loud and belligerent, turned and shoved me again so that I stumbled backward over the curb and almost fell. Then he walked on in mortal ignorance.

I was stunned and I did not act immediately. But I understood as I watched the lurching old man push his way through other pedestrians and cross the street that he had made a fatal mistake. In my mind he was already dead, and so he would be, and was, in actuality. He had left me no choice. As Bailey said, "He hath no power that hath not power to use." So, in a sense, *not* acting against Charles Unger would have diminished my power.

The Eye observed him for several days after that. I would smile as I watched him idly stumble about the neighborhood. He was restless in his retirement, unsure of how to spend his time, not realizing that nearly all of it was already spent. Then one night I parked my car in the usual place, walked into my domain, and waited for Charles Unger to return from a tavern he habitually frequented in the evenings. And after first whispering to him of vengeance and of the wages of sin, I released him from this life.

On my way home last night, I understood that Unger would not be the last of the evil ones to receive swift justice by the hand of the deity. Death is the swift and deserved end for the sinner. To eliminate the wicked is to strengthen the lives of the chaste and the pure. A good god is a just god, and I was determined to be both.

It was not difficult to select the second evil one to die. Peter Cheng I had observed with various young men, some

Chinese and some Caucasian; his homosexual couplings were a mockery of all that is good and clean. And then, one night before his unshaded window, the Eye observed him lewdly exhausting his passion with *two* young men in leather costumes, while an obese Chinese woman looked on, stroking herself. It was bizarre and repugnant. Could I allow Peter Cheng to remain among the living after *this?*

I forgave him as I sent the bullet into his brain and freed him from his sins. I forgave Charles Unger as well; and I will forgive all the others who are to follow.

Oh, I admit again that Martin Simmons was a mistake, and yet I have decided that he, too, deserved to die. He was a fornicator, an evildoer; he brought his evil into my universe, and he paid justly with his life. I have forgiven him too.

The Eye continues to scan the windows of the buildings across the river, even as I dictate these words. Most of the windows are dark now, shades and curtains drawn; most of my children are asleep. The sinners too — some of them. The brief sleep before the final one soon to come.

Do they suspect, any of them, what is in store? Do they sense the higher purpose that is mine, or glimpse the specter of pale horse and rider? There is poetry in death, as every poet knows. Perhaps those about to die can somehow detect the meter of their own imminent demise.

Yet if they do, they ignore it. Far removed (though not so far as they choose to believe) from the primal state, they do not listen to the cells of their own bodies, the ancient silent voices hinting of eternity. They do not really know. And they will not, until the pale horse appears before them, and his name that sits on him shall be Death.

PART 2

SATURDAY
SEPTEMBER 21

9:00 A.M.
WALLY SINGER

When Marion announced that she was going to Brooklyn to spend the day with her sister, Singer barely managed to hide his elation. It surprised him. She didn't get along with her sister; hell, she didn't get along with anybody, the fat cow. But she was upset about the shootings, she said, and she wanted to get out of the neighborhood for the day. She couldn't talk to him; all he cared to do was argue and pick on her. Ellen, at least, was family and would offer a sympathetic ear.

Singer told her he didn't care what she did, and she was gone at 8:45. He waited fifteen minutes, spending the time in the bathroom trimming his sparse beard and daubing himself liberally with English Leather cologne. Then he locked the apartment, rode the elevator downstairs, and went out to the street.

There was an unmarked police car parked at the curb. He'd seen it before, so he knew it belonged to the detectives from the Twenty-fourth Precinct. He didn't like the police much, particularly the sandy-haired cop named Oxman; Oxman's shrewd eyes and probing questions, boring at him as if *he* were guilty of something, had left him with a bad case of nerves yesterday. Still, there was a certain comfort in knowing the law was around. Nothing else was going to happen with the police crawling all over the block.

Singer crossed the street, went up the steps of 1279, and pressed the button alongside the smudged white card that read *2-C Cindy Wilson*. It took a full minute for Cindy's voice to say scratchily from the intercom box, "Yes, who is it?"

"It's Wally. Buzz me in."

"Wally! Yes, just a second . . ."

The lock on the entrance door made a burring sound. Singer pushed inside, climbed the stairs to the second floor. Cindy had the door open and was peering out when he came down the hall. She was wearing a dressing gown over a baby-doll nightgown; her dark hair was tousled and she looked sleepy. Singer's eyes moved over her body as he approached. She wasn't much to look at, really, but she had a damned good body, slender, well filled out. God, it was nice to have a slim woman after all the years with Marian.

As soon as he was inside, she shut the door and threw the dead-bolt locks. Then she turned, put her arms around him, and kissed him lingeringly. Singer let his hands slide over the silky roundness of her buttocks, cupping them, pulling her tight against him. But she wasn't ready for fun and games yet; she broke the kiss, eased away from him. Her eyes, he saw, had purplish half-moons under them, as if she hadn't slept much during the night.

"It's so early," she said. "How did you get out?"

"Marian's gone for the day, visiting her sister in Brooklyn."

He reached for her again, but she placed her hand against his chest. "Wait, Wally. I'm still half-asleep; I need some coffee."

"We can have coffee later," he said.

"No, I need some now. It won't take a minute. I didn't sleep very well and I'm still a little groggy."

She started away to the kitchen. Singer curbed his impatience and followed her, watching the roll and sway of her hips, the outline of her thighs under the thin gown. He could feel heat stirring in his groin. It had been four days since he'd last been to bed with her and he was damned horny. After he'd finally got rid of the detective, Oxman, and come over to see her yesterday, she'd been too upset to do any screwing. He had tried to talk her into it without success, so he'd gone home frustrated. And picked another fight with Marian as soon as she came back, because by then he'd been in a lousy mood and fighting with her gave him a measure of release.

The kitchen was cluttered with dirty dishes, overflowing garbage bags, food remnants all over the table and the floor. The front room, with its worn furniture and piles of movie magazines, was in similar disarray. Cindy was something of a slob, but it didn't bother Singer half as much as Marian's tendencies in the same direction. Everything about Marian bothered him, including the fact that she was intelligent. Cindy, on the other hand, wasn't much in the brains department, and he liked that just fine. He liked having a woman who was his intellectual inferior, a woman he could manipulate, a woman who listened to what he said and thought he was somebody important.

She put coffee water on to boil. Sitting at the table, she brushed crumbs off onto the floor and then ran spread fingers through her hair and yawned. "God," she said, "I can't seem to wake up."

"Why couldn't you sleep last night?"

"You know why. The shootings . . ."

THE EYE

"Stop worrying about that. Nothing's going to happen to you or me."

"But don't they make you afraid?"

"No," he lied. The shootings did worry him, did make him a little afraid, but he wasn't going to tell her that. Or Marian or anybody else. The way he felt was nobody's business but his own. "The police will find out who's doing it. They'll get him."

"You really think so?"

"I really think so."

She yawned again. "I took a cab home last night," she said. "I can't afford it, you know, but I just couldn't come on the subway."

Cindy worked as a waitress at a restaurant on Columbus Avenue near Lincoln Center, from four to eleven, five days a week. That was where Singer had first met her; he'd gone there with Marian one night for dinner, and Cindy had smiled at him in a more than impersonal way, as if she liked what she saw. He liked what he saw too, and he'd gone back a few days later, alone. She'd been impressed when he told her he was an artist; creative people fascinated her, she said. Then they'd found out they were neighbors—one of those crazy coincidences that happen sometimes in a city like New York. She'd been living across the street from him for almost a year and yet they'd never run into each other before, they'd had to meet by chance at a restaurant.

He'd asked her to go to a movie with him and she'd accepted. After that it was walks in Riverside Park, drinks in a couple of bars on Broadway. And after that, just ten days after he'd gone back to the restaurant, it was afternoons in her bed any time he could get away. Cindy was divorced and she lived alone, so there was no problem there. The only hassle was that her ex-husband was trying to convince her to let him move back in and he kept showing up unannounced. Once he'd almost caught them together. That had been a bad time for Singer; the ex-husband was a truck driver, a big

66

bastard, and mean from what Cindy told him. Singer didn't consider himself a coward, but neither did he go looking for trouble. He was careful now never to see Cindy on Sundays or Mondays, the two days her ex-husband was off work. He said, "You going to take a cab home every night?"

"Until they catch that maniac, I am."

"Do you really feel safer that way?"

"I do. Much safer, even if I can't afford it."

"I'd help you out if I could," Singer lied, "but you know how things are with me."

"Oh, I don't want any money from you, Wally, you know that. I'd feel . . .well, I'd feel cheap if I took money from you."

"One of these days my work will start to sell," he said. "Then it'll be different. For both of us."

"I know it will, Wally. You're a good artist, you really are."

"That's true."

"Every time I look at the painting you gave me, I can feel your talent. I mean, I can actually *feel* it."

Singer suppressed a wry smile. The painting he'd given her was a small still life — a bowl of fruit, no less — and one of the worst things he'd ever done. But she'd gone into raptures over it, and the screwing that day had been extra fine. Giving it to her was a smart move on his part. And Marian had never missed it; she didn't even look at his work anymore.

The kettle on the stove began to whistle. Cindy took it off the burner, spooned instant coffee into two semi-clean cups, added the boiling water, and handed him one of the cups. Looking at her in that gown, with the tops of her breasts showing above the baby dolls, Singer could feel his hands twitch. Christ, but he wanted that body of hers. He felt like a stud when he was around her, a feeling he hadn't had with Marian since the first year of their marriage.

Cindy wanted to talk about the cop who'd been to see her

yesterday, a black cop, she said, very polite, but blacks made her nervous because she had never been able to relate to them. Her father was a bigot, she said, maybe that was why. All the time she'd been growing up, it was nigger this and nigger that. Singer didn't want to hear about the cop; he didn't want to talk any more about the shootings. But he let her babble on until both their cups were empty. You couldn't push her when she was wound up like this; you had to wait until the right moment.

When she swallowed the last of her coffee he locked eyes with her across the table. Then he said, "Why don't we go to bed now?"

"Well. . ." she said, and wet her lips. "You did say we have all day . . ."

"Yes, but I want you. You know how much I want you."

"Oh, yes, I know."

"How much I want to fuck you," he said.

He heard the sharp intake of her breath. It made her hot when he used words like that; she'd told him so, more than once. All a matter of timing, he thought. He had her hooked now. She was ready.

He stood up, reached out a hand. She got up too and came to him, and he kissed her, slid his tongue into her mouth. At the same time he opened the front of her gown, eased his hands down inside the baby dolls and fondled her breasts. The touch of them, soft and firm, gave him an erection. She could feel it pressing against her, and she made a moaning sound in her throat.

"Fuck," he said against her mouth.

"Oh, Wally . . ."

"Fuck. Fuck."

"Yes!"

He pulled her into the cluttered bedroom, saying the word over and over until she tore at his clothes, until they were both naked and she was thrashing under him on the bed,

frenzied, saying, "I love you, Wally, I love you, I love
you . . ."

"Fuck," he said.

9:40 A.M. — E.L. OXMAN

Before driving over to West Ninety-eighth Street, he stopped
in at the Twenty-fourth to check with Lieutenant Smiley. A
couple of veteran police reporters were hanging around the
squadroom, and one of them tried to buttonhole Oxman for
a quote. Oxman ducked him with more politeness than he
felt, went over and knocked on the door to Manders's office.

The lieutenant was in a foul mood. He was getting
pressure from Captain Burnham, from the commissioner's
office, and he spent a couple of minutes chewing Oxman's
ass in turn, demanding results. No new developments had
turned up during the night. Oxman had already figured
that; he would have been notified if anything positive or
negative had happened. About the only other thing Manders
had to tell him was that the undercover officer was all set to
move onto the block; Tobin would be meeting with him later
in the morning for a briefing session. Artie had come in
early, Manders said, and was already over on the street.

Oxman left the precinct house and drove there himself.
The morning sun was still low, glinting off the windows of
the high-rise apartment buildings across the Hudson, when
he parked his car behind Tobin's in mid-block. There was no
sign of Artie; he had a list of people to interview, and that
was no doubt what he was doing. There were a few residents
left on Oxman's list too, but before he tackled them he
decided to have another look at the alley where Martin
Simmons had been found.

When he entered the alley he automatically checked doors
and ground-level windows for security. Both buildings, 1272
and 1274, were well kept up and tight. All the windows on

the first two stories were covered with black-enameled iron grillwork.

He paused to look at the fading chalk outline of Simmons's corpse, felt the sense of futility and sadness that seemed to linger at every murder scene. He shook his head and glanced toward the rear of the alley. But there was nothing to see back there; the lab crew had been over every inch of the passageway without finding a damned thing.

Oxman was about to turn back to the street when the basement door of 1276 opened and the super, Richard Corales, came out lugging a box of trash. Corales was a heavyset, swarthy man with broad Latin features, wearing the same outfit as he had been when Oxman talked to him the day before — jeans, sandals, and a yellow T-shirt with a pack of cigarettes jutting from the pocket. He blinked at Oxman, and "cop" registered on his seamed, flesh-padded face. He scowled.

"Morning, Mr. Corales," Oxman said.

"Yeah. Look, man, I got work to do, you know?"

"So have I. That's why I'm here."

"I already told you everything I know. I don't want to keep answering the same damn questions."

The man's hostility annoyed Oxman, just as it had yesterday. It was obvious that Corales was no mental giant, but that was no excuse for his attitude. Oxman decided to question him again. The hostility might mean that Corales had something to hide; and even if that wasn't the case, he might have unintentionally neglected to report something important because of it. People who disliked the police weren't always reliable or as cooperative as they could be.

"Suppose we talk in your apartment, Mr. Corales," Oxman said. "I won't keep you long."

"But I already told you —"

Oxman gave him a hard look. "You lead the way."

Corales said, "Ahh," in a disgusted voice, banged the box of trash down, and turned back to the door. Oxman followed him down a dim, narrow stairway to the basement; the walls on either side were grayish-green and looked to have been newly painted. There were eight steps.

Oxman took stock of Corales's apartment as he entered; when he'd talked to the super yesterday, it had been in the boiler room, where Corales was making repairs. The apartment was small, inexpensively but neatly furnished. On an old table were a metal ashtray, a pencil and tablet, and a deck of cards, as if Corales was expecting someone for a card game. There was a narrow mantel over a bricked-up fireplace, and on the mantel was a cheap plastic model of a battleship, meticulously painted and authentic looking.

Corales saw him looking at the model. "That's the *New Jersey*," he said. "My old man served on her as a gunner's mate in Korea. Blasted the shit outa them gooks. That's the last war we won." He said it almost proudly, as if his old man had been personally responsible.

"I was in the Army myself," Oxman said.

"Not in Korea. You ain't old enough."

"No. Peacetime army; I never saw any action."

"Yeah. That figures."

Oxman sat down at the table. "Tell me again how you found Martin Simmons."

Corales made a face, but did as he was told. He recited the facts as if by rote. There were no essential variations from his original statement. He had taken some trash out into the alley, noticed Simmons's body lying face down against the wall of the building next door, 1272, and looked at it closely enough to determine that Simmons was dead. He hadn't touched the body, hadn't disturbed anything near it. Then he'd come back here to his apartment and called the police. He'd waited for their arrival out in the alley; nobody else had come into it until the first patrol car arrived.

"Did you hear anything during the night?" Oxman asked him. "A gunshot, voices, anything like that out in the alley?"

"No. I didn't hear nothing. I sleep good when I sleep."

71

"Have you noticed anyone in the neighborhood recently who doesn't belong here?"

"No," Corales said. "Most of the time, I'm right here in this building. I always got work to do, you know."

"Had you ever seen Martin Simmons before?"

"Never. Not until I found him dead."

"Did you know either of the previous two victims, Charles Unger and Peter Cheng?"

"I seen the old guy around a few times. He was always drunk."

"What about Peter Cheng?"

"No. You think I know everybody lives on this block?"

There was a knock on the door. Corales went over and opened it, said, "Hey, Willie, how's it going?" in a pleased voice, and admitted a tall, sloppily dressed man carrying a burlap sack. The man had thick-wristed hands and disheveled brown hair that hung lank over his high forehead.

When he saw Oxman he brushed at the lank hair and asked Corales, "Am I interrupting, Richard?"

"Nah. This here's another cop. He's gonna leave pretty soon."

Oxman identified himself. The tall man nodded. "Good morning, officer," he said. "I'm Willie Lorsec."

"Willie's a good friend of mine," Corales said. The hostility was gone from his face; it had been replaced by a grin and a little-boy look of pleasure and anticipation. "He's a junk dealer."

"Redeemable used merchandise," Lorsec corrected.

"Yeah, right. Willie and me, we play gin together." Corales's grin widened. "I won nineteen straight hands off him yesterday. Ain't that right, Willie?"

"A remarkable winning streak," Lorsec said.

"Yeah. I figure if I can keep on winning, I can get into the *Guinness Book of World Records.* Jesus, wouldn't that be something!"

"I guess it would," Oxman agreed.

72

"Sure it would. Listen, you done asking me questions? Willie and me want to get at them cards again — "

The telephone rang. "Damn," Corales said. "I hope that ain't one of the tenants with a problem." He went over to where the instrument was hooked onto one wall and answered it.

Oxman asked Lorsec, "You live in this neighborhood, do you, Mr. Lorsec?"

"I do, yes. In the next block."

"Then you know about the homicides here."

"Yes. A tragic series of events."

"You wouldn't happen to have been in this vicinity late Thursday night, by chance? The night Martin Simmons was shot?"

"No, I wasn't," Lorsec said. "I seldom go out late. It's much too dangerous on the streets at night, especially now."

Oxman asked him a few more questions, learned nothing, and took down his address in case he needed to talk to the junkman again.

Corales finished his telephone call, came over to stand next to Lorsec. "That was old Mrs. Muñoz in one-C," he said. "She's got trouble with one of her light switches, but I can fix it later. We can still play gin, Willie." He shifted his gaze to Oxman. "So you done with me or what?"

"I'm done with you," Oxman told him. He had watched the super closely when Corales repeated his story and answered Oxman's questions, and he hadn't seemed to be hiding anything. Oxman was reasonably sure that Corales had told him everything he knew. "For now, anyway."

He left Corales and Lorsec to their card game and climbed the fifteen inside steps to the lobby. Counting steps was an idiosyncrasy of his; he'd done it since he was a rookie cop and it had once led to breaking a trumped-up alibi. In the lobby he paused. And his mind shifted again to Jennifer Crane.

He had no reason to talk to her again, after yesterday's

interview. But she'd been in his thoughts off and on all morning, just as she'd been in his thoughts last night. It would be foolish to see her again, unprofessional; he kept telling himself that. He had a job to do here, there were literally lives at stake, and it was no time to pursue a dangerous personal attraction.

All right. He consulted the list of names in his coat pocket, and then took the elevator up to the fourth floor to see if Michele Butler was home.

10:15 A.M. — MICHELE BUTLER

She was standing on the stoop, balancing the bag of groceries in one hand and with the other fumbling in her purse for her key, when the door opened and she was suddenly face to face with Marco Pollosetti. She blinked at him, startled. An impulse to turn and flee seized her; she managed to fight it off. *Stay calm,* she thought. *For God's sake, don't let him see that you're afraid of him.*

Marco grinned at her. He was a scrawny man about her own age with yellowing teeth and odd eyes — small and hard and black, like pebbles set in tarnished ivory. His grin was broad and intimate, and he wore a knowing look on his gaunt face. Michele knew that grin and that look; she had seen them before, three months ago, when she'd had another unexpected run-in with him in the hallway upstairs less than an hour after shoplifting several fourteen-carat gold chains from Altman's.

He had tried to date her a couple of times since he'd moved into the building, and he tried again that day. As always, she had politely refused. After making a joke of his suggestion, to lessen the sting to his male ego, he had started to edge around her and managed to brush against her as he did. Her purse had slipped from her hand, fallen to the floor, and the gold chains had spilled out. She hadn't taken them straight to a pawnshop that time, as she'd done with the ruby ring yesterday; she'd been too nervous and she had hurried straight home instead. It had been one mistake she would never allow to happen again.

His eyes had widened when he saw the chains. Each of them was still price-tagged. The stores always removed the tags when jewelry was sold; Marco must have known that. He'd looked at her in a new way, with an amazed and pleased comprehension as he stooped to help her retrieve the chains and stuff them back into her purse.

"No one else here to see anything," he'd said when they both stood up. "Don't worry."

"Why should I care if there was?" Michele had asked him, too quickly, too much as a challenge.

Marco had shrugged his bony shoulders, and that was the first time he'd grinned at her in his knowing and intimate way. He hadn't said anything more about the chains, that day or since, but he had stepped up his attempts to get her to go out with him.

She wasn't worried about him turning her in to the police. She was sure he was on drugs and that he had an aversion to the law for that reason. And there would be nothing in it for him if he steered the police to her.

Still, she didn't like him knowing her secret. She was ashamed of stealing, even if it was a means to an end, even if it allowed her to buy groceries and pay the rent while she concentrated on more important goals. A man like Marco probably wouldn't understand that. She was also ashamed that she no longer met his advances with a curt but polite refusal; instead, she gave him the impression that someday she might accept one of his invitations. It was a hateful game, and a dangerous one, and that was why she was afraid of him. What if he forced the issue? What if he tried to get her to go to bed with him? She didn't know what she would do if that happened. So she avoided him whenever she could, and prayed that he wouldn't knock on her door some night and demand that she let him in.

75

Now, facing him here on the stoop, she could feel her hands turn damp and shaky. She took a firmer grip on the grocery bag, on her purse. His odd eyes were steady on her face, but she didn't meet them. She couldn't bring herself to look at the knowledge in their hard black depths.

"What's happening, sweets?" he said. "Been out shopping?"

"Yes."

"Get anything good this time?"

"What do you mean by that?"

"At the grocery store," he said. "You know, anything on sale?"

That wasn't what he'd meant; Michele was certain of that. God, why didn't he go away and leave her alone? There was a knot in her stomach, almost as if she were pregnant with her fears.

But she was an actress, a good actress, and this was just another role for her to play. It was the only way she could get through situations like this; it was the only way she had been able to go through with each of her shoplifting forays. She made herself smile and meet his eyes. When she spoke again she put a note of intimacy into her voice.

"I really do have to run, Marco," she said. "I have an audition coming up this afternoon and I have to dress."

"Yeah?" Marco said. "What is it, an off-Broadway play?"

"Yes."

"Still nothing on the Big Street, huh?"

"That'll come later," she said. "I'll get my break one of these days."

"Sure you will. Just like I'm gonna get mine."

"That's right. We're both very good at what we do."

"You don't know the half of how good I am, sweets," Marco said. There was a leer in his voice, but Michele didn't react to it. She was into her role now. Her hands were steady again and the knot of fear in her stomach had diminished.

"No, I don't," she said. "I've never heard you or your combo play."

"You don't know what you've been missing. Come on down to Jazz Heaven in the Village; that's where we're blowing now. I'll fix you up with a table right in front."

"Well... maybe I'll do that."

He grinned again. "Hope you get the part today. Got to pay the rent, right? And you haven't worked in a while."

"I'm not hurting financially. My folks send me money from time to time."

"Sure they do," Marco said, grinning. "Catch you later."

"Later," she agreed.

He gave her a mock salute and went past her down the stoop. Michele let out an inaudible sigh, put her back to the street, and fumbled in her purse again for her key.

Upstairs in her spartan apartment, she put the bag of groceries on the kitchen counter. She had handled the situation with Marco fairly well, she thought. She *was* a good actress. It was maddening that audition after audition the past three months had come to nothing after the promising early stages of her career.

She remembered what Susan Sarandon had told her. Two years ago she had landed a small part in an off-Broadway show starring Susan—Michele and the famous actress had become friendly enough to be on a first-name basis—and Susan had assured her that she had more than enough talent to make it on the stage. All it took was one break, Susan had said; talent would take care of the rest. Michele was convinced that this was true, that all that stood between her and her career goals was one lucky break. Wasn't that the history of every successful actress?

The fact that circumstance had forced her to become a thief, then, was merely a compromise. It had been her only alternative, a necessary evil. How else could she maintain this apartment, keep herself in close proximity to the producers and directors, persevere until that one lucky break finally happened? Prostitution was unthinkable. And a menial job would have devoured her time and led nowhere.

Marco Pollo would never understand these things, of course. Neither would her family — or the police. Especially the police. But, then, why should they even try? It wasn't their job to delve into the psychology of crime or the complexity of a person's dreams. Theirs was a world of stark, clear rules that one either obeyed or disobeyed. A world of consequences.

Restlessly, Michele emptied the groceries from the bag and then poured a glass of milk. She didn't have another audition today; she had lied to Marco. But what if the phone had rung while she was out shopping? She hadn't wanted to go out, but she'd been hungry and there hadn't been anything in the fridge. She hadn't been gone more than twenty minutes. Still, her agent *could* have phoned with word of another casting call . . .

She hurried into the living room, to where the telephone sat on the Chinese chest a former boyfriend had given her. The receiver was in her hand, and she was just starting to dial her agent's number, when somebody rang the doorbell.

The sudden sound made her jump, then made her frown. Now who could that be? Marco again, come back to bother her? She put the telephone handset down, reluctantly, and crossed to the door. There was a peephole in it with a magnifying lens that let you see most of the hallway outside; she put one eye to it, squinting.

A sandy-haired man in his forties, dressed in a business suit, stood there. She had never seen him before. How had he gotten into the building? Visitors were supposed to ring the bell from the stoop outside . . . .

"Yes?" she called through the door. "What is it?"

The man drew something from his jacket pocket, held it up to the outer lens of the peephole so she could see what it was. A badge — a policeman's badge. "Detective Oxman,

Twenty-fourth Precinct," he said. "I'd like to have a few words with you, Miss Butler, if you don't mind."

Fear sparked in her. The police! Had they found out somehow about the ruby ring from Bloomingdale's? Was the detective here to arrest her?

"Miss Butler?"

"What do you want? Why are you here?"

"I'm investigating the homicide on Thursday night," he said. "I just want to ask you a few questions."

Relief came to her with the same abruptness as the fear. The shooting—of course. The police would be questioning residents of the block; they had done it before, after the previous two murders. She hadn't been thinking clearly. Guilty conscience. She had nothing to fear from this detective, nothing at all.

Michele composed herself. *Another role,* she thought, *that's all it is; another part to play.* She opened the chain lock and the dead-bolt lock, arranged her face into an expression of calm concern, and opened the door. "Come in, officer. I'm sorry I took so long."

"Quite all right," Detective Oxman said. He came in, glancing around at the Oriental prints on the walls, the Chinese chest, the bead curtains she had put up as a room divider, and then turned to face her as she closed the door. "Sorry to bother you. I came by yesterday, but you weren't home."

"No, I was out all day. I had an audition down in the Village. I'm an actress, you see."

"Ah."

"Yes. Won't you sit down?"

"Thank you."

"Can I get you anything? Some coffee?"

"No, nothing, thanks."

He waited until she had seated herself on the couch and then sat down in one of the chairs. His questions were simple and direct—had she seen or heard anything unusual on

Thursday night, had she noticed any strangers on the block, had she noticed anyone acting oddly, had she been acquainted with any of the three victims—and as she answered them she found herself relaxing. She wouldn't have thought she could sit here so calmly talking to a policeman the day after stealing a valuable ruby ring. It was training and talent that allowed her to do it.

I really am good, she thought once. *I really am.*

Susan had been right. She *was* going to make it. One day the lucky break would come and all her roles would be on a stage, behind the footlights, instead of out here in the real world. And when that happened, all the other things, the thefts and the guilt and the fear, would be forgotten segments in the part of Michele Butler, struggling actress, that she had once and for too long played.

10:50 A.M. — ART TOBIN

The undercover cop's name was Jack Kennebank. He was in his late twenties, he had long hair and a bushy beard, he was wearing dirty Levi's and a dirty sweatshirt with *Fordham* across the chest, and he smelled. As soon as Tobin sat down across from him in the cafeteria on Amsterdam, the smell came wafting over the table, a mixture of body odor, bad breath, and the gamy clothing. It offended Tobin, making his nose twitch to the point where he began breathing through his mouth.

The smell was one reason why he didn't like Kennebank, but it wasn't the main one. The main reason was that the kid was a hot dog. Kennebank had been on the force six years, the last two in plainclothes working undercover assignments, and already he'd been involved in three shooting scrapes, a knifing, a bar brawl, and a motorcycle chase after a drug dealer. And he had killed two men in the line of duty. He thought he was Supercop, a goddamn evil-smelling one-man crusade against crime. He attracted trouble the way California produce attracted the medfly.

Tobin hated hot dogs. He hated extremism of any kind, and Supercops were extremists; they rocked the boat, they thundered and blundered and eventually got themselves killed or maimed, and along the way they made life difficult for cops who did a better job working within the system. He wished Lieutenant Smiley had assigned somebody else to the undercover job. As it was, with Kennebank on the street, there was no telling what might happen. If anything bad went down, it was Tobin and Elliot Leroy who would take the flak; they were in charge of the investigation and that made them responsible.

Kennebank sat looking at Tobin steadily, waiting, very serious. At least he wasn't brash and flip, a smart-ass; he knew how to keep his mouth shut and his ears open. The problem was with his head. Get that straightened out, Kennebank might have the potential to be a good cop. If he lived long enough.

Tobin said, "You smell like a garbage bin. What's the idea, Jack?"

Kennebank shrugged. "Street image. I'm supposed to be an addict, right?"

"If the situation warrants it. But you don't have to be so obvious. Mostly straight people on that block, Jack; they see you looking like that, get a whiff of you, they'll run the other way. How're you going to find out anything if people won't talk to you?"

"I thought we were after a psycho," Kennebank said, frowning.

"We probably are. What does that have to do with the way you're dressed? The way you smell?"

"Well, I figured it has to be somebody shady. Somebody wiped out on drugs, maybe. I can get into the scene better this way, make a connection on the street. Hey, I've done it dozens of times before."

81

Tobin stared at him. These hot dogs—Jesus Christ! Kennebank was a head case, all right; what brains he had were stuffed up his ass. Every crime in the city was drug-related, as far as he was concerned. And everybody who blew somebody else away had underworld connections. But if there was one thing Tobin had learned in his thirty-two years on the force, it was patience. He said patiently, "The psycho could be *anybody*, Jack. Anybody on that block, anybody in Manhattan. A little old lady pulling the trigger because she thinks she sees Martians."

"Then you don't think the shootings are drug-related?"

"We haven't turned up anything to support that idea. You read the reports, didn't you? Nothing about drugs in the background of any of the victims."

"The psycho could still be a hype," Kennebank insisted.

Some of Tobin's patience was starting to slip; he made an effort to hang onto it. *What we have here,* he thought, *is a reversal of racial stereotypes. Intelligent black man, the authority figure, trying to talk to a stubborn, slow-witted white menial—a white nigger, by God.* White niggers were the worst kind. Tobin had met a lot of them in his time; he knew all about them, he knew enough to write a book called *The White Nigger in New York City.* Only problem was, who would be willing to publish it?

"If you've got preconceived ideas about this case, Jack," he said slowly, "maybe you're not the man for the job. Maybe I ought to ask the lieutenant to send somebody else in."

Kennebank frowned again and looked wounded. "I don't have any preconceived ideas."

"Then how come you keep harping about drugs?"

"Hey, I'm not harping about drugs. I only thought—"

"Don't think, Jack," Tobin said. "Just do what you're told and don't make waves. No hot-dogging."

Kennebank bristled. "I'm not a hot dog."

Yes, you are, Tobin thought. *Big white hot dog wrapped up in a Manhattan bun, and one of these days somebody is liable to take a bite out of you.* But he didn't say it. He said, "Just stay out of trouble. If you stumble on anything to do with drugs, make a report; no arrests. We're after a psycho who shot three men and that's all we're after. Understood?"

"Yeah," Kennebank said. "Understood."

"Good. Now where do you live?"

"The lieutenant made arrangements for a vacant apartment at twelve-forty West Ninety-eighth — "

"I know that; that's not what I meant. Where do you *live?*"

Another frown. "Down in the Village, on Perry. Why?"

"Because I want you to grab a cab, go there and take a bath and change your clothes. Trim that beard a little too. *In*conspicuous, Jack, that's how I want you to look."

Kennebank didn't like the idea. Tobin could see him stewing about it, maybe thinking of registering a complaint with Lieutenant Smiley. But he wouldn't do it. He had ambitions, and he knew that the lieutenant had given Tobin and Elliot Leroy carte blanche on this case. Tobin watched him struggling his way to an understanding of that, an acceptance of it. The bearded face smoothed into a neutral expression and Kennebank shrugged.

"All right," he said. "If that's the way you want it."

"That's the way I want it. The way I also want it is for you to contact either me or Oxman if you come up with anything promising. Don't pursue it yourself until you check with us. Don't confront anybody, don't identify yourself to anybody. Eyes and ears — that's all you're on the block for."

"Okay. Clear enough."

Tobin nodded. *It better be,* he thought. *It just better be.*

When the hot dog was gone, Tobin got a cup of coffee and took it to a different table to avoid the lingering after-smell Kennebank had left behind. He still didn't like the idea of Kennebank being on the block, cleaned up or not. He'd have preferred somebody else, but Lieutenant Smiley had told him earlier that nobody else was available. Kennebank hadn't been in the squadroom then and hadn't shown up by the time Tobin left for West Ninety-eighth; that was why Tobin had met him here at the cafeteria. If Kennebank *had* been around, they could have gotten the clothing thing settled at the precinct house.

Wasted time. Tobin hated that, too. There were a lot of things he hated, he realized—too many things, maybe. But he kept them all locked up inside, hidden from the world. His father had taught him that. His father was a man who had really hated: the white world and the white prejudice that forced him to work as a janitor, to live in a roach-infested Harlem tenement. Tobin hated those things too, but instead of letting the hatred eat him up inside, the way his father had done, letting it turn him into a bitter drunk and a dead man at forty-nine, he had set out to do something about it. Joined the NAACP, joined the police force. Make the changes from within, that was his philosophy. There were some who had accused him of being an Uncle Tom, selling out to the white Establishment, but that was the furthest thing from the truth. He had never been a Tom, never once bent under the prejudice, never once compromised himself or his beliefs. He had *used* the white Establishment, made it bend to *his* benefit and, by extension, the benefit of his race. That was what made him a proud man and a good cop.

He finished his coffee, still worrying a little over that jerk-off Kennebank, and then left the cafeteria and headed back to rendezvous with Elliot Leroy.

THE COLLIER TAPES

Who am I?

Who is Lewis B. Collier?

Someday, perhaps, after my death—for even gods must eventually perish—these tapes will become a matter of public record. It is with that possibility in mind that I now offer the essential answer to the question of who I am.

84

To begin with, we must consider the famous insane and now dead American poet, X. I will call him only X. *All* poets are X. They find that out slowly and painfully, but I divined it from the beginning and exercised caution.

X began his academic life as a twenty-two-year-old instructor at Harvard, and within three years he became a tenured associate professor. That was impressive, especially since X did not even have a graduate degree. Of course, that was in the forties, when things in academia were somewhat looser.

Five years later, under rather strained circumstances, X resigned and went to the University of Michigan as an associate professor. With him went the redheaded bitch temptress who had prompted his troubles at Harvard. At Michigan, X missed tenure by an eyelash after three years of probation and subsequently went to the Iowa Writers Workshop, again as an associate professor. Drink had by this time begun to affect him in ways tragic and visible, and the redhead had been traded for a blonde, two brunettes, and finally a bearded graduate student. X left Iowa and went to the University of Alabama on a three-year contract. At the end of that time, and of several hundred bottles of whiskey, he traveled to Drexel on a one-year adjunct. And after that, he went to Colby College as the assistant to the head of the writing program.

By this time X was no longer young or a poet of promise. He had returned to his two true loves — another redhead and Bombay gin.

In the early sixties, after his thunderous dismissal from Colby, X ended up teaching in the extension division of New York University, a night course in creative writing. And then — ah, this many people might remember — X ended his descent in spectacular fashion, immolating himself and his woman in a Times Square hotel.

The point is, I learned from X; I vowed to become a poet of a different sort. I thought I understood the problem. If

85

you *stayed* at the adjunct level you had no heights from which
to fall and you tended to make less trouble for yourself; also, you were outside the politics of the department and, unlike X, your social life could be your own
business.

So I obtained my Master's Degree and settled into what I
liked to think of as the underside of academia. I had slight
standards, but those standards were absolute. And that was
the key. X's problem had been that he was a promising poet
and a classic alcoholic, a sexual adventurer of catholicity if
not precision; he had adhered to no standards, not in his
rhyme scheme, not in his sexual or his professional life, and
at last it had destroyed him.

I spent my days marking freshman themes written by
disadvantaged youths with burning eyes who were fixated on
computer programming, and I worked on my unpublished
novel while I lived modestly, and I thought I had my life
under control.

I made two mistakes, however.

One was not foreseeing the withdrawal of federal funding
of many of the programs through which I was hired. The
other mistake was Darlene.

The contraction of the universities I might have dealt
with, but Darlene was beyond my powers to cope. She was
an intense girl with a yearning for self-improvement of the
creative sort. Soon after our marriage she became pregnant,
had an abortion, and then informed me *ex post facto* of these
two occurrences. She also informed me that I was a pig and
a liar and an exploiter, among other things, and left me and
the New York metropolitan area itself to live in a feminist
collective in San Francisco. Years later, the collective
became a news story in the *Times* because it had been found
to harbor several sixties fugitives who had operated a bomb
factory. Darlene was among those arrested. But that was her
problem, not mine.

My problem was that I was turned down by the Columbia

School of General Studies, then dropped after a one-semester engagement by a federal arts program funded through NYU. In short, I was out of a job and quite bitter about it.

It was the trust fund that bailed me out. My mother had hoarded it in New York's Chemical Bank, as she had hoarded love in the vault of her heart until her death, and on my thirty-fifth birthday I received enough money not to have to worry about finances for years to come. She who had been the first of X's redheads, and with him sown the seed that was to be Lewis B. Collier, warned me of the doom and dissolution of all poets, and provided for me.

After receiving my inheritance, I stopped sending resumés and studying the Sunday *Times* section advertising faculty positions. I moved into this high rise apartment on the wrong side of the Hudson. Like X, I began to drink. Like X, I began to atrophy.

And then one day, on an impulse I now know was fate, I bought the telescope I saw displayed in the window of one of those difficult to categorize shops on East Fifty-seventh Street.

Soon afterward, I realized that I wasn't like X, who is rather famous in the academic world for his long downward odyssey to oblivion. X fell a long way and learned little; I, on the other hand, moved within a very narrow range and learned quite a lot.

Unlike X, I have not dwindled nor will I dwindle to nothingness. It is not death which I embrace, which fascinates me. The pleasure I derive from bestowing death on the wicked is quite apart from the physical sensations during and after the act. Only the smallest of mortals would think otherwise. It is not that with the death of Charles Unger I discovered that I enjoy ending life — the sensual absorption of the powerless by the powerful, the ultimate communication with the victim.

No, not at all. Unlike X, whose poetry is that of the futile

and the impotent and the damned, I can act out not only my
own destiny but the destiny of others. Because unlike X, I
am destiny. I have been transformed and gifted with true
and total freedom and command.

I do *not* kill because I enjoy it.

I have proved that, haven't I?

12:35 P.M. — MARIAN SINGER

She had not gone to Brooklyn to visit her sister; she'd lied to
Wally about that, the first major lie she had ever told him.
Instead she had gone to Otto Kreig's flat on East Ninth in
the Village.

Marian had never done anything like this before, not once
in all the years she had been married, and she'd been very
tense. Her fidelity hadn't been a matter of morals—she had
helled around quite a bit in her college days—and it hadn't
been that she'd felt any great loyalty to Wally. God knew, he
had given her enough provocation: the way he mistreated
her, ignored her physical and emotional needs; the fact that
at the best of times he simply was not a very good lover. No,
she had remained faithful because she had never met anyone
else who interested her. And after she started to put on
weight . . . well, she was afraid of rejection. She doubted if
anyone would want an overweight, sagging-breasted woman
pushing forty.

Then she had found out Wally was seeing another
woman, that ripe doe-eyed bitch who lived across the street.
She'd seen them together in Riverside Park one day, holding
hands, snuggling up to each other. At first she'd been hurt,
then angry, then resigned. What good it do to
confront him? He might actually walk out on her, as he'd
been threatening to do for years, and then where would she
be? She needed a man, even a poor excuse for one like
Wally. Too much time had passed; she would not do well
alone. So she had determined to grin and bear it, let the

affair run its course. Wally knew which side his bread was buttered on. He wouldn't willingly leave her for a cheap waitress with no money and no prospects.

Even knowing about his affair, she might have remained faithful if she hadn't met Otto two weeks later. It had been at a showing downtown of a prominent sculptor's work that she had gone to alone because Wally wasn't interested. Otto was a German immigrant who had moved to New York from Dusseldorf a few years before — a big powerful man in his forties, with enormous hands and sad blue eyes and a pleasant smile. Like her, he was a sculptor, although he didn't have to eke out a living at it the way she did; he was independently wealthy, the son of a successful furniture manufacturer. He had shown surprising interest in her that day, and later, when she brought some samples to his flat, he had shown equally surprising interest in her work.

A reciprocal affinity had developed in her. She felt flattered by his attention and his praise. He was such a kind, gentle man, self-effacing about his own work — unnecessarily so, she felt. His sculptures, mostly of animals with a touching aura of sadness about them, may have been a little crude, but they showed a sensitivity that she had never been able to capture in her abstracts and commercial pieces.

At first her feelings for Otto hadn't been sexual. Then, one night, she'd had an erotic dream about him, and after that she found herself wondering at odd moments what it would be like to sleep with him. But he had never made a pass at her, never touched her in any way; he was always the perfect gentleman. And of course she could never bring herself to take the initiative. Whenever she saw him — no more than once a week, sometimes at his flat for coffee, sometimes at this or that café in the Village — they talked about art, about neutral topics. Once in a while he seemed to look at her in a special way, as if he, too, wished there could be something more between them, but she could never be sure. She kept telling herself that her fantasies were silly and girlish, classic maunderings of a fat, unfulfilled woman in mid-life, almost laughable. She was lucky to have a friend like Otto, and his friendship was all she had a right to expect. All that had changed this morning. She had awakened next to Wally, looked at him snoring beside her, and remembered the nasty things he had said to her yesterday; then she thought about the killings on the block, the suppressed fear that was in her and that she had seen in the faces of her neighbors. An overwhelming need to get away from there, away from Wally, had seized her, followed by an acute desire to see Otto. As soon as Wally awoke, she had made up the story about visiting her sister, left the apartment, and taken the subway straight to the Village.

Otto had seemed pleased at her unexpected arrival. He'd made a breakfast of hotcakes and sausages for her, listened to her pour out her fears, comforted her. She felt better after that and asked to see his latest sculpture. Now they were standing in his workroom under the skylight, close together but not quite touching, looking at the half-finished fawn with its sad eyes.

When he turned to her finally, the look in his eyes was like that of the fawn, but tempered with something more, something deep and tender. *"Liebchen,"* he murmured.

She couldn't believe her ears. *Darling,* the word meant *darling.* Wally had never called her darling; he had never called her anything except bitch and fat cow. Inside her there was a sudden sensation of melting, and the next thing she knew she was in Otto's arms, kissing him, clinging to him.

When the kiss ended she was trembling with a mixture of fear and tension and desire. "Otto," she whispered, "take me to bed. . ."

"No. No, Marian."

At first she thought it was a rejection. She was a fat woman and nobody's darling, he'd let her kiss him only because he felt sorry for her. . .fitful thoughts, turning her as rigid as one of her abstracts. But his big hands remained on her—gentle, so gentle. And he was whispering to her again, saying other things she could scarcely believe.

"I want you so much," he was saying, "but it must not be this way. You are upset, *meine Teure,* you only turn to me because of your anguish. It is not me, Otto Kreig, you truly want. . . ."

"But it is, Otto, it *is* you."

"I am so afraid it is not."

"Afraid?"

"Dear Marian, *schöne* Marian. . . I want you always, not just for today. I—I love you."

The tension left her suddenly and completely; so did the doubts about him and about this moment. It was the truth, and she felt limp with it, a little awed by it. This was what she had wanted all her life, only this. The tenderness, the gentleness, the genuine caring, all the things Wally had never given her, all the things she had never known and never hoped to know.

"Yes," she said, weeping now, "love me, please just love me. . . ."

1:00 P.M. — E.L. OXMAN

He spent the last twenty minutes of the noon hour comparing notes with Tobin. Neither of them had turned up anything new; they kept walking into blank walls no matter who they talked to. It wasn't a conspiracy of silence, an unwillingness of people to get involved with the police. It was simply that nobody knew anything about the homicides. The psycho, whoever he or she was, had so far done his killing with impunity and without making any apparent mistakes. It was frustrating, and a little frightening even to Oxman. He could understand how the people who lived here felt. A thing like this frayed everybody's nerves, made even the fittest in this little corner of the jungle glance over their shoulders and start jumping at shadows.

Tobin recounted his briefing session with Jack Kennebank, and Oxman didn't blame him for being worried. He didn't like hot dogs any better than Artie did. They would have to keep a tight rein on Kennebank, make sure he didn't screw up. The way feelings were running on the block, one bad blunder could unleash a chain reaction of panic.

Just before they split up again, Oxman phoned the Twenty-fourth to see if Lieutenant Smiley had anything new. He didn't. A computer check of known criminals and individuals with a history of mental disorders who might have lived on the block at one time had turned up a few names; another team of detectives was checking them out. But none of the individuals looked promising. It was a longshot anyway, Oxman thought. Why would a former resident of West Ninety-eighth decide to start shooting people in his old neighborhood?

Oxman came back down the block, hesitated in front of 1276, and then took the seven steps to the brownstone's concrete stoop. He scanned the names on the tarnished brass bank of mailboxes. But he knew which one he wanted long before he read the card that said *3-D Jennifer Crane.*

All morning he had fought off the urge to see her again. But it was a losing battle. The attraction was there, damn it; it was strong, and he couldn't deny it. She was a desirable woman, all the more so for her icy New York veneer. And he was sure there was a spark of interest on her part as well; he had glimpsed it in the blue-green mystery of her eyes, heard it in the way she'd asked him if he would be talking to her again, felt it in the way she'd stood close to him in the doorway just before he left her.

But what was it, really, this mutual attraction? A physical thing, that was all. If it led anywhere, it would be to nothing more than an impersonal roll or two in the hay. He would be just another conquest, another statistic on her private scorecard. He had seen hundreds if not thousands of

Jennifer Cranes in his life. She was like so many New York women, as if somewhere they were manufactured using the same mold. They all wore the same jaded mask and played it light and loose, and you couldn't chip away their veneer no matter how hard you tried. Ice queens. That was his private name for the Jennifer Cranes: ice queens.

What would it be like to go to bed with her? he wondered. *What was it like for Martin Simmons on Thursday night?* The thoughts made him feel uncomfortable. Too long without sex, that was his problem. How long had it been this time...a month? That was too long for any man to go without release. Who could blame him if he did tumble into bed with another woman, a woman like Jennifer Crane?

Well, he knew the answer to that. Beth would blame him, and so would Internal Affairs and the Board of Police Commissioners. Beth, with her inexplicable skull-splitting headaches, running up hundreds of dollars in medical bills while forcing him to live a life of near celibacy. Internal Affairs with their rules about police morals—if they found out about any unprofessional conduct on Oxman's part, they would recommend to the Board of Commissioners that he be indefinitely suspended from the force, without pay.

So hands and mind off Jennifer Crane, he thought. It was absurd that he should even toy with the idea. He had never, not once in nineteen years of marriage, been unfaithful to Beth. What good would it do to start now?

He made himself look more closely at the other names on the mailboxes. Royce, Munoz, Hiller, Pollosetti, Singer, Coombs, Butler, Hayfield. He had talked to all of them already, or Tobin had. No point in bothering any of them again, going over barren ground that had already been covered.

3-D Jennifer Crane.

She's probably not even home, he thought, gone off to *Vogue* for another set of meetings. And then, in spite of himself and all the mental arguments, he reached out and almost violently jabbed the button beside her name.

Thirty seconds passed in silence. He was just starting to turn away, with a vague sense of relief, when the intercom unit clicked and he heard her voice say, "Yes?"

"Detective Oxman," he said. "May I come up?"

An almost imperceptible pause. Then, "Of course," and the buzzer on the thick, enameled door began to whirr.

Oxman pushed inside. He was struck again by the familiar apartment building smells: stale cooking odors, pine disinfectant, human effluvium. "Book you," a piece of censored graffiti on the lobby wall proclaimed. The elevator was on one of the upper floors; instead of waiting for it, he mounted two eighteen-step flights of stairs and made his way down the hallway to 3-D.

Jennifer opened the door immediately when he knocked. As he had yesterday, Oxman took her in with a policeman's encompassing glance. She was appealing, all right: finely boned face, long auburn hair, narrow, graceful shoulders, ample breasts and a slender dancer's body — though her calves were unlike a dancer's, nicely curved but not muscular. She was wearing a pair of denim pants with the cuffs rolled up to just below the knee, and a light green blouse with the top three buttons undone. There was no brassiere under the blouse and the swell of her breasts was clearly visible. He wondered if she always wore her blouse open like that, or if she had unfastened the buttons for his benefit.

"Come in, E.L.," she said. She was smiling, but it was an unreadable smile, showing him nothing of what went on behind it. "You don't mind if I call you E.L.?"

"No," he said, "I don't mind."

She closed and locked the door. "Sit down, if you like."

He sat on the same cream-colored sofa he had occupied yesterday. She took the small beige chair opposite him, clasped her hands over one knee. It was bright in there; the net drapes over the windows were open and slanted sunlight poured into the room, glinted off the chrome frames of the

magazine illustrations on the walls. The sunshine touched
her face as well, gave it a glowing quality. Like sunlight
reflecting off glacial ice, he thought.

She was thirty-one, according to the information she had
given Gaines and Holroyd, but she could pass for twenty-
one; only her eyes, cool green eyes that picked up the green
of her blouse and shone with the color of the sea, betrayed
her age. Old eyes, knowing eyes, falsely placid. What swam
beneath that calm surface? Oxman wondered. He was surprised to find himself feeling a little sorry for her. He knew what
this city could do to a young woman like this; the destruction
could be insidious yet thorough. And yet that only added to
her allure, the aura of icy sensuality she projected.

She smiled at him again. Everything about her was
transformed when she smiled. The coldness seemed to fade;
she appeared older, more her proper age, but less sharply
hewn and much more attractive. "What did you want to see
me about?" she asked.

"A few more questions," he said vaguely. He felt awkward
being here with her, awkward under the scrutiny of her
gaze. *She knows how I feel,* he thought. *She knows.*

"Have you found out anything more about the murders?"

"Not yet, no. I thought you might have remembered
something you overlooked yesterday."

"I'm afraid I haven't."

Oxman shifted position; it was a comfortable couch, but
not for him. "You look well rested," he said. "No trouble
sleeping last night?"

"Not really. Should I have had trouble sleeping?"

"If you felt anything for Simmons, you might have."

"I told you yesterday, I barely knew the man."

"But you were intimate with him just a few minutes before
he was killed."

"You don't have to know someone to have sex with
him," Jennifer said. "Sex is a simple matter of biology. Or
are you old-fashioned about things like that?"

"Maybe I am."

"That's too bad."

"Why is it too bad?"

A shrug. "I prefer men with a more modern outlook."

She's fencing with me, Oxman thought. He didn't like it; he didn't like women who played games. And yet, perversely, it also excited him because he sensed an underlying purpose to the game, an open invitation. The excitement in turn made him angry, at himself and at her.

He said a little sharply, "How about guilt? Don't you feel anything along those lines?"

Something flickered in her eyes, behind the mask, but it was too brief for him to get a reading on it. "Why should I feel guilt?"

"Simmons would be alive now if you'd let him spend the night with you," Oxman said. "Or if you'd never brought him here in the first place."

"If I'd had any idea of what was going to happen, I would certainly not have brought him here, nor would I have asked him to leave as I did. But I didn't have any idea. I can't be held responsible for the actions of others, for something beyond my control."

"That's a pretty callous way of looking at a man's death."

"It's a callous world, E.L. You ought to know that if anyone does."

Oxman didn't say anything. He knew it, all right.

"You must have seen a great deal of death in your job," Jennifer said. "You've probably killed someone yourself— haven't you?"

"Yes. Once in the line of duty."

"How do *you* deal with death? Do you grieve for the person you killed, all the dead people you've seen? Or do you wall it off, view it as a simple fact of life?"

"I wall it off. But that doesn't mean I don't have a lot of sleepless nights."

"Perhaps I'll have a sleepless night or two myself. Does it matter to you either way?"

"I suppose not."

"Life goes on," she said. "And I have to live mine my way; everybody does, including you."

"Tell me something else, then."

"If I can."

"Are you afraid, Jennifer?" It was the first time he had used her name and he tasted it as he said it; the taste was bittersweet. "Three murders on this block in the space of two weeks—does that frighten you?"

"Yes, it frightens me."

"You don't act frightened. You only act cold."

"Is that what you think? That I'm cold, that I don't have feelings?"

"I don't know what to think about you."

"Then don't try, E.L. You don't know me and I'm sure you never will."

"Does anybody know you? Do you know yourself?"

She laughed with what he took to be wry humor. "Good Lord," she said, "psychology? I didn't know policemen were trained in that these days."

"All right," he said, "I'm sorry. It's none of my business." He got to his feet. "I'd better move along."

"No more questions?"

"I guess not."

"But you might have more later?"

"Maybe. Probably not, though."

He took a step away from the couch. Jennifer made no move to get up from the chair; he could find his own way out this time. He crossed to the door, opened the locks. His hand was on the knob when she spoke again behind him.

"I'll be at the Tavern on the Green tomorrow afternoon," she said. "Sketching for a magazine layout. I should be there from twelve o'clock on."

Oxman turned. "Why tell me that?"

"I thought you'd want to know. In case you need to see me again."

Unmistakable invitation; he saw it in her eyes and in her ice queen smile. The palms of his hands were suddenly damp. But he said, "I don't think I will."

"Suit yourself. I'll be there, though, in any case."

"You'd better lock your door after I go," he said gruffly.

"It's always better to play it safe."

"Is it?" she said. "All right, E.L. Good-bye for now."

Oxman went out, shut the door harder than was necessary, and took the stairs down to the lobby. The sweat on him when he stepped outside had nothing to do with the heat.

3:45 P.M. — WILLIE LORSEC

In the basement of 1276 West Ninety-eighth, Lorsec stood rummaging through the big fifty-gallon receptacles under the garbage chute. Richard Corales had given him permission to do that any time he cared to, and he was grateful. He liked Richard. Slow-witted, yes, but gentle and kind and forever willing to help a friend. Richard's passion for gin rummy was a little wearying, particularly now that this morning's two-hour session had extended his winning streak to a phenomenal thirty-seven hands. But that was a minor flaw. All in all, he was a good man and a good friend.

Lorsec fished up a black trash bag tied with white twine. That would belong to the Singers, he thought, and there would probably be little of interest inside. People packaged and disposed of their trash in different and distinctive ways; he could tell just by looking at a bag who it belonged to. Trash, he reflected, as he often did, was endlessly fascinating. One could find all sorts of valuable and revealing items hidden away in it.

With dexterous fingers he opened the Singers' bag and

sifted through the contents. As he had anticipated, there was little of interest. More beer cans than usual; Wally Singer appeared to be consuming large quantities of beer lately. An obnoxious man, Singer. Too bad. His wife seemed a decent sort and deserved better. There was something a little sad about her portion of the garbage: empty chocolate boxes, tear- and mucus-stained tissues, other evidence of an unhappy woman.

Lorsec dropped the Singers' bag into another receptacle and reached again into the one under the chute. The bag he came up with this time was cheap and dark green, tied with a notched plastic fastener. Michele Butler's trash. He opened the fastener and started to search among the sparse contents.

The upper basement door clicked open just then and he heard descending footfalls on the stairs. He looked up. A lithe, muscular man appeared, carrying a bulky trash bag that would be, Lorsec thought immediately, too full to have fit inside the chute. He recognized the man as Benny Hiller, apartment 3-A.

Hiller didn't see him until he reached the bottom of the stairs. Then he paused in a startled way, frowned, and crossed the cement floor warily, holding the trash bag out at his side as though prepared to use it as a weapon.

"What the hell are you doing here?" he demanded.

"I have permission," Lorsec said.

"Yeah? To do what?"

"Hunt for redeemable used merchandise. That's my business."

Hiller's narrowed eyes took in Lorsec's shabby clothing, his unkempt hair, the burlap sack slung over his shoulder. "A goddamn junk collector," he said. "Who gave you the permission? That numbhead Corales?"

"Yes. He's my friend."

"I'll bet. Where is he? In his apartment?"

"No. He had an errand to run over on Broadway."

"And you took the opportunity to start pawing through the garbage. You been here before, doing that?"

"Would it bother you if I have, Mr. Hiller?"

"How do you know my name?"

"I've seen you from time to time. Richard told me who you are."

"He did, did he? Well, who the hell are *you?*"

"My name is Willie Lorsec."

"You live around here?"

"In the next block."

"Yeah? I never saw you before."

"I've lived in the neighborhood quite some time, Mr. Hiller. Perhaps you haven't looked closely enough. Or perhaps it's because you sleep days and work nights."

Hiller's alert eyes got even narrower. "Corales tell you that too?"

"He did."

"What else did he tell you about me?"

"Just that you're employed as a cook at an all-night café."

"Corales talks too much. He ought to mind his own business. So should you."

"I was minding my business," Lorsec said. "That, as I told you, is why I'm here."

"Yeah, well, I don't like it. You don't live in this building; you got no right to be in here alone."

"I'm not bothering anyone, Mr. Hiller."

"You're bothering *me*," Hiller said. "There's too much crazy shit going on on this block as it is."

"You mean the homicides?"

"That's just what I mean. Now suppose you go crawl into the garbage in your own building. And stay there; don't come back."

Lorsec managed to curb his temper. He said evenly, "I don't see that you're in a position of authority here, Mr. Hiller. Richard Corales is the superintendent of this building—"

100

BILL PRONZINI AND JOHN LUTZ

"Corales is a half-wit and I don't care if he gave you permission in writing. You won't have it again, I'll see to that." He took a step closer. "Go on, get out of here. I mean it, Lorsec — move."

"And if I choose not to?"

Hiller made a threatening gesture with his trash bag. "Try me," he said. There was no bluff in his voice, only a kind of controlled savagery.

Lorsec shrugged. "All right, Mr. Hiller, I'll go. But not because I'm afraid of you. Only because I dislike trouble."

He turned, walked across to the stairs that led up to the alley door. There were dead-bolt locks on the door; he slid them back, went out, and shut the door behind him. Inside, he heard Hiller come over and jam the dead-bolts back into place, then the sound of his footsteps retreating.

He stood for a time in the sticky heat of the alleyway, thinking about Hiller. What was in that bulky trash bag? he wondered. Something interesting, he was certain of that, or Hiller would not have acted as he had. The fact that he didn't want anyone rummaging through the contents had been written plainly on his face.

Lorsec decided he would have to have a quiet talk with Richard. Whether Hiller liked it or not, he intended to pay another visit to the basement and the waste receptacles. And to learn what was in that trash bag.

Perhaps it would turn out to be something *very* interesting, indeed.

4:10 P.M. — BETH OXMAN

As she walked down the Fifth Avenue sidewalk, Beth could almost feel the evil emanating from the city. The juxtaposition of great wealth and abject poverty in Manhattan always fascinated her. It was the whole world jammed into one seething, fermenting mass. The harried-looking business types who passed her barely glanced in her

101

direction and would step around or over her if suddenly she dropped dead of a heart attack. The tourists were too busy gawking to notice anything but the traditional sights. The cheap hustlers running three-card monte games or hawking inferior clothing with expensive labels sewn in, the street vendors selling their poisonous food, the panhandlers — these were the only individuals in the crowd who actually *saw* Beth, and then only as a potential sucker.

The city was what had made E.L. what he was — though God knew he'd had a choice — and what had ruined their marriage. If only years ago he had listened to her and decided not to go on being a policeman, to study law instead, everything would be different, and so much better.

Beth stopped on the corner of Fifth and Forty-seventh Street and glanced at her watch. More than fifteen minutes remained before her appointment with Dr. Hardin. A man in a blue business suit callously brushed her aside with his shoulder as he hurried to cross the street against the traffic light. A lanky youth lugging a huge blaring radio on a shoulder strap bumped her with his elbow as he turned the corner. She pursed her lips, controlling her annoyance, and began walking again, moving with the masses across Fifth Avenue.

On impulse she decided to stop in a stylish little ice cream parlor for a chocolate sundae before seeing Dr. Hardin. To hell with the calories: This was something she deserved.

It was crowded. Beth walked to the small tables beyond the counter and sat down, prudently placing her purse in the chair next to her where she could watch it from the corner of her eye as she scanned the people in the restaurant. They were like the people on the street, only perhaps generally better dressed. She didn't like them any better indoors than out.

While she was waiting for the sundae to arrive, one of her headaches flared up. She reached into her purse for the small vial of pills Dr. Hardin had given her, and, contrary to his instructions for the days she was to visit him, shook out one of the capsules and washed it down with a sip of the water the waitress had left on the table.

Her vision wavered with the pain that seemed to pull apart the flesh of her forehead and expose a split and throbbing skull. She lifted the glass to her lips again, sipped, then pressed its chilled roundness to her forehead. That didn't seem to help; nothing helped, not even the pills. A migraine headache wasn't like an ordinary headache; it had to do with the swelling of blood vessels in the head, the building of pressure on raw nerves. Only a person who had experienced such a headache could imagine the pain.

E.L. couldn't, that was certain. More than anything else he was the *cause* of her headaches, her nervous condition. He had never even pretended to consider yielding to her wishes that he take up another profession. During the past nineteen years she had spent most of her nights alone, worrying about who would take care of her if anything happened to him, wishing that she could leave the apartment and go to a nice restaurant, or maybe to the theater, like other men's wives. But a policeman's hours, and salary, prevented her from enjoying the pleasures of life that by all reason should have been hers. Too many nights of sitting and moping, a phone call away from widowhood, had done this to her. E.L. had done this to her. Why should she give him pleasure, grant him her body for his use whenever *he* wanted it? No, she obtained her own most intense pleasure another way now, a more subtle way.

The waitress returned with her sundae. And miraculously, with Beth's first spoonful of ice cream and rich chocolate sauce, her headache disappeared.

E.L. didn't believe the headaches were of physical origin. She knew that; he'd as much as told her so, trying to get her to see a shrink, as if he thought she was a mental case. Well, let him think it. What did it matter? She was the only one who understood just how physical her headaches were. You could certainly tell the difference between physical and imagined pain if it were occurring in your own body. Well, she wasn't *quite* the only person who understood. Dr. Hardin knew her pain was real. He wasn't like the other physicians who had recommended seeing another sort of doctor. Dr. Hardin was expensive, but that was because he knew his business. Instead of solitude and lies, he prescribed medicine. Wasn't that what a doctor was for, to heal the sick by administering to the body? The very suggestion that her sick spells were not actually migraine headaches was infuriating as well as false.

Beth realized that she was devouring the sundae as if she were in an eating contest. Already it was three-fourths consumed. She forced herself to place her spoon in the dish between bites, to make her self-indulgent treat last as long as possible. She still had time, and even if she were late, Dr. Hardin would understand. He always did.

Later that evening, when she returned home, E.L. was waiting for her, sitting at the kitchen table eating a roast beef TV dinner — the kind with the watery mashed potatoes and dyed bright green peas. Trying to make her feel guilty for not being there when he got home, no doubt; he was always trying to do that to her, after ruining her life.

"What did Dr. Hardin say?" he asked, feigning interest, hunched like a weary vulture over his dinner.

Beth tossed her light blazer onto a chair near the kitchen door, walked all the way into the kitchen and opened the freezer compartment of the refrigerator. "He said I was about the same," she told him. "He gave me some more medicine."

"What kind of medicine?"

"How should I know?" Beth snapped. "I don't read Latin."

"You don't have to read Latin, Beth; all you have to do is ask what's in the prescription and what it's for."

"It's for my headaches."

He put down the roll he was about to tear in half. "Hardin has the reputation of a Doctor Feelgood," he said.

"And what is that?"

"A doctor more interested in getting you to come back than in making you well."

"That's nonsense," Beth said. "I should know, if anyone does."

E.L. nodded, which meant that he was refusing to continue the discussion. It was one of his more infuriating traits, leading her into an argument and then abruptly withdrawing after he had angered her. Once she had been tolerant of that in him, but no more.

"I'd have put a dinner in for you," he said, "only I wasn't sure what time you'd be home."

She decided not to answer him. She placed a turkey dinner in the oven, adjusted the thermostat to 350 degrees, and then went into the bedroom to change into slacks and a blouse.

E.L. followed her, stood close behind her and watched in the dresser mirror as she slipped off her skirt and panty hose. "I thought about waking you last night when I got home," he said.

"I'm glad you didn't. I wasn't feeling well."

He touched his fingertips to the back of her neck, caressed lightly. "How do you feel tonight?"

"I don't have a headache." She watched him smile, saw the look she knew too well come into his eyes. "But the medicine I took at Dr. Hardin's office made me a little sick to my stomach. I think I might have diarrhea."

"Beth . . ."

"I don't want to talk right now," she said.

He withdrew his hand, nodding. She saw the change in his eyes, the fading of desire. And something else this time, a curious kind of resolve, as if he'd just reached some sort of decision. He left the bedroom, not in anger but with a sort of resigned purpose.

105

The hell with him, she thought as she stepped into her slacks and worked them up over her ample hips. *Let him suffer for a change. It's his turn now.*

11:15 P.M. — CINDY WILSON

She was exhausted when she left the restaurant. Saturday nights were always the busiest and tonight it had been a madhouse, all the tables full from seven o'clock on, customers demanding attention every second. The muscles in her legs felt knotted; it was going to be so good to sit down in a taxi, and even better to crawl into bed. She was too tired to spend another sleepless night worrying about the murders. She'd fall asleep right away tonight.

And she could sleep late in the morning too, stay in bed all day if she felt like it. Sunday was her day off. *Never on Sunday,* she thought, and smiled, and then giggled as she remembered that she had spent most of *this* day in bed with Wally. That Wally, he was insatiable. She had never known a man who liked sex as much as he did. He was really good, much better than Vern, much better than any of the other men she'd been with before and after her marriage. He knew how to arouse a woman, saying fuck all the time, getting her so hot she thought she would burn up sometimes.

She wondered if she really loved Wally. She told him she did when they were in bed, and she felt she did at other times too, but the rest of the time she wasn't sure. Maybe it was just sex. He was attractive and such a good artist and he treated her well enough, but he had that frump of a wife. It made her a little uneasy to be seeing a married man, particularly because there didn't seem to be much future in it.

Oh, he talked about leaving his frump and moving in with her, marrying her, but that was just talk. She'd heard that kind of talk before. He didn't have any money and neither did she, not enough to support both of them. And he was afraid of Vern too. He probably didn't love her; she couldn't remember him ever saying he did, not even once. Just sex for him, she supposed, although she was pretty sure he did care for her at least a little bit. That was the way men were. But it was all right. It was such terrific sex, and they had fun together in other ways, and she was learning all kinds of things about art and the intellectual side of life. So what if he didn't love her? So what if she decided she didn't love him? You had to live for the moment, you had to enjoy yourself the best way you could, for as long as you could. It was just all right the way it was.

Getting a cab on Saturday nights could be a problem, but she was lucky tonight. One was just letting off a fare when she came out of the restaurant, and she hurried over and slid inside before anybody else could beat her to it. She let out a sigh as she leaned back against the seat. Boy, she couldn't remember being this pooped. That Wally. Four times today—four times! No wonder she was so tired. Between Wally and the madhouse tonight, she didn't have a single ounce of energy left.

She stretched her legs, wiggling to get them into a comfortable position. Last night she'd watched the meter, fretting because of the cost, but tonight she didn't; she closed her eyes instead. She knew what the ride would cost—two and a half dollars, plus that damned fifty-cent surcharge the city had granted some taxi companies on evening fares. No tip; she couldn't afford a tip. Well, at least her own tips had been good at the restaurant, better than usual on Saturdays. Anyway, it sure relieved her mind not to have to walk down Ninety-eighth while there was a maniac on the loose shooting people. It made her shiver every time she thought about it.

The ride home took less than ten minutes. Cindy's eyes were open when the cab drifted around the corner from Riverside Drive, and she sat up on the seat to scan the sidewalks on both sides of Ninety-eighth. They were

107

deserted. That was also a relief; another sigh came out of her as the driver pulled up in front of her building.

She squinted through the sheet of protective plexiglas that bisected the cab, looking at the meter. The amount was the same she had paid last night. She opened her purse, took three dollar bills from her wallet, and put them into the little try in the plexiglas. The driver muttered something when he scooped it out, but she didn't hear what it was. Probably grousing about the lack of a tip. Well, that was his problem. If it wasn't for that fifty-cent surcharge, she might have given him a quarter.

She scanned the sidewalk again before she opened the door. Still nobody around. Then she found her keycase, got the front-door key ready. When she stepped onto the sidewalk she slammed the door quickly and hurried up the stoop, looking both ways as she did. Behind her, she heard the cab's gears mesh and the sound of it gliding off.

Bending a little, because it was dark on the stoop, she fumbled the key nervously, before she managed to slot it. Three seconds later she was inside and the door was shut behind her. *Whew,* she thought, *home at last.* The light in the lobby was dim, too dim, she thought. She'd have to talk to the super about that, get him to put in a bulb with more watts or whatever it was. A brighter bulb on the stairs too; there were too many shadows over there. She only lived on the second floor, but she wasn't going to walk up those dark stairs, not if she could help it. She started across to the elevator instead.

She had taken four steps when the man came out of the shadows underneath the staircase.

Cindy heard him before she saw him, the scrape of his shoe on the floor. Sudden terror made her wheel in that direction, and when she did her eyes bulged at the looming shape of him — and the gun, oh God the *gun* exposed in his hand. She opened her mouth to scream, but he was on her too fast; he clapped his free hand over her mouth, used his body to shove her back into the wall. The hard muzzle of the gun jabbed painfully into her stomach, took away her breath, then gouged the skin between her breasts.

"Slut," he said. "Whore. Death to the wicked and the unclean."

She wet herself. She couldn't think, she couldn't move, she couldn't scream, there was only the warm wetness flowing out of her and down her legs, only the terror—

"Whore," he said again, and pulled the trigger.

11:32 P.M. — JACK KENNEBANK

Cats, Kennebank thought disgustedly. *Goddamn stray cats.*

He was in the alley between 1277 and 1279, back near where it dead-ended at a high board fence. He'd been walking along the sidewalk out front, checking things out, making himself a target if anybody had any ideas, and he'd heard sounds in the alley. So he'd drawn his service .38 and made his way back here, nice and slow through the alley's stink with all his senses sharpened. And it had turned out to be nothing more than a couple of raggedy-ass cats yowling at each other over a rat or something. He hated cats. He'd have liked nothing better than to put a bullet in one of the little bastards, do the city a favor.

Reluctantly he slid the .38 back into its belt holster under his jacket and let himself relax in stages, until he felt loose again. Nothing going down so far, but it was still early. Probably too soon for the psycho to go on the prowl again, although you could never tell with psychos. Even so, there might be other shitheels roaming around on the block. Muggers, dope dealers, they were all over the streets on Saturday nights. With a little luck he would run across one of them, collar him and take him out of circulation.

Artie Tobin had told him no arrests, no late-night hunting trips, but the hell with Artie Tobin. Calling him a hot dog, ordering him to go home and change his clothes and take a bath—it was goddamn degrading, that was what it was. He

109

had nothing against blacks, he worked with blacks and drank with them and got along just fine, but Tobin was one of the uppity ones. Thought he knew everything, thought he could boss whites around just because he had seniority. The hell with him.

Kennebank had gone home and changed his clothes and cleaned himself up, he'd done that much, but he was damned if he'd stay cooped up in that vacant apartment the lieutenant had set up for him. What could he do cooped up in there? What good was an undercover man if he only went out during the day and spent his nights keeping surveillance from an apartment window? The people on this block, the people it was his sworn duty to protect, were a lot better off with him out here where he could respond immediately.

So he'd slept for a couple of hours after dinner, gotten restless and then come out at ten o'clock. And he'd stay out, patrolling the neighborhood, moving around the park, until at least two, maybe three, if nothing went down before that.

Kennebank made his way back through the darkness toward the alley mouth. He was ten feet from it when he heard something — a flat popping sound, muffled, that came from somewhere inside 1279. Gunshot? Christ, it sounded like a gunshot! His body went taut again; without even thinking about it, he drew the .38 and broke into a run, holding the weapon down along his right leg.

There was nobody anywhere near the front of 1279. Kennebank veered over to the stairs, pounded up them. Two steps from the top he saw the front door jerk open, the dark figure of a man come barreling out. He tried to sidestep, but the two of them were on a collision course; the man's shoulder caught Kennebank in the chest, spun him off balance and into the doorjamb. The man let out a startled grunt and something jarred loose from his hand, made a series of metallic bumping sounds on the concrete stairs.

Kennebank staggered, lost his footing and went down on his right hip. The man was three-quarters of the way down

110

the stairs, frozen for an instant in profile, as if he wanted to come back for whatever he'd dropped. Kennebank still had possession of his .38; he scrambled around, up onto one knee, and threw his right arm out. Light from a streetlamp glinted off the weapon's surface.

"Hold it right there!" he yelled. "Police officer!"

The man wheeled, jumped, and hit the sidewalk running.

The street was still empty of pedestrians and traffic; Kennebank squeezed off a shot, heard it sing off the pavement at the man's heels. Cursing, he heaved to his feet and plunged onto the stairs. Halfway down, he saw what it was the man had dropped: a small caliber automatic. He checked himself just long enough to scoop up the piece by its barrel, not taking his eyes off the running man, and jammed it into his jacket pocket as he charged down the remaining stairs two at a time.

Lights were coming on in some of the flanking windows; faces peered out anxiously from behind curtains and drapes. But Kennebank's attention was full on the fleeing figure ahead. The man had a fifty-yard lead, but he ran awkwardly, swaying like a drunk, darting looks over his shoulder. And he was heading across Riverside Drive, where there was nothing but the park and the Henry Hudson Parkway and then the river. With a sense of exhilaration, Kennebank knew he could catch him — *would* catch him, the son of a bitch.

By the time the suspect reached the strip of park that bordered Riverside Drive, Kennebank had narrowed the gap between them to twenty-five yards. Then he saw the man stumble, lurch sideways and sprawl onto his side. Kennebank's lips pulled in flat against his teeth. The chase was over now, there wasn't any way the guy could get lost before Kennebank got to him.

The suspect gained his feet again, stumbling. Kennebank was right behind him, and when he shouted, "Freeze!" the man looked back once, took three more uneven strides that brought him up near one of the park benches. And then he obeyed the command, leaned forward with one hand on the back of the bench. The heavy rasp of his breathing was audible above the hiss of traffic on the Parkway.

Kennebank approached him, taking it slow and easy; he was hardly winded himself. Was this the psycho? If so, Christ, what a collar this would be! The biggest collar so far — a promotion for sure.

"All right, buddy," he said. "Move your legs back and spread 'em — "

The man whirled instead, and there was a gun in his hand — another gun, he'd been carrying a *second* piece. Kennebank was so astonished that he hesitated for a fraction of a second, and that hesitation cost him everything. The gun flashed, he heard the roar at the same time he felt a sudden numbing impact in his chest. Then he was falling, and the trees and the dark sky whirled above him. He didn't feel the ground when he hit it; he didn't feel anything except the lingering vestiges of astonishment.

A second piece, he thought dully, *I didn't figure that, it never even occurred to me.*

Hot dog, he thought. *Hot dog.*

Then the dark sky seemed to collapse, and the blackness smothered him.

PART
3

SUNDAY
SEPTEMBER 22

When Oxman neared West Ninety-eighth on Riverside Drive he saw the crazily parked patrol cars with their flashing red, yellow, and white dome lights, the portable kleig lights the men from the crime lab had set up over on the park strip, the officers prowling around, the knot of onlookers and media people being held at bay on the street. And there was more of the same on Ninety-eighth itself, in front of the corner building, 1279. He had approached such scenes often in his career as a policeman — too damned often. They were all oddly similar, like Greek tragedies. But this one was even grimmer than most, because it involved the shooting of a cop.

Lieutenant Smiley had called him with the news a few minutes before midnight. "All hell just broke loose, Ox," he'd

said in a voice that trembled with rage. "That goddamn
Ninety-eighth Street psycho just hit again—two shootings
this time. One of the victims was Jack Kennebank."

"Jesus! Is he dead?"

"No, but he's in a bad way. The other victim wasn't that
lucky. Woman named Cindy Wilson. A woman, Ox. A
woman and a cop."

Oxman had got the particulars from Manders, hung up
the phone, and sat for a few seconds on the edge of the bed,
massaging his sleep-gritty eyes. When he'd reached up to
switch on his dim reading lamp Beth had whined beside
him, "You have to go out, I suppose?"

"Two more shootings on West Ninety-eighth Street," he'd
told her. "One of them was a policeman, an undercover
officer named Jack Kennebank."

"Oh, *God!*" she'd said.

He'd stood up and begun to dress hurriedly, knowing
what was coming. As he slipped his pants on, Beth had
started to complain that she couldn't get back to sleep. As he
was tying his shoes, she'd said she was getting a headache.
By the time he put on his jacket, she'd been sitting up with
her hands pressed to the sides of her head and harping at
him for waking her and subjecting her to such unbearable
agony.

Oxman had left without saying good-bye. He wished he
could feel sorry for her, but he found it impossible. The only
people he could feel sorry for right now were the victims of
that lunatic on West Ninety-eighth Street.

He braked his car and pulled to the curb behind the
angled shape of the meat wagon. Now he was part of this
particular Greek tragedy. He got out and hurried up the
dozen steps of 1279, to where a big uniformed patrolman
was stationed to keep out everybody who wasn't there on
official business. Oxman knew the cop, an Irishman named
Chaney, so he nodded and walked on past without flashing
his shield.

The murder had taken place in the lobby, near the elevator. The victim was still there, sprawled out inside the obligatory chalked outline; through the knot of police technicians around the body, Oxman could see Cindy Wilson's waxy gray face and staring eyes, the blood drying on the front of her clothing. He turned away.

Tobin was already on the scene, and so was Lieutenant Smiley. They were standing off to one side, grim-faced and angry-eyed. Oxman crossed over to join them.

"Hello, Ox," Tobin said gravely. No wry needling humor tonight; the shooting of Kennebank had knocked that right out of him. Tobin hadn't liked Kennebank—not many people had, including Oxman—but Kennebank was a cop. And when somebody shot a cop, every other cop went dark inside for a little while.

Oxman nodded to his partner. He asked Manders, "Any word on Kennebank yet?"

"No. He's still in surgery at St. Luke's. Carletti's over there standing by."

"Do we know what happened?"

"Part of it," Manders said. "The way it looks, Kennebank came on the scene here just after the killer shot Cindy Wilson, as he was leaving the building. Kennebank pursued the suspect, caught him over in the park and got himself blasted as he was making the arrest. His gun had been fired once—Kennebank's, I mean. No sign he hit anyone."

Oxman rubbed his chin; the beard stubble there made a scraping sound. "Kennebank's a hot dog, but he isn't stupid. If he caught the man, how did he get himself shot?"

"Looks like the perp had two guns," Tobin said. "There was a thirty-two caliber Harrington & Richardson automatic in Kennebank's pocket. Evidently the psycho dropped it on the stairs outside and Kennebank picked it up before he gave chase. It figures to be the weapon used to kill the Wilson woman and the other three victims. So Kennebank assumed the guy only had one piece, and he got careless."

"Christ," Oxman said, "if that thirty-two belongs to the killer, then maybe it can be traced. It might even have his fingerprints on it."

"Yeah," Manders said. "Lab's got it now; we'll know pretty soon. But don't hold your breath, Ox. No matter how crazy this bastard is, he's not dumb; packing a spare piece proves that. I don't see him using a gun registered in his own name. And for all we know, he was wearing gloves tonight."

"Then nobody got a look at him except Kennebank?"

"Not that we've been able to find so far. Several people saw him running away and Kennebank chasing him, but they were all inside their apartments looking out through the windows. All they saw was a dark figure in a coat and hat."

"Who was the first to reach Kennebank?"

"First patrol car on the scene."

"Was he conscious?"

"No. And he didn't regain consciousness at any time before they took him into surgery at the hospital." Manders lit a cigarette, expelled a violent cloud of smoke. "We'd better hope he makes it, that's all. If he doesn't, and if we don't turn up anything on that thirty-two automatic, we're right back where we started. Only with two more murders on our hands and the whole fucking city up in arms. As it is, you know what the media's going to do with this, don't you?"

"I've got a pretty good idea," Oxman said.

"Yeah."

Oxman glanced over again at the sprawled body of Cindy Wilson. The photographer and the assistant M.E. were finished with it now and it was being ignored. There was something heart-tugging about all the men in the lobby milling about and talking, not even bothering to look anymore at the small, still form curled on the floor. She was inanimate now, something other than what she had been in this world, transformed with one bullet from animal to mineral in Twenty Questions games.

He sighed and asked Manders, "Anything in here?"

"No. No sign of a struggle; the bastard probably caught her by surprise. Walked right up to her and shoved the gun into her chest and blew her away. She didn't even have time to scream."

"Random victim," Oxman mused, "or was he after her specifically?"

"Could be either way," Tobin said. "She lived upstairs in two-C, worked nights as a waitress over on Columbus and usually got home about eleven thirty. The guy could have known her habits."

"How did he get into the building, I wonder."

Tobin shrugged. "Maybe he lives here. Or maybe he followed somebody else in earlier. Or rang somebody's bell. Just one more thing we'll have to try to run down."

"A woman," Manders said. "I don't like that at all. Bad enough this lunatic starts killing men, maybe cops, but now that he's after women..." He shook his head in angry frustration.

"Well, at least we know it's a *man* we're after," Tobin said. "That's something."

"It's not very much. Goddamn it, we've got to find him before anybody else—"

The assistant M.E. had come over and he asked Manders if it was all right to release the body. Manders growled an affirmative. Two ambulance attendants were standing nearby with a black plastic body bag unzipped; when the assistant M.E. gestured to them they converged on what was left of Cindy Wilson like white-clad vultures eager to be at their carrion.

Manders said, "I'd better go deal with the media. I want you two on this thing twenty-four hours a day from now on. Understood? No off-duty time for any of us until we've got the psycho behind bars."

Oxman watched him follow the ambulance attendants out with their burden. When he looked back at his partner Tobin said, "No witness to the shooting of the Wilson woman, but a man named Gerald Jackson, up in one-A, heard the shot. He's one of those self-defense nuts; he came flying down the stairs with a loaded shotgun. He was the one who saw Kennebank pick the thirty-two up off the front steps. But by the time he got outside, the killer was too far away for him to identify."

"Where's Jackson now?"

"Up in his apartment. Want to go hear it from him?"

"Yeah."

Gerald Jackson was a small, wiry man in his late thirties, with a ferretlike face and a head of bushy, prematurely white hair. He invited Oxman and Tobin into his apartment, where they declined his offer to have a seat. Oxman felt uncomfortable in the apartment. It was incongruously furnished in rattan and heavy dark wood, and there was a sparseness about the place that seemed unfriendly. The only wall hangings were framed bulbous glass displays containing stuffed specimens of squirrels and quail perched lifelike among plastic foliage. No doubt these were Gerald Jackson's personal hunting trophies. Against one wall, near the door, leaned a gleaming pump-action shotgun.

"I always keep it there," Jackson said. He'd noticed Oxman staring at the weapon. "Ain't nothing better for taking care of an intruder than a twelve-gauge. And it damn near paid off this time, having it handy. A half-minute earlier and I'd of bagged Cindy's killer. Say, how's the cop that got shot?"

"Critical," Tobin said.

"Damned shame."

"I know you've been through it before, Mr. Jackson," Oxman said, "but would you mind telling me exactly what you saw and heard earlier tonight?"

Jackson didn't mind. His beady ferret's eyes glowed and he slipped his hands into his hip pockets. He enjoyed telling his story, refining it before an audience. He'd be telling it for years.

"I was making a snack in the kitchen," he said, "about eleven thirty — I know that because I was timing a pizza I'd just put in the oven — when I heard the shot downstairs. It wasn't loud, and maybe nobody else in the building paid any attention if they heard it, but I know what a shot sounds like. So I grabbed my twelve-gauge and ran down the stairs to the lobby. When I got there I didn't see much at first in the dim light, except that the front door was just swinging shut and there were two guys out on the stoop.. They collided and one guy got knocked over; the other run down the stairs.

"I got to the door just in time to see the guy who'd been knocked aside aiming a pistol and yelling for the other to halt. He identified himself as a police officer, so I didn't try to interfere. The other guy started to run; I couldn't see him very well because it was dark. He was just a big guy, wearing what looked like a windbreaker — "

"No identifying characteristics?" Oxman asked. "Anything at all that might help us find him?"

"I'm afraid not," Jackson said apologetically. "Just a big guy, like I said. Well, anyhow, the officer squeezed off a shot and then started chasing the big guy. I run outside myself and watched them head across Riverside Drive, into the park. I figured I'd better stay out of it, except to call the police like any good citizen. So I came back inside, and that's when I damn near tripped over poor Cindy."

"Did you know Miss Wilson well?"

"Naw, not very. We used to say hello in the hall or the lobby, that's about all; she was the friendly type, you know?"

Oxman nodded. "Is there anything else you can tell us that might be of help, Mr. Jackson?"

"I guess not," Jackson said reluctantly.

"Well, if you think of anything, you let us know. We may want to talk to you again. If you don't hear from us, there'll

121

be a statement for you to sign at the precinct house later today. We'd appreciate it if you'd go down and sign it."

"Sure thing. Say, you think I'll need to testify in court?" He sounded eager.

"Maybe. We need to arrest somebody first."

"There ain't no doubt in my mind that will happen," Jackson said, ushering them out, smiling encouragement.

"He's some cowboy, isn't he?" Tobin said when they were out of earshot halfway down the stairs.

"Yeah," Oxman agreed. But he was thinking, ironically, that it would be all over now if the cowboy had reached the lobby seconds earlier, seen the killer standing over Cindy Wilson, and blown him to hell with that twelve-gauge shotgun.

THE COLLIER TAPES

I am calm now.

I was not calm when I returned from across the river; I was quite agitated, badly frightened. I undressed in my bedroom and immediately took a hot shower, surrounded myself with roaring water and fogged glistening tile. The bar of soap cupped in my hand and gliding over my body, the needles of warmth pounding my tense back muscles, soon began to soothe me. And it was not long before the anxiety and the fear were washed away, swirling down the drain with the residue of the filth from the streets where I walked tonight.

When I stepped from the steaming security of the shower stall and toweled myself dry I understood that the worries which had plagued me on the drive home were groundless. I have nothing to fear from the police. I am *God,* and what has God to fear from the likes of them?

It is true that the thirty-two caliber automatic I dropped and lost is the weapon I used in all my executions; the police will have it now and they will soon discover that fact with their ballistics tests. Ah, but the gun is not registered in my name. It cannot be traced to me. I bought it, just as I bought my second weapon, the thirty-eight caliber revolver the foolish policeman who chased me tonight did not suspect I carried, from a man of shady reputation in Pennsylvania four months ago. I obtained his name from an acquaintance, in the most casual fashion, and I did not give the gun-seller my real name when I approached him; nor did he ask for identification. He was only interested in the money I offered him.

Fingerprints? Yes, my fingerprints will surely be on the automatic; I did not expect to lose it, so I did not take the precaution of wiping its surfaces or of wearing gloves. But I have never been in the armed services, never acquired a police record, never held a civil service job, never been fingerprinted in my life. Let the police check. Let their computers hum. My fingerprints are on record nowhere!

What happened tonight, the unforeseen interference of the undercover policeman — for that is what he certainly was; the police are clever, if heavy-handed and inept — what happened was unfortunate, and might have been tragic. But I was not apprehended. I was able to strike down my pursuer with an unexpected suddenness and fury. If the lightning is turned away, even the thunder shall slay them. I am destiny. I am the Angel of Death.

As I speak I cross to the balcony door, step out, and move to where the Eye waits on its gaunt tripod, insectlike. A random thought strikes me: Would any of this have happened had the university granted me tenure? But that was another, a mortal life. A place of fools, better behind me. Like my marriage. All part of a past that was only preparation for something more fitting, something cosmic and grand.

I focus the Eye. The sharp angles of buildings, the hazy night over the river, impede my view. Sweeping, multicolored lights cast wild shadows in the park across from

West Ninety-eighth Street, before the building where Cindy Wilson lives...lived. In the distant clash of light, magical shadow-shapes come and go — the policemen, the onlookers, the media, all those who have come to look with awe and trepidation upon my work. On Riverside Drive, the Eye sees the twin white beams of an approaching car. It turns into Ninety-eighth Street, stops at the wash of colored light. Another police car? Yes: the arrival of the man in charge of the police investigation, Detective Oxman. He steps from the car, hurries up the front stairs of 1279, disappears inside.

Detective E.L. Oxman. What do the initials E.L. stand for? The newspapers have not said, nor have the radio or television announcers. E.L. Oxman. Not a name that suggests mental alacrity. A name to loathe.

A man to loathe too. The Eye has told me that.

For the Eye has seen the way he looks at Jennifer Crane, the lust and longing in his policeman's eyes. And the Eye has seen, too, that E.L. Oxman is the personification of the forces which threaten me. Or *believe* they threaten me. If I so choose I can snuff out Oxman's life as well, cancel his remaining days, his future arrests and fornications. On West Ninety-eighth Street, in my universe, he is mine.

Lights are on in Cindy Wilson's apartment, although the drapes are drawn so that the Eye cannot see inside. No doubt the police are searching it, seeking clues. Laughter roils within me, rises to a soft giggle. The only clues they will find are evidence of the unclean slut's relationship with the married artist, Wally Singer.

E.L. Oxman. The name continues to repeat itself inside my head, over and over, like words from a popular song. Oxman. Oxman, Oxman, Oxman. Why do I hate it so? Why does it begin to make me feel nervous again now, to bring back a tiny measure of my earlier fear?

But I must not worry. Oxman cannot harm me; on the contrary, it is I who can harm him. And perhaps a small

124

measure of fear isn't altogether undesirable. Now I have been warned.

And so, soon, shall Detective E.L. Oxman.

7:30 A.M. — WALLY SINGER

Cindy was dead.

Cindy had been murdered last night, right across the street.

Sitting at the kitchen table, staring out blindly through the window, Singer still had trouble believing it was true. God, he could still hear her laugh, hear her moan, feel her slim, warm body moving frantically against him. He shuddered as he thought of that flawless body being cut open for autopsy, embalmed. It was almost indecent, as if something of *his* were being violated.

He shut his eyes, pressed the heels of his hands against his throbbing temples. There was an awful taste in his mouth, as if something foul had slept there. Hangover. All the beer he'd drunk last night, before going to bed and then afterward, when he'd happened to be standing at the open window in the bedroom, taking a little fresh air, and all the commotion started outside.

Christ, he'd seen what had happened over in the park, that cop getting shot. Well, not *seen* it actually, nothing he could really identify, just dark figures running and the muzzle flash of the gun when it went off. That was bad enough, and had led him straight to the refrigerator for more beer to settle his nerves. But then the cops had shown up in full force, with sirens blaring and lights flashing and that stupid cow Marian had gone out into the crowd in front to find out what had happened and then come back a while later to tell him it was Cindy who'd been killed.

His first reaction had been numb shock. He'd grabbed another beer quick and taken it into the bathroom, to hide the

125

shock from Marian. But she knew anyway. Hidden behind her dismayed features was knowledge of the affair with Cindy and maybe satisfaction that somebody had ended Cindy's life. Singer had been able to tell that by looking at her, by the way she'd acted. Goddamn her, she knew!

Then he'd thought of something that had made him feel even sicker, so sick his stomach had actually convulsed. There were several items in Cindy's apartment that linked the two of them, that would lead the police right to him. Marian would know for sure about the affair, then. And even worse than that, the police might think *he'd* had something to do with Cindy's murder, with all the other murders.

Wildly, he'd considered trying to sneak over into Cindy's apartment and take back the painting he'd given her, the other things of his that were there. But it was an insane idea; the police were all over the place, and if he were caught trying to get in or out, it would look twice as bad for him. No, there wasn't anything he could do. Except wait. Just sit and wait for the police to come.

He was still waiting. And the fact that they hadn't come yet made him feel a little better. They'd have found the painting and his other stuff by now, and if they hadn't rushed right over to talk to him, it had to mean they didn't consider him a primary suspect. He was no longer as worried or frightened as he'd been last night. Hell, he had an alibi for the time of the shooting, didn't he? He'd been right here with Marian all evening, he'd been standing at the bedroom window watching the real murderer shoot the undercover cop. They couldn't pin anything on him . . . .

Marian frumped in from the bedroom, wearing a suit, a pair of gaudy earrings, and too much makeup. "I'm going," she said.

He scowled at her. "Going where?"

"I told you that last night, Wally."

Yeah, she had. Going down to Emil's shop in the Village

to talk to a guy who was interested in commissioning a sculpture, a Kraut friend of some other Kraut she knew. The guy owned a brauhaus over in Jersey and wanted a metal conversation piece for the outside fountain in the beer garden, a bird or something. How about a piece of crap, Singer thought.

He said, "Don't hurry back."

"I won't." She paused and gave him a long, funny look. "You'd better be civil to me from now on, Wally," she said.

"What's that supposed to mean?"

"You know what it means," Marian said, and turned out of the doorway. He heard the muffled tattoo of her shoe heels on the floor, then the door slam as she left.

Singer got up, poured his cup of cold coffee into the sink, and refilled it from the pot. Then he sat back down at the table. He felt a little relieved that Marian had left before the cops showed up; now he wouldn't have to face both them and her at the same time. But why *hadn't* they come? Were they trying some subtle form of psychological pressure by not showing up before now? You could never tell what the police might do. Sometimes they refused to give up on an idea that they got into their heads, hounding people without mercy. That sort of thing, Singer knew, could cause even an innocent man to confess just to get them off his back. And that one detective, Oxman, was like a dog with a bone.

The apartment seemed empty, hushed, now that Marian was out of it. He glanced over at the telephone. Was it all a crazy dream? If he picked up the receiver and dialed Cindy's number, would he hear her live, warm voice?

Cindy's dead.

She was murdered last night, right across the street.

He shuddered again. This wasn't a dream, at least not one from which he would awaken. This was a bright, sunshiny morning in the real world. This was his life. This was it.

8:15 A.M. — MARCO POLLO

The little cunt stole things. Marco knew that as surely as he knew high-C from F-flat. Sweet-ass Michele was some actress; her one facial expression seemed to be guilt. It'd be conviction city if she ever tried her act on a judge and jury.

Marco grinned. He was mellowed out from some of the good Mex weed he'd bought from Freddie the reliable. He lay stretched out on his back on the bed, hands clasped behind his head, ankles crossed, comfortable. It was a pleasure lying here thinking about Michele. Much better than thinking about the shootings, which were what had been in his head when he woke up forty-five minutes ago. Two more last night, one of them an undercover pig. Good thing he'd been blowing with the combo at Jazz Heaven, else he'd have been home, right here in the middle, when all the shit went down. Then he'd really have been spooked. Bad enough to hear about it at the club, have to come home at three fucking A.M. all wired up because some crazy was running loose with a piece in his pocket. Hell, he'd needed that first joint this morning bad. Who could blame him, man?

But now he was feeling all reet, all reet, thinking about sweet-ass Michele. His grin broadened. But hey, why only *think* about her? Why not go *see* her? She'd be home this early.

Yeah. Ask her where she got rid of the things she stole. It was damned important to have a reliable fence these days. The pigs were on to all the amateurs in the business; you needed a pro if you didn't want to get busted. And Marco didn't want Michele busted, at least not until he'd had the chance to bust her himself.

He got up from the bed. Should he have another joint before he went upstairs, maybe a hit on some of that good coke? Nah, better not. He didn't want to get stoned, not with the pigs all over the place. They hadn't been around to talk to him again, but they would be, sooner or later. His stash was safe enough, in the false pipe behind the radiator, but if the pigs saw him stoned they'd hassle him. Who needed that?

Marco took the stairs up to the fourth floor and did the old shave-and-a-haircut on Michele's door. He heard her moving around inside, then stop moving near the door as she looked out through the peephole. He laid a smile on for her, playing it casual. And just like he knew she would, she opened right up.

Usually she acted kind of surprised and flustered when they met, but this time she was ready for him with a big bright smile. Marco tried to remember that acting was her life—not that she could ever fool him. As far as he was concerned, she'd had an X on her ass from the time he found out how she earned her part-time money.

She looked tasty standing there in the doorway, long blond hair pulled back and up in some kind of fancy braid across the top of her head. Wearing a pair of tight—real tight—jeans and a silky tan blouse that did good things for her tits. Marco gave her another grin, a cozy one this time.

"I don't want to borrow a cup of sugar," he told her.

She caught on right away and invited him in, trying to hide her reluctance.

Marco looked around. Not much of a pad, the only funky touch the Chinese chest in one corner. He wouldn't mind having that chest himself; maybe he could work something out with her. He plopped his bony body down on the sofa, saying, "I thought you might be scared, so I figured I'd keep you company. You know, give you some moral support."

Michele crossed the room with a long nonchalant stride, her chin tucked in, her eyes level. When she stopped near the sofa she fired a cigarette with a silver lighter that worked on the first try, squinted at him over the flame. She was doing Lauren Bacall, Marco thought. He loved it.

"I'm not scared," she said.

"No, huh?"

"No."

"Pretty awful what happened last night. Right across the street. Could of been you or me, you know?"

"I suppose so."

"So, like I said, I was worried about you."

"I can take care of myself."

"Can you?" He kept grinning at her, holding her eyes until she had to look away.

"Would you like some coffee?" she asked. It wasn't what she'd wanted to say, though. She'd wanted to tell him to leave, only she didn't have it in her.

"Sure, why not?" Marco said.

He watched her walk into the kitchen: an actress's trained walk, graceful and with a rhythmic switch of her ass beneath the jeans. He loved that, too.

"Cream or sugar?" she called from the kitchen.

Just you, sweetheart, he thought. But he called back, "No. Black's okay."

In a minute she came back with a steaming mug of black coffee, handed it to him. He set the mug on a glass ashtray on the end table. He never touched the stuff. Caffeine could fuck a guy up.

"None for you?" he asked.

"I've had mine."

"So," he said, "why don't you sit down?"

"I'd rather stand. I've been sitting all morning."

"Uh-huh." He watched her. "You know," he said casually, "dozens of really good musicians graduate from Julliard every year. Almost every one of them winds up teaching high school music somewhere, or in some other line of work altogether."

Michele stood looking at him with a puzzled frown; Lauren Bacall was gone. "What does that mean?"

"It means I'm a musician, and I know how tough it is to make it as an actress. We're the same, you and me, same as same can be."

She smiled faintly. "Nice song title."

He didn't smile back. Serious time. "We both do what we have to sometimes, for our art. It's not like when other people do the same things. I understand that, Michele."

She didn't answer; he thought he had her on the fence.

"I just wanted you to know I see where you're at and I'm in the same place. I figured you could use the understanding. I know I could."

Something seemed to change in her. Marco picked up the vibes, high-pitched and subliminal. He felt like a fisherman whose cork had bobbed.

"It's tough for anybody with talent," he said. "Compromising don't come easy for people like us. I had plenty of chances for straight jobs, and good ones, but music is where I'm at and where I'm staying."

"I feel exactly the same way about acting," she said. "Not that I wouldn't take a strictly commercial job. That's part of the profession, I guess."

"Oh, sure, tell me what I don't know. Listen, I done trumpet background for a dog-food commercial once. So what? Thing is, I ain't sitting behind a desk, and you ain't wearing down your fingers in a typing pool. The breaks will come. They got to. And one break is all the difference."

"I know."

"Meantime," Marco said, "we get by any way we can, no rules, no moralizing. But you got to be careful, you know what I mean?"

"Careful?"

"Sure. The heisting's not the dangerous part. What's risky is getting rid of the stuff. Where do you fence it?"

Her face closed up again for a second, then smoothed into an expression of innocence. "I don't understand," she said.

131

"Come on, Michele. You don't have to pretend with me. I know all about it."

"All about what?"

"I'm your friend," he said. "People like us, we got to stick together."

She was silent. Just kept looking innocently at him like Shirley goddamn Temple.

"So you don't want to talk about it, that's okay with me. But if you hock the stuff, you're getting cheated. I know a couple of guys maybe could get you a better price. Just keep that in mind."

"You're not drinking your coffee," she said.

"Who needs it? Why don't you come over here and sit down?"

She stayed where she was. But he still thought he had her. She was no dummy; she knew the score. It was go down for him or else.

"Or maybe you'd rather I leave?" he asked, confident of her answer.

Only she surprised him. "Yes, maybe you'd better," she said. "A friend is coming over in a little while and we're going out."

Shit, Marco thought. He hadn't expected this, and he didn't know quite how to play it. He could force the issue, but that wouldn't be cool; with a bitch like this, you didn't want to come on too strong or she'd spook. The whole idea was to screw her, and she knew that as well as he did. She'd give in sooner or later; she didn't have any choice. So what difference did it make if he waited a while longer? Pussy was always better when you had to work for it a little.

"Okay," he said, getting to his feet. "No problem. Like I said, I'm your friend. We're gonna be real good friends, you and me. Real good."

"Yes. I'm sure we are."

She went over to the door and opened it. He made sure he

132

brushed against her when he passed by, felt the swell of one of her tits against his arm. Nice. In the hallway he said, "Soon, huh, Michele?"

She shut the door in his face, but gently, smiling as she did it. Marco laughed when he heard the locks click into place. *Some sweet piece, all right,* he thought. And then he went back up to his own pad to smoke some more dope and think how good it was going to be when he finally balled her.

8:20 A.M. — E.L. OXMAN

He had grabbed a couple of hours' sleep at the precinct house, on one of the cots in the Swing Room downstairs, and he was in the men's lavatory shaving with a borrowed razor when Tobin, who lived nearby and who had gone home to sleep, came into the restroom. Oxman caught his partner's reflection in the mirror and nodded to him. Tobin was neatly dressed as usual, looking ready for a board meeting of conservative bankers.

"Bunch of reporters and cameramen hanging around out front," Tobin said as he walked to one of the stand-up commodes and urinated. "What's this place coming to?"

"What's this city coming to?" Oxman said seriously.

"Yeah. Any word on how Kennebank's doing?"

"Not that I heard. Which has to mean he's still alive."

"That's something, at least. How about on the thirty-two automatic?"

"There wasn't when I sacked out, and nobody came in to wake me about that, either. If there's any news, you can bet it's negative."

Tobin zipped up his pants. "You seen Lieutenant Smiley?"

"I haven't seen anybody but me, in this mirror."

"Not a pretty sight, eh, Elliot Leroy?"

So we're back to Elliot Leroy again, Oxman thought

133

sourly. But he had to agree with Tobin's comment. There were dark pouches beneath his eyes, an unfamiliar gauntness to his cheeks. His hair was oily and lay close to his head. He put down the razor and splashed cold water over his face to wash away the excess lather. Shaving made him *feel* a little better, anyway.

"Let's go see if Manders is in," he said.

Tobin nodded, finished drying his hands and effortlessly hook-shot the wadded paper towel into the wastebasket.

"You should have played pro basketball with a shot like that, Artie," Oxman said.

"Sure. We all got rhythm and a natural talent for basketball. Not to mention peckers a foot long."

Oxman ignored that. He led the way to the crowded squadroom, across it to Manders' office.

Lieutenant Smiley was in, leaning back in his desk chair, talking on the phone. He waved for them to sit down. Tobin sat. Oxman elected to stand. He listened to Manders say, "Sure, sure, okay, sure thing," and then watched him hang up the phone.

"Fucking newspapers," Manders said then.

"The media howling all over the city like they're howling around here?" Tobin asked.

"Damn right. And they're not the only ones; you should hear what the goddamn Deputy Commissioner said to me a little while ago. I ought to sue the bastard for slander." Manders sat forward, rested his elbows on his desk blotter. His sleeves were rolled up; there was a dark coffee stain on the left one. "All right, here's the official line. I gave the papers a quote: 'There were no fingerprints on the gun Officer Kennebank recovered; the serial number of the weapon is being traced, however, and police are hopeful that it will lead them to the identity of the perpetrator of these crimes.'"

"How much truth is in that?" Oxman asked.

"Hardly any. Ballistics confirmed that the thirty-two is the murder gun, and there were prints on it, all right, nice fat latents; but when we ran them through the FBI computer we got zilch. You know what that means. The killer has no police record, he's never been in the military, he's never held a civil service job."

"Which narrows the list of suspects down to several million people," Tobin said.

"Yeah."

"What about the serial number?"

"Filed off. The lab used acid to bring it out again, but it's not going to do us much good. In the first place, it's an old piece; Harrington and Richardson quit making that model years back. And in the second place, the serial number was filed off a long time ago, not recently. The perp probably bought it hot; he sure as hell didn't get it off a reputable dealer. So how are we going to trace it?"

"Damn," Oxman said. "Right back to square one."

"Well, we do have a clear set of prints and the psycho doesn't know we've got 'em. Neither do the cranks." It was standard police procedure in homicide cases to withhold some vital piece of evidence from the media, not only so it could be used to throw the perpetrator off guard, but as a means of eliminating from suspicion the legion of weirdos who routinely confessed to well-publicized crimes. Five cranks that Oxman knew about had already confessed to the West Ninety-eighth Street shootings. "If we could just get a handle on who he *might* be, we can use the prints to nail him down."

"It's not much, lieutenant."

"It's something," Manders said. "Don't run it down."

Tobin asked, "What's Kennebank's condition?"

"Still critical."

"How about the detail working over on West Ninety-eighth?"

"Gaines phoned in a little while ago," Manders said. "The close search of the Wilson woman's apartment turned up something, but I don't think it'll lead us anyplace we want to go. Wally Singer's name and telephone number was in her address book, and there was also a painting signed by Singer. And some men's underwear monogrammed with W.S., would you believe it?"

"I've met Wally Singer," Oxman said. "I believe it."

"He's also married, right?"

"Right."

"Never trust a guy with his hair in a ponytail," Tobin muttered.

"Gaines talk to him about Cindy Wilson?" Oxman asked.

"No. I told him not to. I want you or Artie to take care of that. Let him sweat for a while."

"I'll do it," Tobin said.

"Okay. Ox, you go over to Brooklyn and talk to the victim's ex-husband, Vernon Wilson. The word is he still wanted her and hung around bothering her."

Oxman said he would.

"It could be the old game of making the intended victim part of a series of killings to divert suspicion," Manders speculated. "It doesn't smell that way, but we've got to check it out. If Wilson and Singer have alibis for the time of the shooting, make sure they're tight before you back off."

One of the Lucite buttons on his telephone began to blink. He picked up the receiver and punched the button. As he listened, his hound-dog features went pale; tobacco-yellowed fingers tightened around the receiver. After a time he thanked the caller and replaced the receiver. His mouth was a blanched thin line between sagging jowls.

"What is it, Lieutenant?"

"That was Carletti at Saint Luke's Hospital," Manders said. "Kennebank died five minutes ago without regaining consciousness."

THE COLLIER TAPES

Oh, I will admit that when I heard on the radio this morning that Jack Kennebank, the undercover policeman I shot, still lives, I felt fear again. And still feel it. He looked upon my face and might identify me. I could go to the hospital and attempt to end his life once and for all, but he will be closely guarded, untouchable in a labyrinth of danger. Oh yes, they're waiting for me there.

I am pacing as I dictate, five steps east, five west, digging my fingernails .into my palms hard enough to feel the warmth of my blood. Martyr's blood, as from the nails of the crucifixion.

Must it come to this always? Must mortals drag the gods down to their own base level?

As I pace, there is a cold tightness in my stomach that draws me forward like a bow, an ache so deep and attuned to the subtle currents of my body that it goes beyond mere physical suffering. My anguish is more than human, and it has, to a lesser degree, been with me always. Does nothing begin or end that isn't paid for in pain?

Nothing?

And yet, as Euripides said, "The divine power moves with difficulty, but at the same time surely." I must console myself with such thoughts. I must reaffirm my strength and my purpose.

For I am the power and the glory, and vengeance is mine. Detective Oxman will find that out. They will all find that out soon enough.

Vengeance is mine!

10:35 A.M. — ART TOBIN

Two minutes after he walked into the Singer apartment, Tobin had Wally Singer pegged. A white nigger. A bumbling, shuffling, honky Stepin Fetchit full of whines and "Yassuhs" that might have been funny some other time, some other place. But Tobin wasn't laughing today. In the first place, a cop was dead. A bad cop, maybe, a foolish cop, but a cop just the same. And that made this case personal. In the second place, an attractive young woman was lying down in the morgue with a bullet wound in her chest and a tag on her toe. Bad enough that a psychotic killer had wasted three men on this block, but now the crazy bastard was after the women too. And in the third place, Singer was too pathetic to stir any feelings in Tobin beyond dislike and a mild disgust.

Singer sat on the edge of his chair, leaning forward; his jaw kept moving from side to side, spasmodically, so that the whiskers on his chin twitched, rabbitlike. The beard suited him, Tobin thought wryly, except that it should have been white. A white spade beard for a white spade.

"I swear to God I was right here when it happened, officer," Singer was saying in his whiny voice. "My wife Marian was here with me. Ask her, she'll tell you."

Tobin watched the man sweat, watched him wring his hands together like a woman. Singer was scared through and through, and that was all he was. He didn't seem to feel a damned thing for the dead woman; his own ass was all he cared about. Too bad it wasn't *him* lying down in the morgue with a tag on his toe.

"Let's talk about Cindy Wilson," Tobin said at length. "Do you admit you were having an affair with her?"

"Yes sir, I admit it. I wouldn't lie to you."

The hell you wouldn't, Tobin thought. *You'd lie your peashooter off if you figured it'd do you some good.* He said, "How long had you been seeing her?"

"A few weeks, that's all."

"How often?"

"A couple of times a week."

"When did you last see her?"

"Yesterday. We...spent the day together."

"Where?"

"In her apartment."

"In bed?"

Singer got to his feet, jerkily, and moved around behind the chair. Tobin half-expected him to start tap-dancing— break into some kind of whiteface vaudeville routine. Bo fucking Jangles. Instead he made a sudden appealing gesture and said, "You won't talk to my wife about this, will you? I mean, she already suspects something was going on, but...well, she doesn't know for sure. You won't say anything to her?"

"That depends."

"On what?"

"On how cooperative you are."

"I'm being cooperative, aren't I? I don't have anything to hide."

"Everybody's got something to hide, Mr. Singer."

"Not me. No sir, not anymore."

"Answer my question," Tobin said. "Did you and Mrs. Wilson spend the day in bed?"

"Yes. We...yes."

"What time did you leave?"

"A little after three. Just before she went to work."

"She worked from four to eleven, is that right?"

"Yes. At the Little Switzerland restaurant, on Columbus."

"Did you stop by there at any time last night?"

"No. Why would I do that? I spent all day with her...."

"Did you call her at the restaurant?"

"No."

"Did she call you for any reason?"

"No. She knew better than that."

"You spent the evening where, Mr. Singer?"

"Here. Right here."

"All evening? You didn't go out?"

"Not once," Singer said. "I came straight back here after I

139

left Cindy's. Marian got home a little after six; she was out in Brooklyn with her sister all day."

"So your wife was with you from six o'clock on?"

"Yeah. We ate dinner, we watched TV for a while. She went to bed around ten, to do some reading."

"What did you do?"

"Watched some more TV."

"What time did you go to bed?"

"Around eleven."

"You sure it wasn't later than that? After you got back from across the street?"

Singer looked startled, and then frightened. "Jesus, you don't think *I* killed Cindy, do you? That's crazy. Why would I do a thing like that?"

"Maybe you had an argument with her. Maybe she wanted to break off the affair — "

"No! She didn't want to break it off; she wanted me to leave Marian and marry her. She loved me. . . ."

"But you didn't love her, right?"

"What difference does that make?"

"Maybe it was you who wanted to break things off, and she wouldn't let go. Threatened to tell your wife, expose the whole business."

"That wasn't the way it was! Officer, please, you've got to believe me. I didn't kill her. *I didn't kill her!*"

Singer was twitching and jerking so badly now that it almost looked as if he were dancing. He was fascinating to watch because he was such a perfect stereotype; Tobin felt like pulling a few more of his strings just to see what else he would do. But he didn't see much point in it beyond his own amusement. He didn't like Singer worth a damn and he wished Singer was the perp because nothing would have given him more pleasure than to nail such a classic white nigger — but this boy wasn't the one they were after. A whiny little coward, yeah, but not a killer and not a psycho. Tobin

140

could feel that deep down in his gut, what the media liked to call a "policeman's sixth sense."

Another goddamn dead end.

11:45 A.M. — E.L. OXMAN

Oxman found Vernon Wilson painting the outer rear wall of his modest apartment building in the Bensonhurst section of Brooklyn. Wilson worked steadily, in blind mechanical strokes, like a automaton. He didn't seem to want to stop working even when Oxman introduced himself and flashed the shield.

"I'm here about your ex-wife," Oxman told him gently. "I'd like to ask you a few questions."

"Figured somebody would be around sooner or later," Wilson said. He was a big man, not tall but paunchy and barrel-chested, with muscle-corded forearms. The forearms bulged as he began again to stroke the paintbrush over the rough clapboard wall. "Ask what you want."

Oxman went through the routine questions, using them to size up Wilson's reactions as well as his answers. The big man's eyes were red-rimmed and his voice was the dull monotone of sadness and shock. Oxman had seen plenty of grieving people in his career and he could recognize genuine grief when he saw it. Vernon Wilson's grief was genuine.

And he had a good alibi for last night. He'd been at a special Teamsters Union meeting to discuss the pension fund, then had stopped at a bar on the lower West Side of Manhattan with half a dozen friends from Dillard Trucking, where he worked; Wilson and his buddies had knocked down beers until well past midnight. The friends would swear to his presence, he said, as would the bartender, who had argued baseball with Wilson. Oxman made a note of the friends' names, the location of the bar. The union meeting didn't figure into it, having been adjourned before ten P.M.

141

By the time Oxman was finished with Vernon Wilson, and left him to his grief-induced painting, it was almost noon. Jack Kennebank's death was on his mind as he drove back across the Brooklyn Bridge into Manhattan. A kind of heavy pall had settled in Manders's office, in the squadroom, in the rest of the precinct house as the news circulated. Oxman had felt it before, been a part of it before. What it was was a hundred men, a hundred cops, thinking the same dark thoughts: *It could have been me. Next time it might be me.*

It was some job, being a cop, Oxman thought. At least Beth was right about that, even if she didn't understand what held men to the job. And when something like this happened, when one of your own was killed, it made you think about how short life was, and about how it could be cut even shorter unexpectedly. Time on this earth was something not to be wasted. The more of it you'd spent, the less there was left of it to be squandered.

He took the FDR Drive along the East River to Fifty-ninth Street, and then switched on his turn blinker and listened to it tick away seconds as he exited. He drove straight to Central Park, left his car not far from the Tavern on the Green.

He found Jennifer Crane easily enough. She was sitting cross-legged on the grass in the sun, sketching the restaurant from an oblique angle. Oxman said hello to her, and she glanced up from the sketchpad on her knees and smiled briefly before she went on working. More an artist's preoccupation than unfriendliness, he judged.

Oxman walked around behind her and looked over her shoulder. She was working deftly and neatly in charcoal. The elegant glass-enclosed restaurant on the edge of the park had never looked so good.

"Very nice," he said.

"Thank you, E.L."

"I wasn't sure if you'd be here, after what happened last night."

"I always keep my promises," she said. "Besides, it's much more pleasant here than cooped up inside my apartment."

He watched her silently for a time, mesmerized by the darting, economical movements of her hand that were transformed into imagery.

"Have you had lunch?" he asked her.

"No." She extended her right elbow, and the hand holding the charcoal made a series of delicate upward sweeps. "Is that an invitation?"

"It is."

She motioned with her head toward the Tavern on the Green. "In there?"

"No, that's too expensive for a policeman's wallet."

"An illustrator's too." Jennifer flipped the cover on her sketchpad and looked up at him. The grass was still slightly damp from a recent watering and had left faint damp spots on her skirt. Her long auburn hair glowed with deep, rich highlights in the sun; her cool green eyes were flecked with brown. Oxman let himself acknowledge the fact that she was beautiful. If she was ice, she was also fire.

"I know a pretty good place over on Fifty-fourth that's open Sundays," he said.

"Fine." She stood up, brushed off her skirt, and tucked her sketchpad and an artist's portfolio beneath her arm. "Is this going to be an official interrogation?"

Oxman could feel the direction of his life subtly changing. *Let it change,* he thought; he was like a ship that had been too long becalmed, ready to go wherever a cool, fresh wind might carry him.

He took Jennifer's free arm and they began to walk. "Not an interrogation," he said, "and as far from official as you can imagine."

He thought of Kennebank. He thought of Beth. Then he became aware of the sun touching the right side of his neck and face with life and warmth and promise.

And he thought only of Jennifer Crane.

12:15 P.M. — RICHARD CORALES

Corales spent all morning avoiding the police. He knew about the new murder last night, some woman across the street; he'd heard all the racket after midnight and he'd heard Mrs. Muñoz and Mrs. Hayfield talking about it in the hallway this morning. So he knew the police would come around again, hassling him, asking questions he couldn't answer, and he just didn't want to deal with them anymore. What did he have to do with shootings and crazy people? Nothing. Nothing at all.

Besides, he had other things on his mind. Like his winning streak at gin rummy. Thirty-seven straight hands now — thirty-seven! That was incredible; that was something for the *Guinness Book of World Records,* all right. It made him tingle all over every time he thought about it.

How much longer would the streak last? Could he make forty, forty-five straight? Even fifty? Fifty straight *had* to be some kind of world record; if he could get to fifty, he'd ask Willie to help make out an application to the *Guinness Book.* He'd be somebody then. And he'd be able to prove it, too. He'd carry a copy of the *Guinness Book* with him everywhere he went, and when somebody he'd never met before asked what he did, he wouldn't say "I'm a maintenance super-intendent" like he had to now; he'd say "I hold the Guinness record for the longest gin rummy winning streak."

Playing gin with Willie, establishing his world record — that was how he'd wanted to spend this Sunday. He'd felt lucky when he got up this morning, real lucky. He'd just been itching to get started. But no, there was that new murder, and the police all around, and then Willie had called up and said he couldn't come by after all, like they'd planned, because he had some other things to do. It wasn't fair. It just wasn't fair.

Right after Willie's call, Corales had taken his toolbox and his passkey up to the Royces' apartment on the fourth floor and locked himself inside. The Royces were out on Long Island for the weekend, and they'd been after him for days to fix their toilet because it didn't flush right and their kitchen faucet because it leaked. The doorbell rang once, but he hadn't answered it. He'd fixed the toilet and the kitchen faucet, then turned on the TV for a while, keeping the sound real low, to watch the Giants and Eagles game. His own TV was black-and-white; the Royces' was color. Football was always better in color.

The only reason he left the apartment was because he was hungry and he didn't want to sneak anything out of the Royces' refrigerator. He wasn't a thief. He thought he'd slip down to his own place, get some cold cuts and a loaf of bread and a couple of beers, and then come right back upstairs and watch the rest of the game.

But no sooner did he get down to the basement than here came Benny Hiller, from 3-B. Hiller hadn't followed him down; he'd been in the basement, over by the garbage cans. He looked angry, too, like he wanted to hit somebody.

"You and me better talk, Corales," he said.

"Sure, Mr. Hiller. What about?"

"That friend of yours, Lorsec. You let him in here again last night, after I called you?"

"Well, I guess I did," Corales said sheepishly. "I didn't see no harm in it, Mr. Hiller. Willie's a good guy and he's got to make a living same as the rest of us — "

"I told you I didn't want him prowling around in here. He doesn't live in this building. I don't even know who the hell he is."

"He's a junk collector," Corales said.

"Yeah? For all I know, he's the bastard who's been offing people on this block."

"Willie wouldn't hurt anybody. He's my friend; we play gin rummy together. Did I tell you about my winning streak, Mr. Hiller?"

"I don't give a shit about your winning streak," Hiller said. "I told Lorsec and I told you that I don't want him nosing around, and now I find out he's been back at the trash again. That pisses me off, Corales. *You* piss me off."

Corales frowned. He was starting to get a little pissed off himself. Hiller had yelled at him last night too, on the telephone; he didn't like to be yelled at. He didn't like people saying they didn't give a shit about his winning streak, either. His winning streak was important. It was a lot more important than Willie poking around in the trash, looking for things to sell, and a lot more important than how upset Mr. Hiller was.

He said, "I don't have to do what you tell me, Mr. Hiller. You don't own this building."

"That's right, but I know who does. You want me to go to him, tell him you been letting strangers in without permission?"

"You wouldn't do that," Corales said, feeling a twinge of apprehension.

"The hell I wouldn't. You let Lorsec in here again, let him steal something else, and I'll see to it you're out of a job."

"Steal something? Willie didn't steal nothing. I was with him the whole time."

"He pawed through my garbage, took some things."

"What things?"

"Never mind. Just things he had no right to take."

"But you threw 'em away, Mr. Hiller. Otherwise they wouldn't of been in your trash. It's not stealing to take things a person has thrown away."

"Quit arguing with me, dummy. I say he —"

"Don't you ever call me dummy."

Corales said it quiet, but his hands were bunched into fists now and Hiller could see how angry he was. Hiller backed up a step, like maybe he wasn't so sure of himself after all, and said, "All right, forget I said that."

146

"Don't ever say it again." Corales was satisfied, but still angry. "I'm not a dummy."

"All right. But what I said before still stands. You let Lorsec in here again, I go to the building owner."

Corales didn't say anything. He'd have to think about what he was going to do; until he made a decision, he'd be better off to keep his mouth shut.

"One more thing," Hiller said. "Where does he live?"

"Who?"

"Who do you think? Lorsec."

"Why do you want to know?"

"I want to talk to him."

"What about?"

"About what he took from my garbage. He told me he lives on the next block. Which building?"

"I don't know," Corales said.

"Come on, Corales. Which building?"

"I don't know. I got to go now, Mr. Hiller. I'll remember what you said; I won't forget none of it."

He opened the door to his apartment and went inside. When he came out again five minutes later, loaded down with the bread and cold cuts and beer, Hiller was gone.

On the way back upstairs, Corales wondered what Willie had taken from Hiller's trash. He hadn't noticed anything in particular and Willie hadn't offered to show him, as he sometimes did when he found an interesting item. What could it be that would get Hiller all stirred up like that? Trash was trash, wasn't it?

Corales couldn't figure it out, so he quit thinking about it. There was no point in worrying about things you couldn't figure out. The murders, that was another example. And the cops. No, it was better to think about things you understood, good things, things that made you happy. Like sandwiches and beer and football on Sunday afternoon. Like a thirty-seven hand winning streak at gin rummy that would maybe turn into a fifty-hand winning streak and put him in the *Guinness Book of World Records.*

He was smiling by the time he let himself back into the Royces' apartment, feeling good again, feeling lucky again. *Willie,* he thought, *I sure do wish you were here.*

3:10 P.M. — JENNIFER CRANE

On the way back from lunch, sitting alongside E.L. Oxman in his car, Jennifer felt an odd mixture of exhilaration and unease. On the one hand he was an attractive man and the thought of going to bed with him, now or later, was tremendously exciting. But on the other hand, he stirred things inside her, resurrected feelings and emotions that she had long ago buried. She could care for him, and that frightened her. She had cared for no man, no other person, since Zach; she must never let herself care for anyone except herself.

So far in this budding relationship, she was in complete control. She had manipulated E.L., seduced him mentally as she would seduce him physically; it was a game she had played many times with many men and she was very good at it. But she sensed that the situation could turn around on her, so subtly perhaps that she wouldn't even know it was happening until it was too late. He was a strong-willed man, intelligent, with a great deal of depth; he could be manipulated for a while, but he could not be controlled indefinitely. She had known men like him before, and always, always, she had broken off with them while she still held the upper hand. Yet she had felt little for any of them. They were just men, warm bodies on cold nights, hard hot flesh to fill the cavity of loneliness. It was different with E.L. Oxman. The seeds of caring had been sown inside her for the first time in nine years and it would not take much to make them sprout.

It amazed her that she could have nascent feelings like this after so many years. After what Zach had done to her. She had told herself often enough that she hated men, and she still supposed that this was true. So how could something like this happen to her? She hadn't let her guard down, hadn't changed her outlook, hadn't lost any of her bitterness or her resolve. How could it happen?

The murders, she thought, that's how. The death of Martin Simmons had shaken her far more than she had let on to E.L., more than she had let on to herself at first. A man she hardly knew, a man like a hundred others she had picked up and brought home; but a man who had gone from her bed and her body to his death a few minutes later. It wasn't her fault that he'd been killed. She had told E.L. that and she believed it. There was no way she could have known what would take place after she asked Marty to leave; she was innocent, she had done only what it was her custom to do. Nonetheless, his death had shaken her, opened her up inside, made her vulnerable again.

She glanced over at E.L. He was looking straight ahead, both hands on the wheel—a competent driver, with a hint of both power and aggression in his handling of the car. *I should break it off with him right now,* she thought. *No sex, don't even let it go that far.* But just looking at him built up a prickling heat between her legs. God, she wanted to go to bed with him! It was an almost overpowering need, and the very intensity of it added to her sense of unease. It was dangerous to want a man that badly, because that was the way she had wanted Zach in the beginning.

Zach. Thinking of him again, in spite of herself. Big all over, thickly muscled, incredible in bed. Six times one night, orgasms by the bushel—incredible. Strong macho personality, easygoing most of the time but with a mean streak, a dark side she'd only been partly aware of before she got pregnant. Her fault, the pregnancy, because she'd forgotten to get her prescription for the Pill refilled. His rage when she told him, his rage when she said she wanted to have the baby. The fights. And then the beating, using his fists, hitting her over and over in the stomach until she began to hemorrhage, and then leaving her there on the floor, bleeding, to crawl to the phone and call an ambulance to come and take her to the hospital. She had never seen him again after that night. Which was a good thing, because if he had tried to come near her she would have killed him. She would have murdered him the way he had murdered her baby....

"...wrong?"

Jennifer blinked and looked at E.L. again. "What did you say?"

"I asked if something was wrong. You had a funny look on your face."

"No," she said, "nothing's wrong. I was just thinking."

"Anything you want to talk about?"

An urge to tell him about Zach and the baby came over her. She fought it down. Too personal, too painful — no. She had never told anyone about that period in her life; the last person to tell would be this man. *Keep it superficial,* she thought. *He's enough of a threat already.*

"It's not important," she lied.

He held her gaze for a moment, the way he had over lunch. As if he were trying to peer through her eyes to see what thoughts lay behind them. Other men had looked at her that way, but not quite so penetratingly. There was a kind of implacability in his look, the eye of authority that refused to be denied knowledge — a man who laid out dotted lines for himself and then followed them. He wanted to get inside her mind as well as her body, and she was not sure she could keep him from doing that, keep herself from giving in. And that, even more than the seeds of caring, was what made her afraid of him.

She looked away, through the windshield. They were just turning onto Ninety-eighth Street now. The sky was a bright blue and hot sunshine bathed the crowded street, made the air shimmer with heat waves; and yet the brownstones had a shadowy, vulnerable look, crouched together like frightened animals. Imagination, she thought. But a coldness had touched her and would not go away.

E.L. drove past a remote camera crew from one of the TV stations that was filming on the block, a knot of curiosity seekers watching them, and slid the car to the curb just ahead of her building. He set the handbrake, but made no move to shut off the engine. Jennifer knew what that meant, and she thought: *Damn, damn* — because the heat in her loins was demanding and she did not want to spend the rest of the afternoon alone. But she let none of that show in her expression. And she made the invitation anyway, because it was part of the game she had established between them.

"Come upstairs with me, E.L."

"I can't, not right now. I still have work to do."

"Yes, I know you have. I'll be home this evening. Or will you be working all evening too?"

"That depends," he said slowly. "Maybe not. If I can get away . . . do you want me to call first?"

"That's not necessary. Just come by."

"All right. If I can."

"If you can. I enjoyed the lunch, E.L."

"So did I," he said.

Jennifer got out of the car and walked around the front, letting him look at her through the windshield. When she stopped on the sidewalk on his side, his eyes met hers again, briefly; then he nodded and pulled away. She watched the car until it swung out of sight on West End Avenue. The heat in her loins and the heat from the sun made her feel as though she were burning.

As she turned toward her building she found herself looking across the street at 1279, where Cindy Wilson, a woman she had not known at all, had been shot to death last night. The coldness she had felt in the car touched her again, like something made of ice being pressed against the fiery skin of her neck.

Preying on women now, she thought. Just like Zach. Four men and one woman so far.

And who's next?

Which of us will he go after next?

3:55 P.M. — E.L. OXMAN

The call came in ten minutes after Oxman returned to the Twenty-fourth.

He was sitting in Lieutenant Smiley's office, listening to Manders bitch. About the media—there was a copy of the *Post* on his desk, with a scare headline that read: POLICE STYMIED IN WEST 98TH MURDERS. About the flack he was getting from the mayor's office and the commissioner's office. And about the lack of any positive leads. Vernon Wilson seemed to be off the list of suspects. So did Wally Singer; Tobin had phoned in a negative report earlier. The checks on known criminals and individuals with a history of mental disorders who had lived on West Ninety-eighth during the past ten years had also proved negative. As had the lab analysis of the clothing of Cindy Wilson and Jack Kennebank. As had the minute examinations of both murder scenes.

"The citizens over there are scared shitless," Manders was saying. "Half of them have called in here or to the commissioner's office demanding protection. And I don't blame 'em. If I lived on that block I'd feel the same way myself."

"What about putting in another undercover man?"

"Yeah. I've already made the arrangements—two men, not one. I pulled Tolluto off another case, and the Six-seven is loaning us one of their best men." Manders lit a cigarette, coughed, and glared at it. "Goddamn coffin nails," he said.

"So why don't you give them up?"

"I've been trying for months. I could do it if it wasn't for things like this that keep coming up. Everybody shits in the Two-four these days and all the shit gets dumped on me."

Oxman didn't say anything. Manders was a chronic complainer; if you didn't encourage him, his individual tirades were usually short-lived. Besides, Oxman had enough on his mind as it was. The investigation, mainly, but also Jennifer Crane. Images of her kept flickering across his mind like slow-motion film clips, at least half of them vividly erotic.

"Maybe the undercover team will do some good," Manders said. "Kennebank, poor bastard, flushed that psycho once; it could happen again. But don't count on it."

"Why not?"

"Because the commissioner ordered me to step up patrols in the neighborhood," Manders said. "The residents want all the protection they can get, and that means they want to see blue uniforms. So we're giving them blue uniforms—three patrol cars cruising the area at staggered intervals, round the clock."

"For how long?"

"Hell, who knows? We can't keep it up indefinitely; we just don't have the manpower to spare. Fact is, too much police visibility is liable to drive the psycho into a hole somewhere until we back off. Then if he hits again, we'd be right back to square one. But the commissioner says undercover cops aren't enough, we've got to minimize the risk to public safety, and who am I to argue with the goddamn commissioner? If it was up to me—"

There was a knock on the office door and one of the other detectives, Ed Slater, poked his head inside. "Call for you, Ox," he said to Oxman. "Might be important—some guy who says he wants to talk about the shootings on Ninety-eighth."

"He give his name?"

"No. Just asked for you and wouldn't say anything else."

Oxman got to his feet. Manders said, "It's probably another goddamn crank. But go ahead and take it in here, Ox." He pushed the phone across his desk.

"Line four," Slater said.

Oxman picked up the receiver, punched the lighted Lucite button for line four on the unit's base. "Detective Oxman speaking."

"Ah, yes, good afternoon, Detective Oxman." Male voice, soft-spoken, cultured. "This is God calling."

"What?"

"You heard me correctly. I am the Lord God and Conscience of West Ninety-eighth Street. I am the Angel of Mercy and the Angel of Death. Cindy Wilson found that out last night. So did Jack Kennebank, when he attempted to interfere in the Lord's work."

Oxman clapped a hand over the mouthpiece and said in a sharp whisper to Slater, who was still standing in the doorway, "Trace this."

Manders came up out of his chair, scowling around his cigarette, as Slater disappeared. "Who is it, Ox?"

Oxman shook his head. The voice in his ear was saying, "Don't bother to put a tracer on this call. I know all about tracers; I know approximately how long one takes. I won't be on the line that long."

"Just who are you?"

"I told you that. I am God—the Angel of Mercy and the Angel of Death."

"Did you kill all those people on West Ninety-eighth?"

Manders said, "Christ! If it's another nut—"

Oxman flapped an impatient hand at him. Manders shut up, but he came out from behind the desk and lumbered into the squadroom. He went straight to Oxman's desk, jabbed at the phone, and hauled up the receiver. Oxman could hear the faint click on the line, and so could the caller; but the voice was talking again and it didn't pause.

"Yes, I killed them. I *executed* them. You think I've done

154

murder but I haven't; I have sent down my wrath in the name of righteousness, I have punished them for their sins. Vengeance is mine."

"Why? What did Cindy Wilson and the others do to you?"

"They offended the universe in which they live; they offended me. They were sinners, and the wages of sin is death. Do you understand?"

Oxman understood, all right. A raving lunatic. But the question was, was he a harmless crank, one of the confessors, or was he the psycho? If he was the psycho, it was as bad as they'd feared and maybe worse; a psychotic with a god complex was the worst kind.

"How do you know they were sinners?" he asked. He kept one eye on Slater out at his desk trying to hustle up the trace. "You live on that block, is that it?"

"God resides in the heavens," the voice said. "The sins of my children are plain to me; I know them all through God's Eye. No sins can escape the notice of God's Eye, Detective Oxman. Not even yours."

"What are you talking about?"

"If you enter my domain, you must act according to my laws and my commandments. You and all your cohorts. Otherwise you will die as the others have died, at my discretion."

"You can't kill all of us," Oxman said. "If you know what's good for you —"

"If you know what's good for *you,* Detective Oxman, you will not challenge me. I am stronger than you. You can't prevent me from cleansing my universe; you can't stop me. The fingerprints on the weapon you found are useless to you; my fingerprints are on file nowhere on this earth. Nor will you be able to trace the serial number. So I will continue to strike as I choose. Be prudent, or the next to feel my wrath will be you."

The line clicked and began to hum emptily.

Oxman jammed the handset into its cradle, pivoted, and

hurried out into the squadroom. Manders, his basset-hound face pulled into a tight grimace, was on his way to Slater's desk, where Slater was talking into the phone. But Oxman knew even before Slater glanced up and shook his head that there hadn't been enough time to trace the call.

Manders said, "Shit," and turned to Oxman. "What do you think, Ox? He could have been a crank guessing we couldn't trace the prints or the serial number on that thirty-two."

"I don't think so. Cranks don't make guesses like that. And, anyway, we said we didn't find any prints, remember? No, my gut feeling says he's the one."

"Yeah," Manders agreed, "mine too. That kind of motive—the god stuff, punishing sinners—fits pretty good. If it was him, calling you is his first big mistake. It gives us the motive, and it says he thinks he's untouchable no matter what he does or what we do. I like that; it means he's liable to get careless."

"That's one way of looking at it," Oxman said. "But he's damned cunning, whoever he is; the way he's handled himself so far proves that. It could be he's got a reason for feeling secure."

"Like what?"

"I don't know. Some sort of edge, some way of monitoring what goes on on that block."

"Which means he has to be one of the residents."

"It figures that way."

"Somebody you talked to personally, maybe," Manders said. "You have a hard time with anybody over there? Hassle anybody?"

"No. Why?"

"That warning right at the end. The crap about you being prudent or you might be his next victim. It sounded personal, like maybe he's got something against *you*."

"So it did," Oxman said musingly.

"Why would he single you out?"

"I'm in charge of the investigation; that was in all the media. I could be a symbol, a kind of potential anti-Christ in his eyes."

In his eyes.

Oxman frowned. He had already begun replaying the conversation in his mind, looking for a lead, anything significant. And now he remembered the voice saying, "The sins of my children are plain to me; I know them all through God's Eye." Why phrase it like that? Why eye singular instead of plural? Why not "I know them all because I've seen them with my eyes"?

"I guess that's possible," Manders admitted. "But I still say it sounded personal. You watch yourself when you're over on that block, Ox. I've already lost one cop; I don't want to lose you too."

"You won't lose me, don't worry."

"I get paid to worry," Manders said. "And I'm worried plenty right now. You just watch yourself, you hear?"

Oxman nodded. But he was thinking: God's Eye.

What could the caller have meant by God's Eye?

5:10 P.M. — BENNY HILLER

It took Hiller most of the afternoon to find Willie Lorsec.

After the run-in with that shitbrain Corales, he'd canvassed the blocks between West End and Amsterdam looking at mailbox nameplates; none of them carried Lorsec's name, so Hiller still didn't know which building the junkman lived in. It had to be one of them, though, because Lorsec himself had let it slip that he lived there. Maybe he didn't put his name on his box because he didn't get much mail. Or maybe he didn't want anybody to know where he lived; he wasn't listed in the Manhattan telephone directory, either.

Hiller couldn't shake the feeling that Lorsec was up to something, that collecting and selling junk wasn't his only scam. Blackmail, maybe; that was the possibility that worried Hiller the most. Lorsec had been too damned interested in Hiller's trash, so interested that he'd come back last night after Hiller threw him out and made off with that fucking ring case and the labels and ID tags Hiller had cut out of the fur stoles he'd heisted over on the East Side last week. What the hell would a junk collector want with labels and ID tags? No, Lorsec must have put two and two together and come up with a fix on Hiller's real occupation. The bastard was up to something, all right. And Hiller intended to find out what—on *his* terms, not Lorsec's.

But it was his own goddamn fault. He should have flushed those labels and tags down the toilet, taken the empty ring box over and dumped it in the river. Only, Christ, who'd figure anybody going through your garbage? Even when he'd chased Lorsec yesterday, he hadn't figured the bastard would be back; so he'd left the stuff in his trash sack and shoved the sack to the bottom of one of the cans. That had been his big mistake. It was mistakes like that that could land him in jail, if he screwed up in a way that would bring the cops down on him.

Well, he'd fix things with Lorsec, one way or another. And he'd be careful not to make any more mistakes in the future. He'd been burglarizing places for six years now, on an average of one or two a month—over a hundred scores so far—and he'd never taken a fall. Come close a couple of times, like with that guy over on Sixty-ninth the other night, but he'd always managed to come away clean. He was good, one of the best in the business; even his fence, Bud Gould, said that, and Bud had been around a long time. He had luck, he had the power. Nobody was going to take that away from him.

He kept wandering around the neighborhood, looking for Lorsec, avoiding the cops and reporters and curiosity seekers crawling all over Ninety-eighth Street. The cops didn't bother him much, though. A couple of detectives had been around to talk to him again about the shootings and he'd handled them all right, no problem; as far as they were concerned, he was a short-order cook — and if they'd bothered to check him out on that score, Hymie Dorman would have covered for him. Hymie ran an all-night café down on Sixth Avenue, and he was a friend of Bud Gould's; they'd had an arrangement for three years now.

No, it wasn't the cops that made Hiller nervous. It was Lorsec, not knowing what the nosy bastard was up to. And it was the shootings, five now, including that undercover cop. Who wouldn't be twitched over a thing like that? If the law didn't find the psycho pretty soon, he'd move out of this neighborhood, maybe get a bigger place over on the East Side, move up in the world. He could afford it; he had a nice little bundle tucked away in a safe deposit box at Chase Manhattan. Yeah, maybe he'd do that in any case. He'd been living here three years, and people on the block were getting to know his face. So were the cops, with all these killings. It just wasn't a good idea to keep hanging around.

Damn cops, anyway, he thought. They were supposed to protect the public from weirdos with guns. They were just no damn good when you needed them.

When he finally found Lorsec it was in an alley between two buildings on Hiller's own block, near West End. Hiller had been walking along West End, because he didn't want to make himself conspicuous by confining his search to Ninety-eighth, and he saw Lorsec when he came back around the corner. The junkman, his burlap sack bulging in one hand, had just come out of the basement door of the brownstone on the left, with a guy in a baseball cap who was probably the building's super.

Hiller backed up to the corner and leaned against a lamppost to light a cigarette. Maybe Lorsec, when he left the alley, would do some more foraging elsewhere on the block. But sooner or later he'd have to go home, and Hiller would be right behind him when he did.

It was another five minutes before Lorsec showed. He headed east, across West End, with the bulky burlap sack slung over his shoulder, like a seedy Santa Claus with his toybag. He wasn't expecting anybody to be following him, so he didn't look behind him and he didn't see Hiller casually cross over into Ninety-eighth Street. Halfway up the block, Lorsec climbed the stoop to one of the brownstones, used a key to open the front door, and vanished inside.

Hiller walked over to Broadway, crossed the street, and came back on the opposite sidewalk. Lorsec hadn't reappeared. Hiller went up the stairs, looked at the bank of mailboxes on the stoop. There were eight apartments in the building, and seven of the boxes had nameplates; the one that didn't had to be Lorsec's. Hiller made a mental note of the apartment number — six — and then walked back down to the street.

He cruised the block another time, but Lorsec still didn't come out. All right. Now he knew where the junkhound lived. He could go in there and face Lorsec, lay some heavy trouble on him, but he wasn't ready for that yet. He had to get that ring case and those labels and ID tags first, destroy the evidence, put himself in the driver's seat. And that didn't figure to be too difficult, not for somebody like Benny Hiller.

Hell, he was one of the best burglars in the business, wasn't he?

6:20 P.M. — MICHELE BUTLER

She was going to have to sleep with Marco. There was simply nothing else she could do.

He'd let her put him off this morning, left without pressuring her, but he wouldn't be that accommodating again. He was determined to have her body, and if she didn't give in, she was sure he would turn nasty — hit her, maybe even rape her. He was that kind. And there wouldn't be anything she could do about it, because if she complained he would go to the police and tell them about her shoplifting. Not in person, not Marco; anonymously. But it would be enough — the police would investigate, the whole ugly truth would come out. She would be put in jail, disgraced. And that would be the end of her acting career.

The thought of jail, of losing her career, was even more repugnant than the thought of going to bed with Marco Pollosetti. So she would have to do it, just as she had been forced to steal. For her safety, for her art. She had accepted that while he was here, looking at her with his hot funny eyes, and yet she hadn't been able to bring herself to go through with it. Not yet, not today. She needed more time to prepare herself for that particular role.

It would be the most demanding role she had ever undertaken, a true test of her acting skills, because she had to handle it in such a way that it would be a single performance only, no encores. Once with Marco would be all she'd be able to stand. She had to be an unsatisfactory bed partner, yet do it in such a way that he would be convinced she wasn't holding back; she had to make him believe she hated sex, not him. That she was frigid.

She paced the apartment, chain-smoking; she couldn't seem to sit still. She'd gone out all day, up to the Cloisters — just a place to go to get away from this neighborhood, this place where a madman prowled and murdered. If only she could move somewhere else, somewhere safe, somewhere Marco couldn't find her! But she couldn't. She had no money, she had nowhere to go except right here.

She stopped pacing to butt out her cigarette. *I should eat something,* she thought. Instead she lighted another cigarette — and found herself staring at the door, listening for sounds in the hallway. A coldness rippled through her.

Don't let him come tonight, she thought. *Please God, don't let him come tonight...*

8:15 P.M. — E.L. OXMAN

Fifteen minutes after he arrived at Jennifer's apartment, Oxman was in bed with her.

There was no pretense, no buildup, no game-playing like there always had to be with Beth even on those infrequent occasions when she was in the mood. Jennifer made drinks for both of them, and they drank them without making small talk, looking at each other, and when they were finished she took his hand wordlessly and led him into the bedroom. He thought once: *I shouldn't be doing this.* But the thought vanished when she kissed him. She knew how to kiss; her mouth was soft, her tongue hot and searching. Not like Beth. Nothing at all like Beth. And she undressed him while he did the same for her; Beth had never done anything like that in all the years they'd been married. And her hands. . . Jesus, it was like being caressed with something electric. And her body, all soft curves and planes, silky, nipples protuberant and hard, all of her hot and pulsing, demanding and entreating at the same time.

When he entered her the softness and wetness that surrounded him, clasped him, was like a shock; he heard her cry out, then murmur, "Yes, oh yes!" against his ear. They began to move together, slowly. He was afraid he would come too fast, an old problem that Beth always exploited, but Jennifer was too experienced to let that happen, as if she sensed the concern in him. Her motions, the touch of her hands sliding over his back were careful, rhythmic. "Relax," she whispered. "Relax, go slow."

He fondled her breasts, fastened his mouth over one nipple and sucked hard as she pulled him deeper into her, still in that slow careful rhythm. He felt his orgasm building, thought *No,* tried to ease out of her, but she held him, not moving for several seconds, stroking his buttocks until he was ready to move again. Each time he climbed near the crest, she did the same thing—squeezing, opening, holding him still for a while, letting the pressure in both of them wane so they could build it up again slowly. On and on, on and on. The feelings in him were exquisite, almost painful; he felt as if he were drowning in her. He couldn't think, didn't want to think. On and on, on and on...

Finally she began to move against him more urgently, a stunning collision; her nails dug into his buttocks, she lunged up to meet his thrust with a small cry, and he felt the faint flutters of her orgasm; her mouth sought his, captured it, moaned into it. And he came with her, not so much a climax as a series of explosions that left him panting, sent after-tremors rippling through his body.

They clung to each other, damp with sweat, still joined. "Oh God, that was good!" she said. She nibbled at his earlobe. "Fantastic, for the first time."

He couldn't speak.

"I think I came three times," Jennifer said. "Three times in ten seconds."

He made a move to withdraw from her, because Beth always wanted him out and off right away, but she clutched at him with her hands and tightened her vaginal muscles, saying, "No, not yet." They lay that way for a while, Oxman with his face buried against her neck and one hand holding her breast. Then, when they were both breathing normally, she said, "Now you're getting heavy," and let him ease away from her and roll over onto his back.

The bedroom lights were still on; he hadn't even noticed. He squinted against the brightness, watched her reach over to the nightstand for a cigarette. She looked soft in the aftermath of sex, he thought, no longer the ice queen; the fire had melted away her glacial veneer. Her eyes had a sloe look when she fluffed up her pillow and leaned back to light her cigarette. *Who are you?* he thought, looking at her. *Will the real Jennifer Crane please stand up?*

She offered him a cigarette, but he shook his head. "They

really do taste good after sex, you know," she said. "Or don't you smoke?"

He shook his head again.

"You haven't said a word, E.L. What's the matter? Didn't you like it?"

"I liked it. I haven't been screwed like that in a long time."

She smiled. "Neither have I. You're very good."

"So are you."

"I've had lots of practice. What's your wife like in bed? Or does it bother you to talk about her when you're in bed with another woman?"

He gave her a sharp look. But she wasn't being caustic; she was being frankly curious — the modern woman, holding nothing sacred. "I've never been to bed with another woman," he said. "You're the first since I took my marriage vows."

She raised an eyebrow. "How long have you been married?"

"Nineteen years."

"My God. That's a long time to be a faithful husband. You must love her a lot."

"No, I don't," he said, surprising himself. "I don't love her at all."

"Does she love you?"

"I don't think so."

She seemed to study him. "Then why stay married to her? Why stay faithful?"

"I guess I'm old-fashioned. You try to make the best of a situation, good or bad. And every marriage has a momentum of its own." He paused. "I didn't want to complicate my life."

"Do I complicate it?"

"I don't know. Maybe you do."

"Why go to bed with *me*, then? After all this time?"

"I suppose I was ready for it. Overdue."

"Is that the only reason?"

"You're an attractive woman," he said. "I don't know you, I don't understand you, but you're damn desirable."

"The feeling is mutual." She took a deep drag on her cigarette. "Do you want to know me, E.L.?"

"I'm not sure."

"I'm not sure I want to know you, either. You could complicate *my* life."

He hadn't been prepared for that; it surprised him as much as his own candor about Beth. It was the first time she had let any of her feelings show through the mask. More games? He didn't think so. She was being honest, and the honesty frightened him a little. It meant she felt there was more here than just a casual roll in the hay — the same thing he felt, and wasn't sure he wanted to acknowledge even to himself.

"I thought it was strictly sex with you," he said. "I thought you didn't get involved."

"I haven't. And I don't want to."

"Neither do I."

"So then we won't, will we?"

"No," he said. And thought: *She's lying and so am I.*

And the telephone rang.

Jennifer kept an extension in the bedroom, on the nightstand, and when the bell erupted it made them both jump. "Nice timing," she said ironically. "But I don't think I'm going to answer it."

"It's your phone."

It kept ringing. Ten times, eleven, twelve. "Damn," Jennifer said. She jabbed out her cigarette in the nightstand ashtray, caught up the receiver, and said hello. Then the skin of her forehead puckered; she said, "Just a minute," and looked at Oxman. "It's for you."

He stiffened. "What? Nobody knows I'm here."

"This man does, whoever he is. He says he knows you're here and he wants to talk to you."

Oxman took the receiver from her, waited until she had lifted the base unit off the nightstand and put it between them so he wouldn't have to lean over her to talk, and then asked into the mouthpiece, "Yes? Who is it?"

A familiar, cultured voice said, "This is God, Detective Oxman."

The hairs on Oxman's neck prickled. His hand tightened around the receiver, but he didn't speak.

"I warned you this afternoon," the voice said with self-righteous anger. "No sins can escape the notice of God's Eye. Thou shalt not commit adultery. Fornication is a sin, and the wages of sin is death."

"How did you know I was here?"

"You have broken one of my commandments; you have offended me. My wrath shall be swift and merciless, Detective Oxman, this I promise you."

The line went dead.

Oxman cradled the receiver, swung himself out of bed. Jennifer was looking up at him in a puzzled way. "What's the matter?" she said. "Who was that?"

He didn't want to frighten her; he said only, "I don't know."

"Well, what did he say?"

He shook his head at her, caught up his pants and put them on, and walked into the front room. There was a feeling of confusion inside him, and he didn't like that; it was the first time in years that he had been caught so completely off guard. He needed time to get his thoughts straightened out, to decide what to do.

He was pacing when Jennifer appeared in the bedroom doorway. She had put on a thin negligee, not bothering to close it, but he didn't even notice her nakedness.

"E.L., what is it?"

"Go make some coffee," he said. "We'll talk when it's ready."

She hesitated, biting her lip. But the edge of authority in his voice kept her from arguing; she disappeared into the kitchen.

He knew he ought to get out of there, do something — but what? He had no idea where to look for the caller. And suppose the son of a bitch decided to come after Jennifer as well as him? Suppose he was waiting outside, watching? He could make a try for Oxman, but he could also wait for Oxman to leave and then make Jennifer his target. He was a god-complex psycho; you could never tell what one of them would do. Damn it, he couldn't leave her alone, not now. Like it or not, he would have to tell her about the call, warn her of the danger.

Bad situation — bad. And all his fault. He shouldn't have come here, shouldn't have slept with her; he was a *cop,* for Christ's sake. Now that he'd underestimated his adversary, both of their lives were in jeopardy.

Oxman paced to the windows. Jennifer hadn't drawn the drapes; visible beyond was the panorama of headlight chains on the Parkway, the moonlit river, the lighted windows in the buildings on the Jersey shore. But he didn't really look at those things, any more than he had looked at Jennifer's nakedness moments ago.

How did he know I was here? Oxman thought. *Saw me come into the building? But I could have been on an official visit; I could have come to see anybody who lived here. And how did he know I'd been to bed with Jennifer?*

How did he know?

PART 4

**MONDAY
SEPTEMBER 23**

She was alone in bed when she woke up. At first she thought E.L. had gone, slipped away without saying anything to her, and she felt disappointment; but then she heard him rattling around in the kitchen, smelled coffee percolating. She sighed, smiled faintly, stretched. The sheet fell away from one of her naked legs, and she reached down to draw it over her again. The air conditioner was still on and the bedroom was cool, almost cold. Still half-asleep, she ran her tongue around the inside of her mouth, burrowed down deeper under the bedclothes.

Her first thoughts were pleasant: E.L. and the sex last night. But the ones that immediatcly followed were disturbing. The relationship with him was already more than sex, and it could be *much* more if she allowed it. She was letting herself become involved, and she was angry at herself for that, but at the same time it was exciting and seductive and she seemed powerless to prevent it. She wondered if it was the same way for E.L., decided that it probably was.

And then she remembered the phone call, what E.L. had later told her it meant. She tasted the fear again, metallic on her tongue, and she was wide awake. It was as though the psycho killer had been right there in her bedroom last night while they were making love, listening to their cries of passion and leering at them out of the shadows. The image of that was horrifying. How could he have known what they were doing?

And what if it wasn't just E.L. he intended to come after next? What if he wanted to kill her too?

Jennifer shivered and sat up in bed. From outside she could hear the swish of passing cars, an occasional angry horn blast, the louder, deeper bass hum of a laboring bus or truck. It was like listening to the separate parts of a monstrous organism coming to life, engulfing, absorbing the people trapped within it for yet another day. And she was one of them. The damned city was going to absorb her one way or another, she thought, until there was nothing left of her but a memory.

She got out of bed, still shivering, and put on her robe and slippers. In the bathroom she splashed warm water on her face, rinsed her mouth with Listerine, and ran a comb through her sleep-tousled hair. Then she went out into the kitchen.

E.L. was sitting at the table, his big hands folded on the bare formica, staring over at where the coffeepot was perking with increasing vigor on the sideboard. But he wasn't seeing it. His eyes had a remote look; he was so preoccupied that he didn't even know she was there until she put her arm around his shoulders and kissed him lightly on the cheek. Then he blinked and looked up at her, gave her a wan smile.

"Morning," he said. "How'd you sleep?"

"Not very well. You?"

"Not very well."

"What time did you get up?"

"About twenty minutes ago. I've got to leave pretty soon."

"I know. Do you want some breakfast?"

"No. Just coffee."

The pot on the sideboard had grown silent; the aroma of brewed coffee filled the kitchen. Jennifer got two cups out of the cupboard, poured coffee, added cream to hers. She remembered that E.L. drank his with sugar and got the sugar bowl down, carried it and the cups to the table. She sat opposite him, watching as he spooned sugar into his coffee.

"I have to tell Lieutenant Manders about us," he said.

"Why?"

"Because of that phone call. Because I'm a cop. Because you might be in danger."

She understood what he was saying and she nodded. But she also understood what the admission might mean for him; she felt a vague sense of guilt. "What will he do?" she asked. "I mean . . ."

"I know what you mean. It depends. Report me to Internal Affairs, maybe. But not right away; this case is too important. He won't let it become public knowledge for the same reason."

"I wouldn't care if he did."

"I guess I wouldn't, either."

"Are you going to tell your wife too?"

"Maybe. It doesn't matter to me if she knows."

"It's that way between you?"

"It's that way and has been for years. She wants it that way."

"I shouldn't be glad, but I am," Jennifer said. "Small of me, I guess."

"Only realistic."

She sipped her coffee, burned her tongue. When would

173

she learn? She put the cup back down, brushed an errant strand of hair from her eyes. Her gaze kept clinging to him. God, he had a good face — not handsome but strong, gentle. Something stirred inside her, old feelings, old tendernesses, that she had forgotten were part of her emotional makeup.

"E.L.," she said softly, "don't let him do anything to you."

"Nobody's going to do anything to me. Or you. Don't worry."

"Do you really think you can find him before he — before anybody else gets hurt?"

"I'm sure as hell going to try." He sipped his coffee. "I'd feel better if you'd agree to move out of here until we do get him," he said.

"We went all through that last night. I swore off running a long time ago, when I found myself on my own. I live here, E.L. If I run from here, I run from part of myself."

"Christ, don't get philosophical on me," he said. "This is an apartment in Manhattan, nothing more — — "

"Damn it, E.L., I'm not talking about this place, any *place*, and you know it. What I'm not going to run from is my fear. If you don't understand that . . ."

E.L. raised his hand and then lowered it gently, requesting calm. "Take it easy. I do understand."

"Then don't ask me again to leave."

"All right. But don't you take this lightly; meet me half-way. Lock your door when I leave. Don't go out today and don't open the door for anybody but me or another policeman. And don't answer the phone. If I want to call you I'll let it ring three times, hang up, then call back."

She nodded. "If that's what you want. I have work to do, so it won't be a problem today. But I can't stay a prisoner here forever."

"You won't have to, believe me."

He finished his coffee, pushed his chair back and stood. "I'd better go now," he said. "I'll be back as soon as I can.

And I'll either stay here with you again tonight or see to it that another officer does."

Jennifer managed a small smile. "I'd prefer you, E.L. It would be too much trouble breaking in another cop."

She went with him to the door. He kissed her, and she held onto him for a moment, her body· tight against his, while he stroked her hair. "Remember what I told you," he said, and a few seconds later he was gone.

After setting the locks, she returned to the kitchen and poured more hot coffee into her cup. She was a solitary person and she had always liked being alone, but now the apartment seemed empty, full of small odd sounds, vaguely oppressive. E.L. occupied a lot of space, she thought, so that his absence left a kind of vacuum. And it wasn't just physical space that he occupied, either; it was also space inside her. The image of his strong, gentle face lay vivid in her mind.

She wondered, with a sense of awe, if she were falling in love with him.

8:20 A.M. — BETH OXMAN

Beth knew long before E.L. finally called her—though she couldn't say how—that he had spent the night with another woman.

They had been polite at the precinct when she'd phoned earlier and asked for her husband, saying that he wasn't available at the moment but would be back soon. Lieutenant Manders himself had told her that. She disliked Manders intensely and expected him to lie. What would he have said if she'd asked him point-blank why E.L. hadn't come home last night? Why he hadn't even called to explain his absence? But then, those questions would have prompted another lie, of course. Only another lie.

And now the phone had rung, and it was E.L. She'd known it would be, just as she knew he'd been unfaithful to her. Another of her headaches flared as soon as she heard his voice from the receiver.

"I meant to call you," he said. "I'm sorry I didn't."

That was a laugh, Beth thought. A lie and a laugh and not very original. He'd made it impossible for her to respond sexually to him at home, so he'd been out rutting with one of the sluts he ran across almost daily in his work. Yes, she was certain of it now.

She tried to keep her voice calm, but it was vibrant with her fury. "You never spent the night away from home before without phoning. It's the least a policeman's wife can expect, a simple phone call."

"You're right, I should have called. . ."

"You were with another woman, weren't you."

A pause. "Beth, not over the phone. . ."

The resignation, the weariness in his voice added fuel to her anger. His guilt was so *obvious*. "How else, damn you! You're not here to talk to in person." She realized she was gripping the receiver so tightly that her fingers ached, and she forced herself to relax her arms, her upper body. Tension was the worst thing for her; Dr. Hardin had told her, had warned her about the effects of stress. But it was E.L. who was causing her tension, causing all her problems. Why should she suffer all day today, waiting for him? Hadn't she, in one way or another, been waiting for him all her married life? "I don't want to wait until tonight to discuss this, E.L."

"I don't think I'll be home tonight, either."

She felt her throat tighten. "Your work, I suppose," she said acidly.

"Yes. You know how serious this case is ——"

"You can't fool me," she said. "You never could."

"Beth. . ."

She hung up on him. She hadn't really planned it; her right arm snapped downward in a paroxysm of anger and slammed the receiver back into its cradle.

176

Beth sat for a long time on the bench near the phone, trembling, watching her fingers flexing and unflexing as if there were solid matter in her hands which she was slowly pulverizing. He hadn't actually denied being with another woman, so he had been. She knew him well enough to be sure of that. And she hated him now as she had never hated him, with a force like hell's own fury.

She stood suddenly — a reflex action, like slamming down the receiver minutes before. Not this time, she told herself. *Not this time.* She had put up with E.L.'s insensitivity and ingratitude for too many years. This was the final indignity.

She walked into the bathroom, stood before the washbasin and ran cold water over her wrists as Dr. Hardin had instructed her to do when she became flushed and overwrought. It helped; she was aware of the slowing of her heart. She could think more clearly now.

It *would* be different this time, she thought. She would be the one making the decisions, controlling her own life. When E.L. finally did come home — if he ever would — he would find her gone.

Beth gazed up at her reflection in the bathroom mirror as she made her decision, looked into the tortured depths of her eyes. And she knew that this time she meant it. Something in her had stretched and broken, and a part of her life was over.

She stood leaning with both hands on the washbasin; now she was completely calm, with the same sense of loss and acceptance that she'd felt long ago at her father's funeral. She would go to her mother's. Her mother understood how she'd suffered with E.L. Her mother would —

A flash of pain struck behind her eyes, without warning. She straightened, waiting with clenched jaws for the full force of the headache to assail her. Only it didn't, not yet. Slowly, carefully, as if balancing something fragile on her head, she walked from the bathroom and back out to the front room. She would call Dr. Hardin, explain to him that she was in the midst of a crisis. He would tell her what to do.

Halfway to the phone, she stopped and lifted a hand to her forehead. The pain had vanished as quickly as it had come; the headache hadn't taken hold. Always they started this way, and always once they started they struck with full and debilitating force. But not this time. Why?

Did freedom from E.L. mean freedom from the pain she'd so long endured?

She glanced again, lingeringly, at the telephone, weighing whether or not she should call Dr. Hardin. She had an appointment with him for tomorrow, she remembered. She could discuss things with him then, get a refill for her prescription if she needed it and if he felt it was necessary.

She hurried back into the bedroom and began to pack.

8:45 A.M. — E.L. OXMAN

Oxman was preoccupied as he entered the Two-four, trying to frame in his mind the words he would speak to Manders. They were difficult words, but they had to be said; it was his duty to tell the lieutenant about the phone call last night, about the psycho's threat against him. And he also had a responsibility to Jennifer, to protect her, to keep her safe; he cared for her more than he was ready to admit just now. So there had never been any real question in his mind of what he must do, no matter the consequences to his career and his personal life. It was only a matter of summoning his resolve and facing the music.

He had already done that once, with the phone call to Beth from a public booth near Ninety-eighth Street, and it had been easier than he'd anticipated. Beth already suspected the truth, had divined it through some wifely intuition; and the fact was, he simply didn't care. The marriage was over, had been over for a long time. The severing of the final threads was only a formality; he was sure Beth understood that as well as he did, now.

Lost in thought, Oxman didn't notice Drake raise a cautioning hand as he passed by the muster desk, or hear him call out. He went upstairs without counting the steps, and he was five paces inside the squadroom before he realized that it was much more crowded than usual, before he heard Manders' voice droning in a significantly official tone. Too late, Oxman saw the TV minicamera. And Manders and several milling members of the media saw him.

The shoulder-mounted minicam turned its round blank eye toward Oxman. A newsman from one of the local TV stations called out his name. *Shit,* Oxman thought. But there was nothing he could do now except to put on an official face of his own and let the vultures descend; he'd already lost his chance to avoid them.

There were at least a dozen media people in the squadroom. Oxman recognized some of them: Charlack from the *Times,* Barry from the *Post,* handsome David Nicely from WCTV. Even Barbara Marchetti from *The Village Voice* was there.

"The lieutenant says you're working several avenues of investigation on the West Ninety-eighth Street homicides," Nicely said, edging his way closer. Microphones were thrust at Oxman from every angle. "Are you making any real headway, Detective Oxman?"

"We think so, yes."

"Can you be more specific?"

"I'm sorry, no. Not without possibly acting in a way detrimental to the investigation."

"Do you personally think the killer will strike again?" Barbara Marchetti asked.

"I think he'll try."

"How can you stop him? He picks his victims at random, doesn't he?"

"It would seem so. But we've taken certain preventive measures."

"What are they?" somebody asked.

Stupid bastard, Oxman thought. *What the hell kind of a question is that?* But he said, "I can't tell you that, for obvious reasons."

Charlack asked, "What do you think this psycho's motive is? Have you got any leads along those lines?"

Oxman glanced over at Manders, who gave him an almost imperceptible headshake. That meant he hadn't told the media about yesterday's phone call; the god-complex angle was pure sensationalism, and there wasn't any benefit in letting the media spread it around.

"We have some theories as to motive, yes," Oxman said, "but I'd rather not discuss them at this time."

"Do you have any suspects so far?"

"No, but we expect that situation to change shortly." He was sweating from the hot glaring lights for the TV minicams. He wondered how long Manders had been putting up with this.

"Is there a sex element involved?" a woman asked.

God, Oxman thought. He said, "We don't believe so, no."

There were more questions, a rush of them, most of the same mindless ilk as the one about a sex element. Oxman fought them off manfully, sweating all the while, until Manders finally came to his rescue.

"That's all for now, ladies and gentlemen," the lieutenant told them. "You already have my statement and the written statement from Captain Burnham, and we've got work to do here. You'll be notified if there are any new developments."

He began ushering everyone to the door, none too gently. One of the men carrying a minicam stumbled and almost fell. "Jesus, get off my feet!" someone else said. And then they were gone, and Manders came back and steered Oxman into his office and shut the door.

180

Oxman sank into one of the chairs, wiped his damp forehead with his handkerchief. "Those bastards are relentless," he said.

"Now you know what I've been going through. Ladies and gentlemen, my ass! They'd all love for me to keel over dead right in front of them to add spice to the story." Manders sat down behind his desk and glared across at Oxman. "You didn't shave this morning. I like that. Gave the media the impression you were up all night tracking."

"I didn't shave because I didn't go home last night," Oxman said. "I spent the night in Jennifer Crane's apartment."

"I know."

Oxman frowned. "You know?"

"Tolluto saw you go into her building a little before eight last night. Your car was still parked there when he toured the neighborhood at midnight. The relief from the Six-seven phoned in about an hour ago that you'd finally left the building." Manders shrugged. "It didn't take much detective work on my part to figure out where you'd spent the night."

Oxman nodded silently, glad now that he'd decided to confide in Manders. Lieutenant Smiley wouldn't have liked it if he'd come up with a lie, or if he hadn't said anything at all. And Oxman was also glad Tolluto was that alert; it was some small comfort to think of him undercover in the neighborhood, doing his job, with Jennifer there alone.

"You sleep with her, Ox?" Manders asked in a neutral voice.

"Yeah." Then, a bit defensively, "You want reasons, excuses, an hour by hour account?"

"None of those things."

"I'm not the first cop to sleep with someone involved in a case," Oxman said. Which was a stupid remark; he knew that as soon as he said it. He wouldn't be the first cop to take a bribe, either. Or to go berserk and shoot up the precinct house.

"You wouldn't be the first cop never to make Detective First Grade, Ox." That was more to the point. Manders shrugged, shook his jowly features sadly. "What I ought to do," he said, "is report you to Internal Affairs right away. That's what the book calls for."

"Is that what you're going to do?"

"I don't know yet. Outside of your job, it's none of my business. But as it pertains to the case . . ."

"It isn't going to affect my investigation," Oxman said.

"No? Internal Affairs would probably think otherwise. In fact, they'd probably suspend you."

"Do you want me off the case, Lieutenant?"

Manders sighed. He started to light a cigarette, decided against it, and ground it unlit into the ashtray on his desk. "No," he said, "that's not what I want. *If* I can count on you."

"You can."

"All right. Just make sure you low-key this affair, if that's what it is. Or was it a one-night stand?"

"It wasn't a one-night stand," Oxman said.

"I didn't think it was. You're not the type. Well, Tolluto won't say anything; neither will anybody else on the force if they get wind of it. But I don't want the goddamn media to find out. If that happens, it's out of my hands. Understood?"

"Understood." Oxman shifted on his chair. "There's something else you've got to know about last night," he said. "I got an anonymous phone call while I was with Jennifer Crane."

Manders raised his head. "The guy with the god-complex?"

"Yeah. He somehow knew what went on between Jennifer and me. I don't know how he could have known, but he did."

"What did he say, exactly?"

Oxman related the conversation verbatim from memory. Manders grunted and said, "Why do you figure he called you?"

"Two reasons. The first is that, in his eyes, I committed a sin last night. He wanted me to know he knows about it."

"You think he actually believes he's God?"

"Oh, he believes it. Which makes him all the more dangerous."

"An ego thing like that," Manders said, "usually builds and builds until the perp secretly wants to be caught and stopped."

"Not with this one," Oxman said. "It's an ego trip, just as you say, but he hasn't reached the point of wanting us to know all about him."

"Then what's his second reason for the call?"

"What we talked about yesterday. I think he feels I'm interfering in his bailiwick, that he sees me as the leader of the forces against him. A kind of anti-Christ."

Manders chewed on his lower lip. "If you're right, Ox, then that means he's liable to go after you next."

"Maybe. But I don't think he's ready for that yet."

"Why not?"

"He's taunting me, exercising what he thinks is his greater power, telling me he's invincible and that he'll get me before I can get him."

"So you figure he'll pick another target first?"

"Yes. And I'm afraid it might be Jennifer Crane, because of her involvement with me."

"Makes sense," Manders agreed. "Or at least it could. So how do you want to play it?"

"First of all, I think we ought to have Jennifer's apartment dusted for prints; the psycho could be someone she knows, someone who's visited her. And I want her place swept for bugs, too—he could have planted some sort of listening device in there days or even weeks or months ago. That would explain how he knew what went on last night."

"I'll go along with that," Manders said. "What else?"

"I want to start living on that block full-time," Oxman told

183

him. "That way, if he does decide to come after me I'll be available to him."

Manders scowled. "You're not thinking of moving in with Jennifer Crane, are you?"

"That's just what I'm thinking. We've got to protect her, Lieutenant; I'm the one who put her into this situation, so it's up to me. Besides, with me in her apartment it'll provoke the bastard because it'll look like I'm taunting *him*. It might push him into making a try for me, into making a mistake that'll put him right in our hands."

Manders was silent for a time. Then he said, "I don't like it, Ox. You can't hide the fact from everybody else that you're staying with her. The media is liable to find out —— "

"Let them find out," Oxman said. "It wouldn't be the first time a cop moved in with a potential target in a homicide case. We can concoct a cover story along those lines."

"I still don't like it," Manders said. "If you're that worried about the Crane woman, get her to move out temporarily. That makes more sense. . . ."

"Maybe, but she won't leave. I've already talked to her about it." Oxman spread his hands. "Under the circumstances, my way is the only way to handle it, Lieutenant — the only way to force this psycho's hand."

Manders was silent again for several seconds before he said, "You could screw yourself up bad, Ox. You know that, don't you?"

"I know it. But I don't see any other way."

Another doleful sigh. "I guess I don't either," Manders said. "At least not for the time being. Okay, Ox. I'll probably regret this, but. . . go ahead, make yourself the bait. It's your funeral."

"No," Oxman said thinly. "Not mine — his."

THE COLLIER TAPES

I am much calmer today. The nagging fear which plagued me vanished as soon as I learned, via the *Six O'Clock News* last night, that the undercover policeman, Jack Kennebank, died of his wounds. The newscast did not mention whether or not Kennebank regained consciousness first, but I must assume that he did not. If he had given them a description of me, the police would not have suppressed it. They would have brought in an artist to create a likeness, and they would have published it in the newspapers and shown it on television, in the hope that someone might be able to identify me.

Why did I worry? I have nothing to fear from the police. They cannot stop me. Of course they cannot stop me.

I am God, and no man can stand in God's way.

Detective Oxman thinks *he* can, but he is a fool. And a sinner, an evil man. The Eye observed every second of his fornication with the Crane slut last night, his bestial rutting atop her in her lighted bedroom. It was a disgusting exhibition, and it invoked my wrath and fueled my hatred for him. I have hated none of my wicked children as much as I hate this interloper, this fornicator hiding behind the badge of a public official.

That is why I decided to telephone him after his lust had been sated. The others who have died, and who will die, have been given no warning of their fate, and this is as it should be. I forgive them as I destroy them. But Detective Oxman I will not forgive; he is beyond forgiveness, he is the personification of evil. Therefore he must know that his days are numbered, that he cannot mock God and expect to continue to live. He must know that I hold his destiny in *my* hands.

I swore after the Martin Simmons episode that I would not willingly destroy anyone who was not a resident of my universe. But in Detective Oxman's case I must make an exception. He deserves to die by my hand. And so he shall.

Tonight? Shall it be tonight?

I have not yet decided. The Eye will help me decide, as the Eye always does. There is plenty of time.

4:45 P.M. — MARCO POLLO

He was still half stoned when Leon dropped him off in front of his building. There'd been plenty of good dope at the practice session at Jazz Heaven and they'd all been flying high and blowing sweet all afternoon. Too bad Jazz Heaven was dark on Monday nights. The way they were jamming, the combo could have fucked a few minds tonight. Marco's solo on "I Can't Get Started" had been a thing of beauty, man, as fine as anything Bunny Berrigan ever did; he'd been so hot there'd been smoke coming out of his horn. He'd have knocked 'em dead, all right.

Marco entered the building, floating a little, grinning to himself. The elevator was at lobby level, so he decided to take that instead of the stairs. But when he stepped inside and started to punch the button for Two, his hand halted halfway to the panel; he found himself staring at the Four button instead. His grin widened.

Michele, he thought. Little tight-ass Michele.

He hadn't thought about her all day, but now that he did he was suddenly horny. It'd been awhile since he'd last gotten laid, so he was prime, man, ready to jump some bones, and Michele's bones were the sweetest around. If she was home, and if she was alone, he wouldn't take no for an answer this time. Not *this* time.

He pushed Four, rode up, and went along the hallway to Michele's apartment. Nothing happened for about a minute after he rang the bell, and Marco was starting to feel a letdown when he heard her voice say, "What is it, Marco?" His grin came back, then. He knew she was looking at him through the peephole.

"I want to come in. That is, if you're alone."

"I'm alone," she said. "What do you want?"

"Invite me in and I'll tell you."

Michele hesitated for maybe fifteen seconds. But she didn't have any choice; she'd let him in. When he heard the locks rattle finally a giggle came out of his throat. *Oh, baby,* he thought, *tonight's the night!*

She was wearing a lacy, lavender housecoat that made Marco lick his lips when he saw it. Her face was puffy, as if she'd been asleep; the uncertainty, the fear, lay across her features like a pale shadow. Wordlessly, she stepped back so he could enter.

Marco crossed the room and sat down on the sofa, as he had yesterday. Michele followed, stood staring down at him with her arms folded over her tits as if she were cold.

"How come you're dressed like that?" he asked her. "You been sleeping?"

"I was taking a nap, yes," she said. "I didn't sleep very well last night."

"How come? Worried about the woman got murdered across the street? What was her name — Cindy something?"

"Wilson. Cindy Wilson."

"You know her?"

Michele shook her head.

"Sexy-looking lady," Marco said. "You see her picture in the paper? They always put the good-looking ones' pictures in the papers. If something like that happened to you, you'd make it sure with your looks."

Michele shuddered. She paced to a chair but didn't sit down.

"I didn't mean to spook you," he said, amused.

"I know. It's just damned nerve-rattling, all those people killed in the neighborhood. And the police can't seem to do anything about it."

Marco's eyes were on the pale flesh of one thigh, visible where the housecoat had fallen open in front. "Come over here," he said, patting the sofa cushion next to him. "Sit down, relax your bones."

She hesitated. But she knew as well as he did that this was it, they were all through with the bullshit. It was only a couple of seconds before she walked across the room and sat down next to him.

But Marco still had to play it slow and cool; he didn't want to spook her by coming on too strong, at least not this first time. Push the right buttons and she'd respond pretty as you please. "You should of told me you were nerved up about the murders," he said, touching her lightly on the shoulder. "I worry about you, sweets, whether you believe it or not."

She stiffened at his touch, her hands tensing on her knees. Marco didn't remove his hand from her shoulder. He began tracing a circle gently with his forefinger, ever so gently. . . .

"There isn't any reason to worry about me," she said.

"Oh, I don't mean I'm worried about you getting hurt. I'm talking about your little sideline — where you sell the merchandise you lift. I'd hate to see you get nailed because of a word in the wrong ear."

"I don't know what you mean."

"Don't tell me that, Michele." He kept his voice low, sympathetic and patient. He might have been coaxing and disciplining a dog. "Don't tell me that again."

She lowered her eyes. "All right," she said. "But I don't want to talk about it now."

"And I don't want the pigs coming down on my favorite actress." He flashed her a reassuring, candid smile. "That shouldn't be so hard for you to understand."

"I understand, Marco. I appreciate your concern, really I do."

"Good." Marco nodded, gave her a casual caress. "Just remember, I know somebody who'll handle all the stuff you can walk in with. No questions asked, no hassle. I ain't butting into your business, but all you got to do is ask and I'll give you the guy's name."

"I may do that," she said. "I'll have to think about it."

"Think real hard," Marco told her. Then he shook his head in deep, deep concern. "You should of told me about being nerved up, too," he said. He knew how to play on fear, use it to his advantage. He'd been a safe port in a storm plenty of times.

She let out a long, low breath. "I guess I should have."

He moved closer to her, and she didn't pull away. In fact, her body swayed slightly toward his.

"So tell me about your acting," he said, "about your art, about you."

When she'd loved to play dress-up as a six-year-old, he had his arm around her. When she was the most promising student in her high school drama class she was leaning on him, hypnotized by his touch and by her own autobiography that verged on confession. She was starring in college productions when Marco slid his hand down the front of her housecoat, his fingers skillfully manipulating a rigid nipple. By the time she had her first paying role, a small speaking part in a local Ohio production, the housecoat was half off. And when she had landed her first role in an off-Broadway play, they were in the bedroom and naked on the bed with Marco's eager hands all over her.

Every sort of acting honor would inevitably come her way, Marco assured her, panting. There was a natural progression to things.

Oh, baby, was there ever a natural progression to things!

6:10 P.M. — E.L. OXMAN

There was no answer when he called home again from Jennifer's apartment. There hadn't been any answer all day.

Oxman wondered if that meant Beth was just out somewhere, gone for another session with her Doctor Feelgood, maybe — or if it meant that she had left him. She had threatened to leave him before, and on three or four occasions she had actually gone off to her mother's for a few days; but those times she had been upset about his work, what she felt was his neglect of her during particularly difficult cases. This was different. This was another woman, not his job. This, maybe, was the point of no return.

But he simply didn't care. In fact, he hoped that she *had* left him and wouldn't come back, that she would soon file for divorce. If she didn't see a lawyer to end their marriage, he thought that he probably would. He didn't want to live with Beth any longer; and his relationship with Jennifer was... well, he thought he knew what it was, or what it could be. Only he wasn't quite ready to put a name to it, to take the big step into a commitment. It all depended on Jennifer. He couldn't be sure of her feelings because he didn't really know her yet. Until he did —

She came into the living room from the kitchen, interrupting his thoughts. "I put some macaroni-and-cheese in the oven," she said. "Are you hungry?"

"Not very. But I suppose I should eat."

"How about a drink first?"

"I could use one."

"Scotch, bourbon — what?"

"Bourbon. Ice and a little water. But don't make it too strong; I'm still on duty."

She nodded and went back into the kitchen. Oxman sank wearily onto the couch. It had been another long and frustrating day: insignificant interviews, two brief stops to make sure Jennifer was all right, a talk with Tobin, another talk with Lieutenant Smiley. No leads, no new developments of any kind. The tech crew Manders had sent here to Jennifer's apartment had found no fingerprints to match those on the .32 Harrington & Richardson murder gun, nor had they found any listening devices. The question of how the psycho had known about the lovemaking last night was still a mystery.

Oxman kept telling himself that he was close to the truth about the killer's identity and MO, that all he needed was one break—a mistake on the psycho's part, a bit of evidence, something—to get hold of. But the break wouldn't seem to come. The Angel of Death, as the bastard had called himself, still had the upper hand; and that meant he could strike again any time, any place, and they might not be able to stop him. Jennifer returned with Oxman's drink. She handed it to him, then sat down beside him and gave him a wan smile. Looking at her, he thought it was amazing how different she seemed since the two of them had become lovers. The ice queen was gone; in her place was a woman as soft and warm as any he had ever known. This was the real Jennifer Crane, he was sure of that. She had taken off her mask for the first time in a long while, and she had done it because of him and for him. If the mask stayed off, if the ice queen stayed melted, then what they had might be much more than a simple if intense affair. It might be something permanent.

He put his arm around her, drew her close to him. She came willingly, nuzzling his body with hers like a purring cat. This was the way it ought to be between a man and a woman, he thought. This was the way it had never been with Beth.

Jennifer kissed him, ran her tongue over his lower lip. "How would you like to go to bed?" she asked.

"I thought you had dinner in the oven."

"I thought you weren't hungry."

"I'm hungry," he said. "But not for food."

"Uh-huh."

"But I'm also tired."

"Then I'll get on top." The worry in her eyes had vanished for the moment; they held a bawdy gleam now. "So do you want to go screw, or don't you?"

"I want to go screw," he said.

191

8:30 P.M. — BENNY HILLER

From where he stood listening outside the door to the super's basement apartment, Hiller heard Corales exclaim in almost childish glee, "Gin! That's forty straight, Willie! Jesus, forty straight winning hands!"

"You're very lucky, my friend," Lorsec's voice answered. But the junkhound sounded irritated, as if he didn't like losing. Hiller smiled faintly in the basement's gloom. Well, Lorsec was going to do a lot more losing pretty soon, if he had anything to say about it.

Hiller had been waiting ever since yesterday afternoon for an opportunity to get into Lorsec's apartment. But the junkman hadn't been around anywhere. Hiller had watched the street from his front window, had taken half a dozen walks around the neighborhood, but he hadn't wanted to go ringing Lorsec's doorbell. For all Hiller knew, Lorsec was also watching the street. If the junkman suspected what Hiller was up to, he might stash the ring case and the other stuff somewhere outside his pad, assuming he hadn't already done that. So Hiller had been patient, figuring he had nothing to worry about as long as Lorsec didn't try to contact him with some sort of blackmail scam; and a half hour ago, while he was sitting in front of the window again, eyes on the street below, Lorsec had finally shown. When the junkman came up the front stairs and disappeared inside the building, Hiller figured that shitbrain Corales had let him in and that the two of them were in Corales's apartment. He'd slipped down to the basement to make sure. And the way it sounded, Lorsec was going to be here awhile playing gin rummy.

"Deal 'em again, Willie," Corales was saying. "I'm going for forty-one straight now — forty-one and then right on up to fifty. Guinness record book, here I come!"

Hiller backed away from the door, went over to the stairs,

and climbed them silently and lightly on his soft-soled shoes — his jogging shoes, his working shoes. He left the building by the front door, lit a cigarette as he walked east on Ninety-eighth to the brownstone he'd seen Willie Lorsec enter yesterday. Once he got to it he flicked the glowing butt away and then went up onto the stoop.

Getting into the building was no problem. The front door, he'd noted yesterday, had a flush-mounted, five-pin cylinder lock, with a steel lip on the door frame to protect the bolt and strike plate. That meant it was a lock you couldn't loid with a credit card or a shim; it had to be picked. There were two ways to do that: the precision way, using picks and tension bars to spring the tumbler pins one at a time; or with a pick gun, which bounced all the pins at once. Hiller preferred using picks and tension bars, because it was the more reliable method. But it also took time, and the longer he stood on the stoop, fiddling with the front door lock, the greater his risk that somebody would come along and spot him. So he'd taken his pick gun, along with a few other tools he figured he might need; he had them in his jacket pocket.

He made sure the lobby inside, visible through the door glass, was empty and that the street behind him was also empty. Then he got the gun out, slid it into the lock. He spent some time getting it set, working the little knob on top to adjust the spring tension, and when he was ready he pulled the trigger. No problem. All the pins bounced free and the door opened under his hand.

Hiller pocketed the gun, eased quickly across the lobby to the stairwell. When he got to the third-floor hallway he saw that it was deserted. He stopped in front of the door with the numeral six on it, bent to examine the lock. His lips curved in a smile. No problem here, either. Lorsec didn't have a Fox lock or any other kind of dead-bolt; all he had was a cheap mother any kid could pick.

He got an aluminum shim out of his folding kit, slid it in above the bolt and worked it around the door frame and into the crack where the door and jamb joined. He felt for the bolt, found it, twisted the shim down against it, and within another thirty seconds he had the bolt sprung and the door open. He made sure the other two doors that opened off the hall were still closed; then he stepped inside and shut the door behind him.

He breathed easier then. The tough part was over. Tossing an empty apartment was the easy part.

The room he was in was dim, illuminated only by light from a streetlamp outside, but even at that Hiller could see that it was neat and nicely furnished. Not the sort of place he'd have figured for a junkman like Lorsec. He moved quietly through the apartment, using his penlight to examine the living room but keeping it shielded so light wouldn't show in the windows. He searched drawers, beneath cushions, behind drapes, under lamps.

Nothing.

Hiller went into the bedroom and started tossing the dresser drawers. He was surprised at the quality of clothing, and at the fact that half of it belonged to a woman; Lorsec must be living with someone. There was even some pretty good jewelry, and fifty dollars in small bills rolled and rubber-banded beneath a stack of underwear. Hiller helped himself. Why not?

He was stuffing the money into his hip pocket when he heard the noise out in the front room. The back of his neck crawled. It sounded like somebody had opened the door, come inside the apartment.

Hiller started back toward the bedroom doorway—and the front-room lights came on. He blinked, lifting a hand to shade his eyes. Then he was looking at a big man wearing slacks and a light-colored blazer, a guy with a face Hiller had never seen before and a strained, determined expression that Hiller didn't like.

The man was pointing a gun at him.

A cold band of fear pressed tight around Hiller's chest,

binding him where he stood. He stared at the stranger with the gun, confused. Who was he? What the hell was he doing here? Why didn't he say something? Hiller eased his head around, darted a look at the bedroom window. It was barred with wrought-iron: a typical Manhattan window. Hiller knew he should have checked it earlier, found out if there was another way out of the apartment; now it was too late. He looked back at the guy with the gun.

"Hey, listen, pal . . ." he said.

The hand holding the weapon was rigid, the finger tight on the trigger.

"Listen," Hiller said, "all I want to do is walk out of here. All right? I just walk out of here." He took a step toward the man, his hands out in a pleading gesture.

The muzzle flashed. Something slammed into Hiller's chest; the world seemed to reverse rotation, and the next thing he knew was the feel of his fingers clawing into the rough nap of the carpet and he realized he was on the floor. Blood rose in his throat, dribbled out of one corner of his mouth. A long way off, somebody was screaming.

"Why?" he managed to say.

And then he died.

11:00 P.M. — MICHELE BUTLER

The picture on the TV in Michele's bedroom had gone haywire again, merging into a disjointed pattern of flickering diagonal lines that cast asymmetrical shadows over the walls and on the bed where she lay with Marco. The volume was turned off; the TV had served its function as a nightlight to provide the sort of soft illumination that he felt was conducive to sex.

Sex with Marco. Michele shivered, remembering the groping voraciousness of his experienced hands, the sour odors of his frail body and his breath. She had not had to fake frigidity with him; all he had aroused in her was coldness and revulsion. Her skills as an actress had been tested to the fullest, but she thought she had handled it well enough. Cooperated, let him do what he wanted to her twice already, but responded to him not at all. Still, he hadn't seemed to mind. Marco was an animal; all he cared about was his own gratification.

She lay staring up at the ceiling, hating him, hating herself a little for allowing this to happen. The stale scent of her couplings with him hung heavy in the still air of the bedroom. Marco was asleep, lying on his back with his arms flung loosely at his sides, his head thrown back, his hair comically mussed and a little-boy expression on his face. The regular rasp of his breathing was the only sound in the room, and it seemed to grow louder and louder, harsher and harsher, until it began to grate unbearably on Michele's nerves. She had to get away from it, away from Marco, if only for a short time.

She rolled onto her side, trying not to tilt the mattress, then sat nude on the edge of the bed. She stayed there for a moment, making sure she hadn't awakened him; even in the faint light from the TV, she could see that the insides of her thighs were still reddened from the friction of his frantic lovemaking.

Full of traps, she found herself thinking, *life is full of traps. Why does it have to be that way?* She sighed, almost a moan, and stood up.

"Hey, where you goin', sweets?" Marco murmured behind her.

Michele stiffened. Without turning she said, "I'm thirsty and I'm going to get something to drink. Do you want anything?"

"You got any beer?"

"I think so." She seemed to recall two long-ignored cans of Budweiser shoved to the back of the refrigerator.

"That'll do fine," Marco said. "You hurry back, sweets. I feel another hard-on coming on."

She repressed a shudder. Behind her as she padded out of the bedroom, she heard his cigarette lighter click as he lighted another joint.

In the kitchen, she ran some cold water, filled a glass, and drank the water down. She really was thirsty, as thirsty as she'd ever been. Then she opened the refrigerator, and in the bright light streaming from it wrestled with the pull-tab on one of the beer cans until it defeated her. She'd let Marco open it. The cold air from the refrigerator was going to give her pneumonia; her bare feet were like ice.

When she returned to the bedroom he was still lying on his back, with one arm behind his head, smoking his joint and staring at the shadows playing on the ceiling. Michele set the beer on the table by his side of the bed. "I couldn't get it open," she said.

He grinned dreamily. "No problem." The ember of the marijuana cigarette glowed like a red warning light as he took another puff. "You want a joint?" he asked.

"No," she said. He'd kept trying to get her to smoke one with him, or to take a hit off one of his; she had never smoked marijuana and she didn't want to start now, with him, but she almost wished she'd done it, gotten herself stoned. That would have made the past few hours a lot easier to handle.

"Come on back to bed," Marco said.

She returned to the bed, stretched out tensely beside him. She had something of the rigid aspect of a corpse in a funeral home; she knew it and didn't care. He wouldn't notice. She understood now that he saw only what he wanted to see.

"You know, sweets," he said, "you got a lot to learn about sex. Lucky thing for you you got somebody like me to teach you the finer points. You take a blowjob, now—" He stopped speaking. And then he said in a different voice, "What the

197

fuck!" and sat bolt upright in bed, staring past her at the doorway.

Startled, Michele opened her mouth to ask him what was wrong. But her head turned at the same time to follow his gaze, and the question died in her throat; she saw what was wrong.

The dark shape of a man stood in the bedroom doorway. She jerked upright, just as Marco had done, and gaped in disbelief. The man was holding something bulky in his arms: one of the throw pillows from the sofa. It flashed through her mind who he must be; the terror that came rushing into her was paralyzing, greater than any she had even known.

The black figure moved, took on a curious vigor, extended the wadded pillow toward her and Marco like an offering. "The wages of sin," he said softly, "is death."

Michele had a glimpse of the gun he held behind the wadded pillow. She tried to scream, tried to expel her terror, but her throat was too constricted even to allow the passage of breath. She heard Marco whimper behind her—and suddenly he was gripping her upper arm, her hair, yanking her sideways so her body shielded his. But he hadn't moved fast enough.

There was a muted slapping sound. And Marco's head seemed to explode.

Blood spurted from the hole that appeared where his left eye had been; droplets of it splashed hot on her arm, her cheek. Marco's hands released her. His body toppled backwards and the back of his head thunked against the headboard.

Michele screamed.

11:15 P.M. — E.L. OXMAN

In Jennifer's apartment, directly below Michele Butler's, Oxman heard the scream. It wasn't very loud, and at first he wasn't sure what it was. He came up off the living room couch, where he had been sitting and thinking while Jennifer worked on a set of fashion sketches at her drafting board. Hunger had driven them out of bed at eight o'clock, and they'd been up ever since.

His sudden movement caught Jennifer's notice; she stopped working and stared over at him with puzzlement in her green eyes. "What's wrong, E.L.?"

"Did you hear that?"

"Hear what?"

Then, from the floor above, there were hard thumping noises — footfalls, somebody running. Every muscle in Oxman's body went taut. He drew his service revolver, ran to the door, snapped off the locks. He threw the door open, said sharply to Jennifer over his shoulder, "Lock up again behind me!" and rushed into the hall.

As he took a step toward the stairwell, he heard the whine of the descending elevator.

"E.L.!" Jennifer was asking urgently behind him. "What's going on!"

"Get inside and lock the door!" he commanded again. He hesitated for a second to be sure she would comply, then he charged ahead to the stairs and half-ran, half-stumbled down them, racing the elevator to the lobby.

At the second-floor landing, he caromed off the rough plaster wall and almost lost his balance; pain lanced through his shoulder. As he shoved away from the wall, breathlessly started to pound down the last flight of stairs, he heard the elevator door open below, the hollow rhythm of running steps.

The lobby was empty when he reached it, the front door already easing closed on its pneumatic stop.

Cursing violently, Oxman stretched his stride and hit the door running. He'd forgotten how heavy it was and he was nearly knocked off his feet by its resistance. But is swung open, and he was through and out and then down the concrete steps to the sidewalk.

Except for a pair of headlights approaching from Riverside Drive, the street was deserted.

Oxman didn't realize that he had kept on going, out into the street, until the brakes squealed and the approaching car rocked to a stop close by, almost hitting him. He veered away, got back onto the sidewalk. The driver gave him a blast of the horn and yelled something at him, but Oxman barely heard. He kept swiveling his head back and forth, eyes probing the darkness for a sign of anyone on foot.

Nothing. Whoever had come out of the building had hidden himself, or entered another building; had been swallowed by the night.

Oxman holstered his service revolver, stood breathing hard, bent over with his hands on his knees. *Too old for this,* he thought, *too goddamn old...*

When the burning in his lungs eased he hurried back inside the brownstone. The elevator was still at lobby level; he rode it up to the fourth floor. The resident across the hall from Michele Butler, Wally Singer, had his head poked out of the door to his apartment; he pulled it back when he saw Oxman and the door slammed shut. Oxman kept hoping he was wrong about the meaning of the cry he'd heard, the fleeing steps, but when he reached Butler's door he knew he wasn't.

It was standing ajar.

He drew his revolver again, called out, "Miss Butler? This is the police."

Silence from within.

Oxman shoved the door all the way open and stepped inside, dreading what he might find. The only light seemed to come from the bedroom: the flickering, pale light of a television set. He found the switch for the ceiling globe in the living room, flipped it on, and then went slowly into the bedroom.

He smelled the stench of cordite even before the fluctuating light from the TV showed him the two still

200

figures on the bed. There was a reaction in his stomach, the same reaction he'd felt too many times before. He crossed the room, again holstering his weapon, and switched on the bedside lamp.

Blood gleamed in the sudden glow. The naked man, he saw, was Marco Pollosetti; one look at the composition of blood and brain matter on the headboard, like a grotesque Rorschach test, and another at the crimson hole where Pollosetti's left eye had been, were enough to tell Oxman that the man had died instantly. But the Butler girl was still alive. Shot in the chest, smeared with blood, unconscious; he could see the barely perceptible rise and fall of her breasts, and when he pressed his thumb against the artery in her neck he felt a faint pulse.

He found a heavy blanket in the bedroom closet. When he had covered her with it he ran out into the living room, located the telephone, draped his handkerchief over the receiver, and put in an emergency call for an ambulance. Then he dialed the number of the Twenty-fourth.

"This is Oxman," he said when the switchboard answered. "Put me through to Lieutenant Manders."

"Ox," Manders said, within ten seconds, "what the hell's going on there? I just tried to call you, and the Crane woman said you ran out with your gun drawn——"

"Another shooting," Oxman said tersely. "In the apartment above Jennifer's."

"What!"

"Two people shot this time—Marco Pollosetti and Michele Butler. Pollosetti's dead, but the woman is still alive. In bad shape, though. I've got an ambulance on the way."

"Good Christ!" Manders said. "When did this happen?"

"Just a few minutes ago."

"Shit! I thought we had the son of a bitch; I figured it was over."

"Over? What're you talking about?"

"We got a call a few minutes ago," Manders said. "Somebody got shot a little after ten o'clock during an apartment break-in at eleven-thirty West Ninety-eighth. Intruder, not a resident. I figured it must be the psycho."

Oxman felt a sinking coldness in his stomach. "It couldn't have been, Lieutenant. What happened here...it's his work."

Manders cursed again. "Wholesale slaughter, that's what's happening over there. All right. Who found the bodies? You?"

"Yeah. I heard a disturbance up here; that's why I ran out. He used a pillow to muffle the shots, but the Butler woman had time to scream. I heard him leave, chased after him, but by the time I got downstairs he was gone."

"You get a look at him?"

"No. But Butler must have. If the medics can save her, she might be able to give us an ID."

"Christ, I hope so. The media's going to go crazy over this; so are the mayor and the commissioner. Ox, you stay tight. Tobin's on his way to the eleven-twenty squeal, which was where I was going to send you; I'll be over myself as soon as I can."

"I'm not going anywhere," Oxman said grimly.

He rang off and went back into the bedroom. Michele Butler was still breathing; he checked her pulse again to make sure. *Come on, medics,* he thought. *Hurry it up, will you?*

As if in reply, the baying of approaching sirens sounded from outside.

Oxman turned away from the bed, feeling sickened. It always amazed him anew what people could do to one another. It was beyond all reason, totally beyond it; it had to do with the dark recesses of the brain, the hidden dead-end corridors of the mind's labyrinth. Sometimes he thought everybody in this city was insane. That was how he saw it more and more of late — a gigantic, teeming insane asylum.

And there was no way to be sure if he was a keeper or an inmate.

11:45 P.M. — ART TOBIN

Tobin stood tight-lipped and angry in a bedroom in 1120 West Ninety-eighth. He had just hung up the phone; Lieutenant Smiley had called to tell him about Michele Butler and Marco Pollosetti, and about Elliot Leroy almost catching the bloodthirsty motherfucker who'd shot them. Tobin had figured they *already* had the psycho, just as Manders had, when this squeal came in. Now they were right back at the beginning, and with one and maybe two more homicides on their hands.

Tobin still figured that this shooting was tied in with the others somehow; he didn't like coincidence worth a damn. But if it was tied in, it was in a way that he couldn't even begin to understand yet.

The resident of 1120, one Herb Blocker, was seated in the living room with his blond wife Gretchen. They had come home from a late dinner an hour ago and found someone inside their apartment, rummaging around in the bedroom. Blocker was a jeweler in the Diamond Exchange; he had a permit to carry a handgun. He'd had the gun with him. He'd used it.

So it seemed to be a simple matter of a B and E man getting caught in the act and shot. At least, that was the way it looked now.

Only the dead man happened to be a resident not only of West Ninety-eighth Street, but of the block where all the other shootings had taken place. When Tobin had gone into the bedroom after his arrival, to join the uniformed patrolman on guard there, something about the corpse on the floor struck his memory. He'd walked around so he could see the dead man's face and immediately recognized Benny Hiller.

The issue was so damned confused at this stage that Tobin didn't even try to speculate on possible answers. He returned to the living room and listened to Blocker's rambling story. The jeweler had never killed anyone before tonight; he hadn't dreamed of the consequences of such a simple act as aiming a gun and squeezing the trigger. Tobin had killed a man five years ago; he knew how Blocker felt, so he was tolerant. He was still trying to get the man calmed down enough to make a coherent statement when the professionals began to arrive — the lab boys and the photographer, then Smathers, the assistant M.E.

Smathers was a little gray-haired guy who seemed to love his work, which always struck Tobin as not only odd but obscene. He didn't like Smathers for that reason, and because he had once heard the little honky prick refer to a black victim as "another dead nigger."

"Caught with his hand in the cookie jar, eh?" Smathers said as Tobin led him into the bedroom. He grinned and set down his bag. He had on his usual wrinkled three-piece checkered suit and polka-dot bow tie. *A hell of a dresser,* Tobin thought sourly; Smathers was one short step from being a circus clown.

He watched the assistant M.E. walk slowly around Hiller's body, smiling down at it as if he suspected that Hiller might only be faking and would jump up at any second. "He's dead, all right," Smathers said finally, making his customary joke. Tobin had heard it even at the scene of a gruesome auto accident on Broadway that had left its victim decapitated.

"I figured he wasn't only sleeping," Tobin said.

"You want the photog to get in here before I do?"

Tobin nodded. That was the usual procedure: Get the homicide scene recorded on film before Smathers and the lab people did their jobs.

While the photographer circled the room taking his Polaroid flash shots, Smathers moved over to stand by Tobin. "Two more people shot right down the street tonight," he said. "What is this, the last act of *Hamlet*?"

"I wish it *was* a last act," Tobin said.

"I got instructions to run over there after I'm finished here," Smathers said. "Your partner Oxman is already there."

"I know. I've been told."

Tobin had to get away from Smathers. Without saying anything more, he went into the living room to see if Herb Blocker and his wife were calm enough now to give statements. He'd seen all he needed to see in the bedroom. On the way he wondered how Oxman was handling things. He didn't much like the idea of Elliot Leroy moving in with Jennifer Crane; he suspected old E.L. had made himself a conquest, which, if true, was goddamned unprofessional. A man Elliot Leroy's age was too old to let a piece of tail jeopardize his career. Tobin decided he'd talk to Elliot Leroy about it when he saw him, see which way the wind was blowing.

"He's . . . really dead, isn't he?" Blocker asked from where he sat in a low-slung chair. His face was the color of ashes and his hands were still trembling. "I mean, sometimes if you're not a doctor you can be fooled."

"He's dead, all right," Tobin said, echoing Smathers's stale irony. "You shouldn't feel so badly, Mr. Blocker. It could be you in there instead of him."

"Was he armed?" Gretchen Blocker asked.

"No. But that probably won't make much difference. There was no way for your husband to know if he was or wasn't."

"I should have tried to find out," Blocker said miserably. "I shouldn't have just . . . shot him. But he came toward me, he had his hands out in front of him; I thought he was going to attack me. . . ."

"Just take it easy, Mr. Blocker."

Blocker's wife said, "Is Herb . . . in trouble?"

"Some," Tobin said. Blocker wasn't the psycho; he was reasonably sure of that. And because he found himself liking these people, he decided to tell it straight. "But Hiller was shot from the front in your bedroom, so ultimately it'll be ruled self-defense or justifiable homicide, after you thread your way through the legal entanglements. You'll need a good lawyer, even for this."

"Hiller," Blocker said softly. "Was that his name?" It was personal now; he'd killed a man with a name, an actual human being, not just a menacing figure lurking in his bedroom.

"He lived the other side of West End," Tobin said. "When we check I'm pretty sure we'll find out he was a pro."

"You mean a professional burglar?"

Tobin nodded. "He's dressed the part, he's got burglar tools in his jacket pocket, and he got in here without arousing anybody. He was a pro, all right."

"God," Blocker moaned. "Why did he have to pick us? Why *us*?"

Yeah, Tobin thought. *Why?*

He wanted to get the initial stages of this one over with, so he could find out from Elliot Leroy what had gone down there. He said, "I'll need you to answer some questions, Mr. Blocker."

"Yes, sure," Blocker said with a kind of pathetic eagerness. He needed to tell his story now, needed to purge himself of it.

Tobin asked the key questions and sat listening to the same sad story he'd heard so many times in so many places, with only slight variations and always with the same ending.

When Blocker was finished talking, Tobin put Holroyd in charge of seeing to the removal of the body and questioning the neighbors. Then he left the building, decided to let his car stay parked where it was, and hurried through the warm night to where Elliot Leroy was waiting with more death.

THE COLLIER TAPES

Two more of the wicked are dead. Two more blemishes on the face of my universe have been erased.

I quote Swinburne for swine:

> *They say sin touches not a man so near*
> *As shame a woman; yet he too should be*
> *Part of the penance, being more deep than she*
> *Set in the sin.*

I knew Marco Pollosetti and Michele Butler must be the next to be punished for their sins when the Eye observed them copulating on the woman's bed. Pollosetti's thin, hairy buttocks rising and falling in ever-increasing tempo, her legs entwined about him, his mouth fastened like a suckling child on one of her pale breasts. . .it was a disgusting, evil sight. As one, like an obscene beast, they writhed in concert, their motions becoming frantic, their legs flailing as if seeking a foothold in the air. The Eye saw the mindless spasms of their bodies grow to a fierceness, then closed in shame as they finished sating their lust. And I left my apartment immediately and went down into my world and brought them their just reward; I brought them Death, I brought them salvation.

Now the Eye is open again and I watch the police at their futile work. They are Philistines; I will not fall prey to them. Quite the contrary. I prove that and go on proving it, do I not?

And I give lessons even as I wreak my vengeance and deliver sinners to the purifying infinite. Detective Oxman must know by now that the fate of the two young fornicators might just as easily have been delivered unto him and his harlot. How do he and Jennifer Crane feel about that? What are they thinking, even at this moment? Fear haunts by fits

207

those whom it takes. Detective Oxman will not rest easy tonight, for now he surely realizes my power.

Another quote comes to me, my favorite verse from Coleridge's *Ancient Mariner:*

> *Like one that on a lonesome road*
> *Doth walk in fear and dread*
> *And having once turned round, walks on*
> *And turns no more his head;*
> *Because he knows a frightful fiend*
> *Doth close behind him tread.*

It is too bad there isn't time to mail Detective Oxman a copy of that verse. He would certainly identify with it if I did. For he is sure to blanch each time he hears an unfamiliar step behind him in a lonely place, and for an instant at least his bowels will turn to water. The first or second or third time it happens, perhaps, the one who walks behind him will pose no threat. But then, very soon —

Then the one who walks behind him shall be me.

PART 5

TUESDAY
SEPTEMBER 24

7:15 A.M.
JENNIFER CRANE

She couldn't seem to get warm.

She had lain sleepless in bed with the air conditioner off and her electric blanket turned high, alone because E.L. had been up all night, in and out of the apartment; she had taken a shower with the water as hot as she could stand it; twice she had lit the oven in an attempt to warm the apartment, only to have E.L. complain when he returned and shut it off again; she had put on a sweater and a light jacket, still had them on now. None of that made her warm. Her feet felt as though she had been walking barefoot in snow, her hands were icy, little chills kept slithering up and down her back.

It was the fear that had robbed her of warmth; she knew that. She had never been more frightened than she was now, than she had been ever since E.L. came back last night to tell her about Michele Butler and Marco Pollo. But it wasn't just herself she was afraid for; it was E.L., too. And it wasn't just their lives she was afraid for; it was what they had together, the fragile relationship they had begun to build before these new explosions of terror the past two nights.

For the first time since Zach, like it or not, want it or not, she had found somebody who mattered to her, let somebody inside her mind as well as her body. Maybe there was no future for her and E.L. in any event, but then again maybe there *was*. She wanted badly to find out. But if this madness kept on, if they didn't get the maniac soon, she sensed that something terrible would happen. E.L. would be killed, or circumstances would drive them apart in some other way . . . *something* terrible would happen.

She shivered, hugged herself tightly as she paced the confines of her bedroom. E.L. was out in the front room now, with Art Tobin; she could hear the murmur of their voices through the closed door, but not what they were saying to each other. E.L. had sent her in here when Tobin arrived, so whatever it was they were discussing, he wanted it private. But she thought she knew what part of it was, anyway — the same thing she and E.L. had talked about over an hour ago.

He was going to move her out of here, to some other part of the city where she would be safe. And he was going to bring in a policewoman to take her place.

"It's the only way that makes sense now," he'd told her. "You can't stay here; it's too dangerous. That psycho got in and out of this building once. I'm not going to take any chances that he can do it again, no matter how many cops we have in the vicinity."

"But if he's watching the building, he'll see me leave . . ."

"No, he won't. The policewoman will come in uniform, and we'll see to it that she's your size and build; when she gets here you'll change clothes with her. She'll also have different color hair than you, noticeably different, and she'll

212

bring wigs for both of you. You'll be out of here and away in a couple of minutes; if he's watching, he won't have time to notice the switch."

"What about you?" she asked.

"I've got to stay, Jennifer, you know that."

"I want to stay here with you."

"No. I told you, it's too dangerous."

"Damn it, E.L., this is my apartment—"

"Not anymore, it isn't," he said grimly. "It's a command post and maybe it's a trap. It was a bad idea to let you stay here this long; I should have called in a policewoman twenty-four hours ago."

"What if I refuse to leave?"

"Then I'll have you put in protective custody and removed by force. I mean it, Jennifer. This isn't a game."

"My God, don't you think I know that?"

"Then don't argue with me anymore. I'm a cop and I know what I'm doing."

So his mind was made up and she was going: The policewoman was due to arrive by eight o'clock. On the one hand she hated the idea of being forced out of her apartment, of leaving him; of having to sit somewhere in unfamiliar surroundings, holed up under guard, waiting for the phone to ring or somebody to come and tell her it was over one way or another. The idea of all that passive waiting — hours, maybe days — was repulsive. But on the other hand she felt a deep-seated sense of relief. Not only would she be leaving this apartment, she would be leaving this block and the spying eyes and malevolent purpose of a mass murderer. She would no longer have to fear for her own life. Because it could have been she and E.L. who were shot last night, in *her* bed; it could be E.L. who was dead and she the one who was lying unconscious, in critical condition, in the hospital under police guard. E.L. was doing the right thing to get her away from here. At least now she would be *safe*.

Yet she hated that feeling of relief, that desire for safety.

213

Ever since Zach and the loss of her baby, she had wallowed in safety—safe job, safe relationships with men, never allowing herself to step out from behind the high safe walls of aloofness and calculation she had erected. If E.L. hadn't happened to her, she might have remained hidden behind those walls; and it would be much easier for her to go away now, to run from her fear into still more safety. But E.L. *had* happened to her. She was changing, emerging, and she felt naked and vulnerable, and she wasn't sure if she could escape back into that sanctuary she had built for herself. It was that as much as anything else that made her so afraid.

She lit another cigarette—smoking too much too, a full pack already this morning—and paced to the closet door. The muffled sounds of E.L.'s and Tobin's voices still came from the other room. On impulse she turned the knob and cracked the door soundlessly to listen.

"...even some talk about evacuating the entire block," Tobin was saying. "That's how panicked City Hall is this morning. The media's got the whole city on the verge of hysteria."

"If they went ahead with anything like that, it'd screw things up so bad we might never get him. He probably lives on the block himself. And even if he doesn't, he'd just lie low and wait until things cooled down and everybody moved back."

"I know. Smiley talked to the commissioner and got him to see it that way. But they're still talking about cordoning off the block."

"I don't like that either."

"Neither do I. Stepped-up patrols, more undercover men in the buildings—all of that makes sense. But we don't want to scare the perp off by turning the neighborhood into a fucking war zone."

"Yeah. He's out of control as it is, Artie; he's hit two days running and he thinks he's invincible. All he is is lucky. He'll make another try damned soon, and when he does his luck is liable to run out. *If* everybody doesn't panic."

"You think he'll come after you this time?"

"I hope so," E.L. said. "Jesus, I hope so."

"Well, if he does make another try, against you or anybody else, we'd better made sure his luck runs out. Heads are gonna roll in the Department if we don't, yours and mine included."

"Tell me something I don't know."

"It'll be worse than that, too," Tobin said. "The media's got people spooked; everybody's screaming for protection. If that bastard kills again and gets away with it, the city's gonna explode. We'll have armed vigilantes running around, blowing people away on the streets. We'll have riots. I'm telling you, Elliot Leroy . . ."

Jennifer shut the door again, shivering, and went to the overflowing ashtray on the nightstand to jab out her cigarette. Immediately, she lit another. The smoke burned her lungs, made her cough and tears come to her eyes.

You think he'll come after you this time?

I hope so. Jesus, I hope so.

And I hope not, she thought. *Jesus, I hope not.*

Her eyes were still wet from the coughing; she could feel the tears warm on the icy surface of her cheeks. She wished suddenly that she could cry, that she was the kind of person who could sit down and let the emotion come spilling out of her. It would be so good to just sit down and—

And she sat down on the bed and began to weep.

8:10 A.M. — WILLIE LORSEC

Corales stared at him across the table. Richard was standing there with a cup of coffee in one hand and the deck of playing cards in the other; his eyes were bright with disappointment and what Lorsec took to be a kind of desperation. "What do you mean no more gin games, Willie? What do you *mean?*"

215

"Just what I said. You must understand——"

"I *don't* understand," Corales said. "Maybe you don't understand either. I won forty-nine straight hands. One more and I'll have fifty and I can get into the *Guinness Book of World Records.* I got to do it, Willie. You said last night you'd play this morning; you promised me before you left. It's only one more hand!"

"Richard, you're not being practical. Two more people were shot last night, right here in this building. And another of your tenants was killed just up the street. We can't simply go on playing gin as if nothing had happened."

"Why can't we?"

"Because we can't. You knew each of the victims; don't you care that they're dead?"

"Sure I care," Corales said. "I'm sorry they're dead. But they weren't friends of mine, and there's nothing I can do about it. You and me, we got to go on living, don't we?"

"Yes, we do. If we can."

"What do you mean, if we can?"

"Several people have died already," Lorsec said patiently. "Who's to say there won't be more? Who's to say the next victim won't be you or me?"

Corales shook his head. "Nobody'd want to kill us."

"It seemed nobody would want to kill any of the others, either. But they're dead just the same."

"You mean you're afraid, Willie?"

"Of course I am. Aren't you?"

"No," Corales said. "I don't go out at night, and I got locks on my door and a Reggie Jackson baseball bat right alongside my bed. Even if somebody wanted to shoot me, he couldn't do it."

Lorsec sighed. Corales was such a child, such an innocent. Mental retardation was a tragedy for the most part, but in a situation like the one which existed here, and in a man such as Corales, it was also a blessing. Unlike everyone else who lived on this block, Richard could sleep

216

nights—the sleep of the untroubled, the unafraid, the guileless. *His* world had not been disrupted. His world, at least as he perceived it, remained as simple and unencumbered as it had always been.

"So I don't see no reason why we can't play gin," Corales said. "Christ, Willie, I only need to win one more hand. Then I'll be somebody. Don't you see that? I never been nobody in my whole life and now I can be."

"I'm sorry. I really am. . . ."

"You're not sorry at all," Corales said, and there was anger in his voice for the first time. "If you were sorry, you'd sit down and play so I can win one more hand."

"Richard, listen to me——"

"You're afraid of losing any more. That's it, isn't it? You lost forty-nine times straight and you don't want to lose no more."

"That's not so," Lorsec said. Which was not quite the truth. Actually, he *had* become annoyed at losing so many consecutive hands; he was not a man who cared to lose at anything. At first, Corales's phenomenal winning streak had amused him—and he had continued to put up with it because he was genuinely fond of the man. But enough was enough. He had too many things on his mind to want to put up with it any longer.

"Then why won't you play one more hand so I can get into the Guinness Book?"

"Richard, even if I agreed to play just one hand, there's no guarantee that you'd win."

"I'd win, all right. I'd win."

"You can't be sure of that. Can you even be sure fifty consecutive winning gin rummy hands qualifies you for the Guinness Book?"

Corales blinked. "What?"

"Have you checked the Guinness Book, Richard? What *is* the record for most consecutive winning gin rummy hands?"

"No, I never checked it," Corales said. "But it's got to be the record. Nobody could win more than fifty straight."

"Well, then, suppose the record is only forty-eight. Or less. Then you've already established a new record, haven't you?"

"I never thought of that," Corales said, frowning. But then the frown deepened and he said, "I don't care what the old record is. I want to win fifty, I want to see how many hands I can win in a row. Maybe I can make seventy-five, or even a hundred. Maybe I can set a record that nobody'll *ever* break."

Lorsec sighed again. "I think I'd better go," he said.

"Go? You mean you're really not gonna play anymore?"

"I've already told you I'm not. I couldn't concentrate with so much going on outside, so many police in the area——"

"Damn the police! I don't give a shit about the police!" Corales's face was splotched now; his oversized hands were fisted at his sides. "What'd you come around here for this morning, anyway, you don't want to play gin no more?"

"I wanted to see you, that's all——"

"Yeah, sure," Corales said. "And you want me to let you rummage around in the trash some more, right? That's all you ever wanted from me."

"That isn't true. You're my friend."

"Well, you ain't *my* friend, not anymore," Corales said angrily. "Go on, get out of here. I don't never want to see you again."

"Richard——"

"Get out, I said. Get out! And don't come around no more. Go make friends with some other super if you ain't done that already, get your goddamn junk from *him.*"

Lorsec considered standing his ground, making an effort to pour oil on these troubled waters, but the look in Corales's eyes changed his mind. He let out another sigh, inaudible this time, and went to the door.

"No matter what you think now," he said as he opened it, "I'm your friend and I wish you well."

"Go fuck yourself, Willie," Corales said, and slammed the door behind him.

Lorsec started across the basement to the alley entrance. Halfway there, he noticed that Corales had left his tool chest on a wooden stool. He shook his head sadly. *Poor Richard,* he thought. *Always leaving things around where someone could steal them. Such a trusting soul. Such a foolish innocent.*

Lorsec picked up the tool chest and took it back and set it in front of Corales's door. Then he knocked once. He was already on his way back across the basement when Corales looked out.

8:25 A.M. — WALLY SINGER

He couldn't believe it, he just could not believe it.

"Leaving me?" he said. "Leaving me? What kind of bull-shit is this, Marian?"

"It's not bullshit," Marian said. She was still over there at the dresser, methodically taking her clothes out and putting them into her open suitcase on the bed. She hadn't stopped doing that, had barely even looked at him, since he'd come in and caught her at it a couple of minutes ago.

"You can't walk out on me!"

"Can't I? You just watch me."

"Where the hell are you going to go?"

"I'm moving in with a friend in the Village."

"What friend?"

"Someone you don't know. A man."

"Man?"

"A man I've been seeing," she said, neatly folding a skirt. "A man I love and who loves me."

It struck him funny. He threw back his head and laughed, but when he did that the sudden motion aggravated the hangover pain in his temples, made him wince, and cut the laugh into a bark. Christ, he must have drunk half a case of beer last night. But who could blame him? Another shooting right here in the building, right across the hall, that snooty little actress and the junkie musician who lived downstairs;

219

cops all over the place, more questions. It had shaken him bad, even worse than when Marian told him Cindy had been killed across the street.

And now this. Marian calmly packing her suitcase, telling him she was moving out, telling him she was in love with somebody else. Marian? Fat, stupid Marian? It was funny, all right, crazy funny. Nobody in his right mind would want a cow like her.

"Go ahead and laugh," she said. She didn't sound angry; she didn't sound anything except determined. "It happens to be the truth."

"Sure it is. You think crap like that is going to bother me, hurt me?"

"I don't care if it does or doesn't. You've hurt *me* plenty, Wally, and I don't want to live with you anymore or be your wife anymore. That's what matters right now."

He put it into words this time: "Who'd want a cow like you?"

That got to her; pain flickered across her dumpy face. But only for an instant. She still didn't stop stuffing clothes into her suitcase. And she didn't answer his question.

Singer felt a little tug of desperation. Maybe it *was* true; maybe she *had* found somebody to have an affair with. And maybe she really was going to leave him. He still couldn't believe it, but what if it was true? What the hell would he do then?

"You're not walking out of here," he said.

"How are you going to stop me? By force? The building is crawling with police, Wally; all I have to do is scream once and they'll be at the door in ten seconds."

"I'm your husband, goddamn it!"

"Not for long," she said. "I'm going to file for divorce as soon as I can find a lawyer."

"You're crazy," he said. "You've gone off your rocker, you know that?"

"You can keep the apartment and the furniture. I'll send for the rest of my things in a few days."

"Keep the apartment? For Christ's sake, how am I going to pay the rent?"

"It's paid through the end of the month. You'll have to get a job, that's all. It's your problem, Wally, not mine — not any longer."

"You bitch, you can't do this to me!"

"I should have done it a long time ago," she said.

"He talked you into this, didn't he? This bastard you've been sleeping with."

"No, he didn't. I've been thinking about it for days and what happened last night made up my mind. And he's not a bastard. He's kind and gentle; he's everything you're not."

"Who is he? What's his name?"

"I don't think I want to tell you that."

"I got a right to know who you think you're running off with!"

"I'm not running off with him."

"Damn you, Marian, who is he?"

"No," she said. She finished putting the last of her clothes into the suitcase, pulled the lid down, leaned on it, and fastened the catches. "There's fifty dollars in the jar in the kitchen. You'll have to make do with that until you get a job."

He wanted to hit her. God, he wanted to rush over there and smash her fat cow face until it was slick with blood. But he couldn't move; his legs wouldn't work. He just stood there in the doorway with his head pounding, pounding. He couldn't even move when she brushed past him, carrying the suitcase, and walked into the front room.

"I'll get you for this, Marian!" he shouted after her. "I won't let you do this to me!"

"Good-bye, Wally," she said.

Fifteen seconds later she was gone, actually gone.

He moved then, as soon as he heard the front door close. But not far, just into the middle of the studio; he didn't have anywhere else to go. He knew that now, believed it all now, and it was like a hole had opened up and he was being sucked down into it. His hands were shaking; he felt sick to his stomach. And wild inside, trapped. Marian's sculptures seemed to leer at him from across the room, mocking. He tried to make himself go over there and smash them, but he couldn't do that either. All he could do was stand there shaking, screaming at her inside his head.

He couldn't do anything at all.

8:30 A.M. — E.L. OXMAN

Questions kept flashing around inside Oxman's mind like the lighted images in a video game.

He paced the front room of Jennifer's apartment, from the door to the sunlit windows and back again in frustrated movements. He was alone in the room now. The policewoman, Carla Ullman, had arrived a few minutes earlier and was in the bedroom with Jennifer, making the switch of their clothing. Tobin had gone off to continue taking the statements of building residents — a probably futile activity because nobody seemed to have seen or heard the killer last night, as if he were some kind of phantom who could appear and disappear at will. Oxman would do the same as soon as Jennifer left with the uniformed officers waiting out in the hall — and he would take the questions with him, because he couldn't seem to score an answer with any of them.

Why had the psycho gone after Michele Butler and Marco Pollosetti, instead of Jennifer and him? Maybe the telephone call, the threats, of two nights ago had been a smokescreen; maybe the Butler girl and Pollosetti had been the targets all along. Or maybe it was some sort of cat-and-mouse ploy — taunting Oxman again, trying to show him and the police that he could strike whenever and wherever he felt like it, right under their noses. Or maybe it was part of some complex plan his madman's brain had cooked up.

How had he got into the building last night? None of the ground-floor doors or windows had been forced; the lab crew had already established that. And preliminary questioning of the residents had established that none of them had admitted anyone at any time prior to the shootings. Did he live in the building himself? Did he have a key to the main entrance? Court orders had been obtained and searches were being conducted now of each apartment; but even if he did live here, he was too cunning to keep his weapon or anything else incriminating on the premises, and it was a longshot at best that the searches would turn up anything.

How had he got into Butler's apartment? The lab boys had also examined her door and found no signs of forcible entry. Had she left it unlocked for some reason, or forgotten to lock it? Was it possible the psycho was somebody she knew well enough to give a key to?

Had Butler recognized the assailant, either as a friend or neighbor? Or if he was a stranger, could she describe him? Surgery to remove the bullet from her chest had been successful, and the doctors thought her chances for survival were good, but as of fifteen minutes ago, when Oxman had called the hospital to check on her condition, she still hadn't regained consciousness. There was no estimate as to when she would.

How had the psycho known Oxman had been to bed with Jennifer on Sunday night? If he was a resident of the building, it might explain how he'd been aware that Oxman had entered her apartment, but that didn't explain how he'd been aware that Oxman had entered her body. He couldn't see through walls, for Christ's sake. Lucky guess? No, the voice on the phone had sounded confident, righteously offended; he'd *known*. And yet how the hell *could* he have known?

223

Was there a connection between the psycho and the shooting of Benny Hiller? Tobin had ruled out the possibility that the man who'd shot Hiller, Herb Blocker, could be the psycho; Blocker was just a man protecting his home and property against an intruder. Tobin had figured Hiller for a professional burglar, and evidence found later in Hiller's apartment had pretty much confirmed the fact. It could be that Hiller's death had been a coincidence, with no relation to the other shootings; that he'd just gone out on a B and E job and picked the wrong place to burglarize. The only thing wrong with that theory was, professional burglars didn't shit where they lived. The last place any of them would pick to hit would be a building on the same block they called home. But what other reason could Hiller have had for wanting to break into the Blocker apartment? Could it have something to do with the psycho, and if so, *what?*

The constant clamor of questions, the frustration, had given Oxman a headache and wired him up so tight he felt a little crazy himself. What Tobin had said earlier, about the city exploding if there were any more killings on West Ninety-eighth, might be true; they *had* to get the psycho and they had to get him fast. There was some sort of pattern in the answers to all those questions, in everything that had happened so far, Oxman was sure of it. If only he could fit just a few of the pieces together, enough to give him an idea of what that pattern was. . . .

The bedroom door opened and Jennifer and Carla Ullman came out. Oxman stopped pacing to look at them. He didn't have to look twice to see that a switch had been made, but he might have if he hadn't known about it; nobody was going to tell it from a distance. Ullman bore a superficial resemblance to Jennifer—that was why she'd been picked—and with the wigs both of them now wore, and Jennifer in the police uniform and Ullman in one of Jennifer's dresses, they passed well enough for each other.

"All set, Ox," Ullman said. "How do we look?"

"Okay. I think it'll work."

Jennifer came over to him. She had put on some of Ullman's dark red lipstick, and it made her pale face look even whiter, as if it had been drained of blood. Her eyes were puffy; he wondered if she had been crying, and the thought wrenched at him. He had an impulse to take her into his arms, but he didn't want to do that with Ullman watching. He stood still with his hands at his sides, watching her, stroking her with his eyes.

"I don't want to go, E.L.," she said.

"I know. But it's got to be this way."

"Do you know where they're taking me?"

"Yes. A hotel on the East Side."

"The Haverton, Carla said."

He nodded. "You'll be all right."

"Will I? I guess I will. But it'll be a little easier if I can talk to you later, just for a couple of minutes."

"I'll try to call you," he said.

"Do that. Try." She gave him a small smile; he could see the effort it cost her. "I'm ready now."

Oxman resisted another impulse to gather her into his arms. Instead he turned and went to the door and unlocked it. When he opened up the two policemen in the hall came to attention. "Policewoman Ullman is leaving now," Oxman said, just loud enough for his voice to carry; there were people behind the other doors along the hall, and if any of them were listening, the words were for their benefit. "Escort her downstairs, will you?"

"Yes, sir," one of the patrolman said, very casually. A natural actor.

Jennifer came over to the door, gave Oxman one last lingering look, and then stepped out into the hall. He watched her move away with the uniforms, stiff and erect, clutching Ullman's black bag. A knot of something painful seemed to have formed in his chest.

When he closed and relocked the door Ullman said,

"Well," with forced cheerfulness. Nobody had told her there was anything between Jennifer and him, of course, but Ullman knew it anyway; the knowledge was in her eyes. "How about a cup of coffee, Ox?"

"No," he said. "I've had enough."

"You mind if I make some for myself?"

"Go ahead. You're supposed to live here."

She nodded and turned toward the kitchen. And the telephone rang.

Oxman moved quickly over to it, gesturing to Ullman. "You answer it," he said. "If it's somebody for Jennifer, tell him you have a cold or something and can't talk and hang up."

"Right."

Ullman picked up the receiver, listened for a moment, and then held it out to Oxman. "It's Lieutenant Manders."

He took the instrument. "Oxman."

"I'm over at St. Luke's, Ox," Manders said. "Michele Butler just regained consciousness."

"Thank Christ. You talked to her yet?"

"Not yet. Doc's still with her, but he says he thinks we can go in pretty soon."

"Everything still under wraps?"

"Yeah," Manders said. The decision had been made, and the cooperation of the media solicited, to keep Michele Butler's condition a secret; as far as the city-at-large knew, she had presumably died along with Marco Pollosetti last night. If she *could* identify the man who'd shot her, the Department didn't want the psycho to know she was still alive. Or that they had his description until they were ready to circulate it. "What's going on there?"

"Jennifer Crane just left," Oxman said. "That's all."

"Any problems?"

"I don't think so."

"All right. Hang tight; I'll get back to you as soon as I talk to Butler." Manders paused. "You a religious man, Ox?"

226

"Not particularly. Why?"

"Neither am I," Manders said. "But if Butler can't identify the perp, we'd better both start brushing up on how to pray."

9:10 A.M. — MICHELE BUTLER

She lay small and still in the hospital bed, waiting for the police to come in and talk to her. Her thoughts were clear enough, if still a little fuzzy at the edges; she held them in tight check, trying to tell herself that this was just another role she was playing. The bottles and the tubes extending from them into her arm, the bandages across her chest, the sterile white room — these were just props. The scene she was about to play was a scene in a stage production. Or a soap opera. *General Hospital.* Even the dull pain, she told herself, was something she had created herself to enhance her portrayal of a critically wounded gunshot victim.

But she couldn't make herself believe it. The world of acting, of make-believe, the only world she had ever really dwelled in, had been torn asunder; it lay inside her in piles. The real world was where she lived now, and the images of terror that kept rising up in the back of her mind — the dark figure of the intruder, the gun in his hand, the explosion of Marco's head, the spurts and streaks of blood — were real images. Nothing else mattered, nothing else had any meaning. The other world, the make-believe world, was sham and illusion, a place of ghosts and shattered dreams, and the woman who had lived in it had died when it died.

She hadn't died, though; the real Michele Butler was still alive. And she wasn't going to die. That was the first thing she'd asked the doctor: "Am I going to die?" And he'd said no, she was going to be all right. It had eased her, because she was terrified of death. She had never really realized that before. And maybe that hidden fear was why she had wanted so desperately to be an actress: It was a form of immortality. Except that it wasn't. When you died you were dead. What difference did it make to *you* if your image lived on in films or people's memories? Death was death, and life was life. Reality was everything.

The images of last night's reality kept rising, rising; she felt the terror again, tasted it. She couldn't drive it away by pretending, not ever again.

Now the police were there.

She didn't hear the door open, but she felt their presence and turned her head, and saw them standing just inside the room. There were two of them. They came over to the bed, and the taller one with the sad face said, "I'm Lieutenant Manders, Miss Butler. I'd like to ask you some questions about last night."

"Yes."

He leaned down toward her. "The first question is the most important. Did you recognize the man who shot you and Marco Pollosetti?"

"No," Michele said.

"You never saw him before?"

"I didn't see his face very well. It was dark."

"Can you describe him?"

"No. I'm sorry...no."

Lieutenant Manders said, "Damn," under his breath, and glanced at the other policeman. Then he said to her, "Try to remember, Miss Butler. Isn't there anything at all you can tell us about him?"

"He was just a dark shape. It all happened so fast..."

"Was he a big man? Tall? Fat? Thin?"

"Big, I think. Just a man, just...a man."

"Did he say anything before he started shooting?"

"He said...I think it was 'The wages of sin is death.'"

"That's all?"

"Yes. Then he shot Marco. Oh God, he just..."

"Easy, now. Did Pollosetti say anything. Did *he* seem to recognize the man?"

The images were vivid in her mind, now—Marco's head exploding, and the blood, all the blood, and the gun turning to her, and the second flash...

"Miss Butler?"

"No," she said. "No."

"All right." There was a look on Mander's sad face approaching desperation. "Tell me this: Was your apartment door locked?"

"Yes."

"You're sure of that?"

"I locked it myself, after Marco came."

"Then how did the killer get in?"

"I don't know."

"You didn't hear anything from the bedroom?"

"Nothing. He was just...there."

"Who else has a key to your apartment?"

"No one."

"Not even Pollosetti?"

"No. I'd never have given Marco a key."

"He was your boyfriend, wasn't he?"

"God, no. I hardly knew him."

"Miss Butler, you were in bed with the man."

"Yes. I...yes, I was in bed with him."

"A man you hardly knew?"

She averted her eyes. "It was...it was just..."

"Just what?"

She wanted to say, "It was just a casual affair." The lie, the actress's line, was on her tongue, hot and bitter, and yet she couldn't put it into words. Something seemed to be happening inside her, something critical, a sudden overpowering desire to take a step the old Michele Butler, the one who lived in dreams, could never have even considered. And before she could stop herself, she said, "He forced me to go to bed with him."

Manders narrowed his eyes. "Forced you?"

"He would have gone to the police if I hadn't slept with him. He would have exposed me."

"Miss Butler, what are you saying?"

Don't tell him, she thought. *Don't say any more! He'll arrest you, you'll go to jail, Mom and Dad will find out, everyone will know, you can't just confess like this . . .*

"I'm a thief," she said. And the images went away and so did the terror, and it was as if something heavy had been lifted from her; she felt weak with relief, she felt utterly real. "I've been stealing jewelry from department stores and selling it to support my acting career."

11:45 A.M. — RICHARD CORALES

He opened the door of his apartment and another cop was standing out there in the basement, the big black one who'd been around a couple of times before.

Corales cussed inside himself. He was sick of cops. He was sick of getting up in the middle of the night and answering questions and having cops stick a piece of paper in his face that said they could come into his apartment, come right into his *home,* and poke around like he was a crook or something. He was sick of murders and people rubbernecking on the streets and television cameras. He wanted to be left alone so he could do his job. That was all he had now, all he'd ever had and ever would have — just a big half-Puerto Rican building superintendent, nothing special even though he'd won forty-nine straight hands of gin rummy, because that damned Willie Lorsec wouldn't let him win fifty straight and get into the Guinness Book. He was sick of guys like Willie too, who pretended to be your friend so they could get something for themselves. Why couldn't they *all* just go away and leave him the hell alone?

"Detective Tobin," the black cop said, showing his badge. "I've got a few questions, Mr. Corales, if you don't mind."

230

"I do mind," Corales said. "I got to go out. I got to go to the hardware store for some faucet washers."

"This won't take very long."

"Listen, I already told you people. I don't know nothing about what happened upstairs last night. I was sleeping. How many times you gonna come around bothering me?"

"I'm not here about the shooting upstairs," Tobin said. "I'm here about the one up the block."

"Up the block?"

"Benny Hiller. You know about that, don't you?"

"Yeah, I been told. I don't know nothing about that, either."

"You knew Hiller, though, didn't you?"

"Sure I knew him. He lived right here in this building."

"Did you know he was a burglar?"

Corales blinked at him. "What?"

"A burglar," Tobin said. "Did you have any idea that was what he did for a living?"

"Chrissake, no, I didn't have no idea. Was Mr. Hiller really a burglar? No kidding?"

"No kidding. Did you have much contact with him?"

"Contact?"

"See him often, talk to him."

"I'd see him around sometimes during the day, while I was working," Corales said. "He was mostly home during the day. He said he worked nights in some café."

"When was the last time you talked to him?"

"Sunday, I guess."

"Where was that?"

"Down here in the basement. He come down to talk to me."

"What about?"

"He didn't like me letting Willie Lorsec come in and go through the trash."

"Who's Willie Lorsec?"

He's a snake-in-the-grass, Corales thought, *that's who he is.*
But he said, "A junk collector."

"Does he live on this street?"

"Yeah. Between West End and Broadway."

"Are you a friend of his?"

"Not no more."

"How come?"

Corales didn't feel like telling Tobin about the forty-nine straight winning hands; he didn't want to think about it anymore, because it just made him angry. "He wasn't really my friend. He just come around so I'd let him go through the trash."

"To collect junk, is that it?"

"Yeah."

"And Benny Hiller didn't like Lorsec doing that?"

"No, he didn't like it."

"Why not?"

"He said Willie stole some things from his trash."

"That was the word he used, 'stole'?"

Corales nodded. "I told him it wasn't stealing to take things a person has thrown away. But he got mad and called me a dummy. I don't like that. I'm not a dummy."

"Did Hiller tell you what these things were that Lorsec took?"

"No. He never said."

"Do you have any idea what they were?"

"No. Willie took all kinds of stuff; I never watched to see what most of it was."

"What did Hiller want you to do? Get these things of his back from Lorsec?"

"No. He just said he didn't want me to let Willie into the basement no more."

"Did he indicate he was going to try to get the stuff back from Lorsec himself?"

"I guess so. He asked me where Willie lived."

"Did you tell him?"

"No. I don't know where he lives."

"You just told me Lorsec lives in the next block."

"I never been to his place," Corales said. "He always come here to see me."

"Then how do you know where he lives?"

"He told me. And I see him around, collecting his junk."

"What else can you tell me about Lorsec?"

"I don't know too much. Willie told me once he'd traveled a lot and worked at a bunch of jobs, but the onlt thing made him happy was collecting and selling junk."

"Did he tell you where he was from?"

"Someplace up in New England. He never said where."

"Any other personal things he might have told you?"

"I guess not."

"Well, what did you talk about when he came to see you?"

"We didn't talk much about nothing. Sometimes he helped me do some things, carrying boxes and things; the rest of the time he rummaged in the trash or we played gin rummy." Corales pursed his lips. "I'm a better gin rummy player than Willie is. I'm a *lot* better than he is."

"Good for you," Tobin said. "You wouldn't happen to know where Lorsec is now, would you?"

"No. He come around earlier this morning, around eight, but I told him to get out. I don't know where he went after that, and I don't care."

"All right, Mr. Corales. Thanks for your help. I may need to talk to you again later on, so I'd appreciate it if you'd stick close to the building."

"Yeah," Corales said. Christ, weren't they *ever* going to leave him alone?

When the black cop was gone Corales went out through the alley door and up Ninety-eighth toward Amsterdam, where the hardware store was. He didn't look at the people and the police cars and the television cameras; the hell with all of them. And as he walked, he wondered if he'd got Willie

THE EYE

in trouble with the cops. He hoped he had. It would serve Willie right for keeping him out of the *Guinness Book of World Records.*

THE COLLIER TAPES

I have come out onto the balcony to dictate. Down below and across the river, my little universe swelters and writhes under the lash of heat. But up here, there is a cooling breeze and I am quite comfortable. The difference, if I may be permitted a small joke, is as between heaven and earth.

The Eye sits before me, waiting. How beautiful it is in the sunlight! How its brass fittings shine! Sometimes, as now, I am struck by the awesome power it represents, and I feel toward it—perhaps oddly, perhaps not—as I felt toward women in the days before my apotheosis. To touch it is to experience a feeling akin to ecstasy. To blend my eye with its Eye is to know rapture of the purest sort.

Soon I will go to it, and together we shall learn what my flock and what the police are doing this afternoon. But there is no hurry. Nothing those foolish minions of the law can do will affect me in any way. The power that is mine expands within me. I can wreak my vengeance daily if I choose, from now until forever, and they can do nothing except to sit in awe far greater than my own for the Eye.

I need not even wield the sword of justice myself to destroy a sinner, as has been proven by the death of Benny Hiller. God's will is all that is necessary; the hand of a mortal can carry out the deed. I must confess that I laughed when I learned, via the television, of Hiller's demise. How confused the police must be! They cannot comprehend the scope of my power to eliminate evil. Hiller was evil, a common burglar, a predator preying on the just, and I decreed that he must die, and so he died. It is as simple and as awesome as that.

Tonight I will go down among my children again, and when the time is right I will end another iniquitous life.

234

Tomorrow night, perhaps, I will strike yet again. And tomorrow and tomorrow and tomorrow, while the world continues to creep at its petty pace. For God is in his heaven, and he will see to it that all is right with his world.

The time, according to my watch, is twelve-oh-six P.M. Let it be noted.

Detective Oxman has less than twelve hours to live.

12:50 P.M. — E.L. OXMAN

He was on his way back to 1276, after a session with the media and more frustrating interviews with block residents, when he saw Artie Tobin come out through the front entrance. He waited on the sidewalk for Tobin to descend the stairs. The street was deserted, baking under a white-hazed noonday sun that had the look of a boiled egg. Headquarters had decided not to cordon off the area just yet, but they had installed teams of patrolmen on Riverside Drive and West End Avenue to keep curious citizens and the media wolves from clogging the block. What was it Artie had said this morning? Something about the area being turned into a war zone. Yeah. It felt like one already; all that was missing was flak-jacketed troops and barbed-wire bunkers.

"Been looking for you, Elliot Leroy," Tobin said. He squinted up from beneath his bushy brows at the milky haze overhead. "Christ, it's hot."

"And getting hotter."

"Yeah. Anything new?"

"Not a damned thing. The searches of the apartments in there" — he nodded toward 1276 — "were negative; another dead end. You heard about the Butler woman, I guess?"

Tobin inclined his head. "I checked in with Smiley a little while ago. Good news she's gonna be okay; bad news otherwise."

"That's what I meant about it getting hotter," Oxman said. "You turn up anything?"

235

"Well, I got something worth checking out. Too early to tell if it'll lead anywhere. You know a guy named Willie Lorsec, friend of the super's here, Corales?"

"Lorsec. The junk dealer?"

"That's the one."

"I talked to him briefly a few days ago. What about him?"

"Corales told me Benny Hiller was on Lorsec's case about some things missing from Hiller's trash. Seems Hiller was hot to get the stuff back."

"What stuff?"

"Corales didn't know."

"Did he know why Hiller was so hot to get it back?"

"He says not. You get an address for Lorsec?"

"Doesn't Corales know where he lives?"

"Just that it's someplace in the next block. He's never been to Lorsec's place."

Oxman fished out his notebook, scanned through it. "Here we go. Eleven-oh-seven West Ninety-eighth. One of the rooming houses near Broadway, probably."

"You haven't been there either, huh?"

"No. I talked to Lorsec in Corales's apartment and I didn't get around to checking him out again. Maybe I should have."

"Well, eleven-oh-seven's not the building Hiller got himself shot in, that's for sure. I figured there might be some connection between Lorsec and Hiller being in that building last night, but now I don't see how that's possible. I'll go have a talk with Lorsec anyway."

"I'll be back in the Crane apartment if you need me."

"Right."

Oxman entered 1276. Upstairs, he knocked on the door to Jennifer's apartment, identified himself, and added Jennifer's name for the benefit of any listening ears. Ullman let him in.

"Any calls?" he asked her.

"None. It's been quiet, Ox."

236

"You eat yet?"

"Not yet. I can fix something, if you want."

"I'll do it. It's better than pacing."

He went into the kitchen, found some salami and cheese in the refrigerator, some bread and a packet of potato chips in a cupboard, and set everything on the table. He was getting utensils out of the drawer next to the sink when the telephone rang.

Ullman had already picked up by the time he shoved open the swing door. He watched her listen, frown, and then cover the mouthpiece with her hand and turn toward him. "It's for you," she said.

"Manders?"

"No. He didn't give his name."

Premonition touched Oxman. He moved quickly across the room, took the receiver. "Oxman here."

"This is the voice of God, Detective Oxman."

Rage boiled inside him. In all the years he had been a cop, he had never hated any of the criminals he'd had to deal with, not even the drug dealers and the child pornographers, as much as he hated this cold-blooded purveyor of death. He didn't trust himself to speak for a moment, until he had himself under control. Then he said, "What do you want this time?"

"Did you really believe you could deceive the Eye?"

"What does that mean?"

"You know what it means, Detective Oxman. The Eye is all-seeing; nothing can escape the Eye. Certainly not the fact that Jennifer Crane is no longer there."

"What?"

"The woman who answered my call is not Jennifer Crane. Oh, I admit she resembles Miss Crane; the wig she's wearing is quite natural. But God's Eye can see that she is an impostor. A policewoman, perhaps? Yes, no doubt a policewoman."

Oxman's lips peeled in against his teeth; the rage was like a thick, hot mucus in his throat.

"Miss Crane will not escape the wrath of God," the voice said. "It matters not where you've taken her; I will find her, and when I do I will punish her. Just as I will punish you."

"Listen, you goddamn son of a — "

"Blasphemy is also a sin," the voice said calmly. "You are beyond redemption. Death to those who blaspheme God. Death to those who fornicate before the Eye of God. Death to *you*, Detective Oxman. Soon, now. Soon."

There was a click and he was gone.

Oxman slammed the receiver back into its cradle, with enough force to make the bell ring. He wheeled toward Ullman. "He knows about the switch. The bastard *knows.*"

She was staring at him with wide eyes. "But how — ?"

"I don't know how. Did anybody come around while I was out?"

"No, no one."

"And nobody called?"

"No."

"Did you go out, even for a minute?"

Ullman shook her head. "Maybe it was my voice that tipped him. Maybe he's familiar with Jennifer's voice. . ."

"He knows you're wearing a wig," Oxman said, "he knows what you look like. How the hell could he know that if he hasn't seen you?"

Oxman stalked over to the windows, stood staring out blindly. How could he know? Had he been down on the street when Jennifer left, had he got close enough to recognize her? No. He hadn't said anything about Jennifer leaving in a policewoman's uniform, wearing a wig; it was Ullman he'd talked about, Ullman's wig. And he hadn't seemed to know for sure that Ullman was a policewoman; he had said, *A policewoman, perhaps? Yes, no doubt a policewoman,* as if he were speculating on the fact. And if he had seen Jennifer leaving, he wouldn't have waited this long to call up and do his gloating; that wasn't the way his megalomania seemed to work. It was as if he'd just found out about the switch, within the past few minutes. . . .

But that wasn't possible. Ullman hadn't left the apartment by her own testimony, she hadn't had any visitors, she hadn't even had any calls. Could the psycho live in one of the other apartments on this floor, have been peering out through a cracked door and seen Ullman when she opened up five minutes ago? No, damn it, that wasn't it. Ullman had stayed well inside the room, as she'd been instructed to do, and Oxman had slipped in quickly; nobody could have seen her from any of the other apartment doors.

How, then? *How?* The perp wasn't omniscient. And he couldn't see through walls.

Or could he?

Something stirred in Oxman's mind, a budding revelation. And all at once he was no longer staring blindly through the window; he was seeing what lay outside, he was seeing the window itself.

Windows were walls, too; you *could* see through windows.

The psycho kept talking about the Eye, God's Eye. But not as if he meant his own eye; as if it were something else, some independent instrument.

Jesus, binoculars? Was he out there somewhere with binoculars?

Oxman studied what lay beyond the windows — and the idea collapsed. There was no place out there where a man could set up with a pair of binoculars, no hiding places. This apartment was on the third floor; a man couldn't see into it clearly from ground level even if he had a place to hide. And if he'd tried to climb one of the trees, somebody would have seen him; Riverside Drive and the park were crawling with people, with police officers.

Any location beyond the park was too great a distance for binoculars, even the high-powered variety, to be of much use. And there weren't any vantage points out there, either.

239

Just the West Side Highway and the river and then the high-rise apartment buildings on the Jersey shore...

Those buildings, he thought suddenly. *Those high-rise buildings?*

But they were more than two miles distant; nobody in an apartment over there could see this far away. Not with binoculars, not with anything short of—

The Eye.

A telescope?

A goddamn *telescope?*

Oxman spun away from the window. It was a wild idea, it was grasping at straws—and yet it was possible, it explained how the psycho could have known about the sex with Jennifer, how he'd recognized Ullman as an impostor, why he felt so bloody sure of himself. It put the whole pattern together. It explained everything.

Ullman was staring at him again. "Ox, what is it?"

He shook his head at her. Which building? Which apartment out of hundreds? It would take too long to bring the Jersey cops into it, to start a building by building canvass; and if the perp *was* over there, that sort of search was liable to alert him so that they'd never find the Eye or him. But there was another way to check out those buildings. A way to do the checking from this side that might, just might, pinpoint the location of a telescope.

Oxman ran to the telephone, hauled it on its long cord to the kitchen door, out of sight of the windows, and put in an urgent call to the Two-four.

1:30 P.M. — ART TOBIN

Willie Lorsec didn't live in the rooming house at 1107.

Lorsec's name wasn't on any of the mailboxes and when Tobin talked to the landlady she verified the fact that he wasn't one of her lodgers. She had never heard of him. Neither had two other residents of the building Tobin spoke to.

Back out on the sidewalk, Tobin wondered if Elliot Leroy had misheard the address Lorsec gave him, or copied down the wrong number. But that wasn't likely; Elliot Leroy was too thorough and too careful to make that kind of mistake. Which meant that Lorsec had given a false address. Not that that necessarily meant anything. False addresses were an everyday fact of life for certain types of people in the city, and so was sidestepping unpleasant visits from the police.

Still, it made Tobin want all the more to talk to Willie Lorsec.

He checked the mailboxes in all of the other buildings on the block. None of the names was Willie Lorsec. He went back across the avenue and canvassed the mailboxes there. No Lorsec. He talked to half a dozen residents at random; some of them had seen Lorsec in the neighborhood, some of them had spoken to him, but none of them knew where he lived. Tobin cursed silently when he had finished. He was growing weary of this bullshit.

On West End Avenue, he found a public phone that hadn't yet been vandalized and called the precinct. Lieutenant Manders wasn't in. Tobin relayed what he had to one of the other detectives on duty, Birnbaum, and asked him to run a routine background check on Willie Lorsec, junk dealer. Then he dialed the number of Jennifer Crane's apartment, but the line was busy. He debated going up there, decided not to waste the time. He could check in with Elliot Leroy later.

He sighed and went to continue his search.

3:45 P.M. — E.L. OXMAN

"Telescope?" Manders said. "Jesus Christ, Ox, is that what this is all about?"

He had just come into the Harbor Squad offices at Battery Basin, where Oxman was waiting with Deputy Inspector Hoffman of the Marine Division and Lieutenant Jack

241

Roberts from the Police Photo Lab. Manders looked rumpled, like a man who had just been mauled by a pack of wolves; he had spent most of the afternoon in conference with the commissioner and sundry other police brass. Oxman hadn't been able to get in touch with him as a result, so he had gotten his authorization from Captain Burnham. Manders had received the message to come here, but he hadn't been told the details. Few people had been told; the operation was being kept under tight wraps so the media wouldn't get wind of it.

Oxman said, "It may be a pipe dream, Lieutenant, but it all adds up. It's the only possibility we've got that does add up."

"Spell it out for me."

Oxman did that. When he finished Manders was gnawing at his lower lip, his sad eyes thoughtful; he seemed torn between skepticism and hope. "Maybe," he said, "just maybe. But how the hell do we check out all those buildings on the Jersey shore? There must be a few thousand apartments over there."

"That's where I come in," Roberts said. "We're going to photograph them."

"Photograph?"

"Each building, using cameras with powerful telephoto lenses. One series of photographs from a patrol boat on the river; one series from a helicopter. Then we'll do blowups."

"So that's what's going on here."

"Right. If there is a telescope, it has to be set up in a window or on a balcony. The men in the chopper, including one of my photogs, should be able to catch it on film or maybe even spot it."

"If they can spot it, why bother with the photographs?" Manders asked.

"We need to pinpoint the exact location of the apartment," Oxman said. "And we've got to be damned careful with that chopper. The psycho's smart and he's cunning. If he sees a helicopter hovering outside his building, all he has to do is turn that Eye of his on it and he'd see what was up; he'd be long gone before the Jersey cops could get to him. We can't risk more than one pass with the chopper."

"Yeah, I see what you mean." Manders turned to Deputy Inspector Hoffman. "Have the Jersey State Police been alerted, sir?"

"They have," Hoffman told him. "They're standing by."

"When does the chopper go up?"

"We've got one ready to go right now. It'll be in radio contact with the patrol boat."

"I'd like to go along," Manders said in dour tones, "but I've got to meet with the deputy mayor for a press conference at five o'clock." He tugged at an earlobe, glancing at Oxman. "Wouldn't it be better if you were in the chopper, Ox?"

"The psycho knows me," Oxman answered. "Me being in that helicopter is another risk we can't afford to take."

Manders nodded. "You ready, then?"

"Boat's waiting," Hoffman said.

They went out and down the ramp to where the sleek, black-hulled police boat sat in the still water of the Basin. Manders squinted at the windowed pilothouse and asked Hoffman, "How does Ox keep out of sight? The psycho could see into this boat with a telescope just as easily as into the chopper."

"Not with the curtains drawn," Hoffman said.

Manders and the deputy inspector wished them luck, and Oxman and Roberts boarded and entered the pilothouse. The skipper's name was Calder; they shook hands with him. Roberts unlimbered his photography gear and began setting up. Two minutes later, the patrol boat had backed out of its berth and they were chugging out of the Basin, into the sun-struck waters of the Hudson.

Oxman stared out through the windshield at the twin towers of the World Trade Center looming ahead. He was thinking that if he wasn't right about this, the ball would be back in the psycho's court. And more people were liable to die.

4:30 P.M. — ART TOBIN

Was everybody hiding from him?

The thought was in Tobin's mind as he walked toward the pay phone on West End Avenue. Willie Lorsec seemed to have disappeared, maybe deliberately so he wouldn't have to submit to police questioning. It wasn't unusual for a junk dealer like Lorsec to have no permanent address; it could be he was making his home in the subways or parks or Grand Central Station or in the virtually dozens of other Manhattan haunts frequented by the dispossessed. Still, it irked Tobin that he hadn't been able to find him. Even if Lorsec was clean, Tobin intended to roust him a little, put the fear of God into him, when he finally turned him up.

But right now Tobin had temporarily given up on Lorsec and was wondering where Elliot Leroy was. He'd checked at Jennifer Crane's apartment, and Carla Ullman, still on duty there, had told him Oxman had left three hours ago; Elliot Leroy had come up with some kind of hunch, she said, called the Two-four privately, and then had split without telling her what was going on.

So what was the hunch? Tobin wondered. It wasn't like Elliot Leroy to go traipsing off on his own like that, without leaving a message for his partner. Oxman was getting difficult in his advancing years; Tobin would point that out the next time he saw him.

He crossed the street, jaywalking, went to the telephone kiosk, and dialed the precinct. The desk sergeant, Drake, didn't know where Oxman was; no one did, he said. Tobin asked for Lieutenant Smiley, but Manders, too, had disappeared.

"Where *is* everybody?" Tobin asked rhetorically.

"You got me," Drake said.

"Why didn't Oxman or Manders leave a number where they could be reached?"

"Maybe they're not near a phone," Drake suggested. "Maybe they're in transit."

"Transit, my ass. If either of them checks in, tell him I called."

"Sure, Artie. You want to leave a number where *you* can be reached?"

"No," Tobin said. "Let them look for me for a while."

An elderly, scowling woman had come behind him and was now glaring impatiently at Tobin. Her pushiness aggravated him; he decided she could damn well wait to use the phone. He pretended to make another brief call.

"I was talking to my stockbroker," he said when he finally hung up and gave the woman a nasty smile. "The rich are jumping out of high windows all over Manhattan. The market is collapsing."

"So's my arches collapsing," the woman said. "You took long enough on the phone. Ain't you got no consideration?"

Fuck you, lady, Tobin thought and walked away as she lurched for the phone. He was hot. He was irritated. This city and the people in it were a pain in the ass. He'd get out someday; he swore he would.

Where the hell was Elliot Leroy?

4:45 P.M. — E.L. OXMAN

In the cramped pilothouse of the Marine Division patrol boat, Oxman tried to ignore the suggestion of discomfort in his stomach as he listened to the choppy river waves slap at the hull. The small boat rolled and pitched more than he'd imagined it would in weather like this.

With the pilothouse curtains drawn, his only view was out through the tinted windscreen; about all he could see was the hazy sky scratched by a few high wispy clouds. Calder, the boat's skipper, a weathered near-midget, expertly played the

wheel and spoke only when necessary. Which suited
Oxman. The last thing he wanted right now was small talk.

"Approaching Seventy-ninth Street," Calder said without
turning his head. He was hunched forward, peering at the
Hudson's shifting waters and the sparse river traffic.

Oxman didn't say anything. It was Roberts, extending the
aluminum legs of his camera tripod, who answered. "Okay.
I'm almost ready."

Oxman watched the wiry, square-featured photographer
set up his Nikon on the tripod and affix to it a long telephoto
lens equipped with a small supporting arm. "You going to be
able to do this, Jack?" he asked. "Those buildings on the
palisades are still pretty far away." The damned things were
like mountains, Oxman thought; you had to be almost on
them before they became larger to the eye and seemed
closer.

Roberts smiled a professional's tolerant smile. "This is a
two-hundred millimeter lens," he said. "I could use one more
powerful, but the boat isn't the steadiest platform, and a
three- or four-hundred millimeter lens would necessitate a
slower shutter speed and we'd get some blur. This was there
won't be much depth of field, but we'll have sharp definition
when we make our blowups."

"Fine," Oxman said. He didn't really grasp the
technicalities; all he was interested in was a resolution to this
case. He wanted the psycho nailed as much as he'd ever
wanted anything, and he would have to depend on Roberts'
know-how without really understanding it.

The marine radio buzzed and a metallic voice sputtered
something Oxman couldn't understand. Then Calder's
gnarled hand was offering the microphone to him. "It's the
chopper," he said. "Pilot's name is Niebauer."

Oxman accepted the microphone, bracing himself against
the boat's motion. He depressed the button and said,
"Oxman here," into the mike. He didn't know the protocol of

marine-air radio and he decided to play it straight without the NYPD code numbers.

When he let up on the button he could hear from the radio's speaker the pulsing beat of the helicopter's rotors. "We're approaching the river now," Niebauer said, his voice breaking up with the throb of the blades. "We'll be passing over you in about a minute at five hundred feet. Any other instructions? Over."

Oxman could hear the faint pulse of the rotors approaching outside now, not over the radio. He jabbed the transmit button. "No other instructions," he said. "Just let us know if you spot anything. Over."

"Will do. Over and out."

Oxman handed the microphone back. Calder took it, saying, "We're abreast of the Boat Basin now."

Roberts said, "Right." He had his equipment set up and the pilothouse curtains on the Jersey side slightly parted to allow room for the long telephoto lens to peek out. He squinted like a surveyor into the Nikon's viewfinder, then looked up at Oxman and nodded. He had calculated that because of the viewing angle into West Ninety-eighth Street, the Jersey high rise they wanted had to be one of those facing between Eightieth and One-hundred-and-fifteenth. He was ready to start taking his pictures. "Sam Belson's my man in the chopper," he told Oxman as he bent again to the viewfinder. "He's a good photographer; he'll get all the shots from angles we can't cover."

The boat suddenly began a violent rocking. Oxman's stomach did a double flip. He swallowed a bitter column of bile that rose into his throat. "What the hell?" he asked Calder.

"Backwash," the skipper said. "Damn pleasure cruiser running past too close." He spoke as if all the water on earth were for purposes strictly business.

"I can't get my shots if that keeps up," Roberts said. He

had one hand wrapped tight around the tripod leg, to steady the camera. "You'll have to hold her steady."

Calder grunted, adjusted the throttle. The tempo of the engines decreased and the boat lost speed, began to settle into a more even motion.

"Good," Roberts said. "Keep her just as she is." He was kneeling with his eye fitted to the viewfinder, tripping the shutter with a cord and hand control. The SLR shutter gave a loud but smooth *snick,* and the automatic winder whirred and advanced the film to the next frame. There were three more snicks and whirs in quick succession, then several farther apart.

Listening tensely to the intermittent sound of the camera, to the counterpoint beat of the helicopter as it passed overhead, Oxman parted the curtains on the Manhattan side of the pilothouse and stared out at the city. It appeared symmetrical and clean and beautiful from this distance. How deceptive that was, an illusion, like so many things in his life.

Except Jennifer. She wasn't an illusion; she was real, perhaps the most real thing now in the world for him. And she was still in the city, at the Haverton Hotel. A pang of doubt stabbed at him. Maybe he should have moved her all the way out of Manhattan, where he could be absolutely certain she was safe.

Snick-whir!

But there was no way the psycho could know where she was. She hadn't been seen leaving her apartment, and she was registered at the Haverton under an assumed name. She was also under twenty-four-hour police guard. How much safer could she be?

Snick-whir!

And yet the doubt still nagged at him. From the beginning he had underestimated this madman with unsettling consistency; and people had kept on dying. It was almost as if he

248

were in a macabre game, pitted against an opponent with vastly superior skills.

Snick-whir!

Oxman turned away from the postcard view of Manhattan. He could no longer hear the chopper over the pulse of the boat's engines, but through the windshield he had a glimpse of it just up ahead, shining silver against the hazy sky. He ran his tongue over dry lips, fixed his eyes on Roberts's bent back. There was some comfort in the photographer's dedication and skill, in the knowledge that Roberts and Niebauer and Calder, and all the people like them, were on his side. And on Jennifer's.

Snick whir! Snick-whir!

He sat back and tried to will his stomach to settle itself, tried to relax his tensed back muscles. He could do neither. There was still so damned much to be done. Finish the photographing, return to Battery Basin, drive to the Photo Lab, process the film and make the blowups. Even if he was right about the telescope, there was no guarantee that the photos would pick it up or pinpoint the proper apartment. And even if they did find it and pinpoint it, by that time the perp could already be on his way back to West Ninety-eighth for more carnage. . . .

The marine radio gave its metallic sputter. Calder answered, said to Oxman, "Niebauer in the chopper," and handed the microphone to him.

"Oxman. Go ahead, Niebauer."

He couldn't understand what the pilot said; static and the pound of the rotors made the words unintelligible. Oxman pushed the transmit button and asked Niebauer to repeat. This time, he got the gist of the pilot's message — not every word, but enough of them. Christ yes, just three were enough.

". . . spotted a telescope," Niebauer said.

THE COLLIER TAPES

Since my telephone call to Detective Oxman—and how amusing the memory of that call, of the consternation on his face revealed by the Eye! —I have spent the afternoon reading and thinking about evil.

The destruction of evil has become my life's work; know thy enemy in all his forms and guises. Thus, a quiet afternoon studying that which God is bound to defeat on the battlefield, the miniature Argmageddon of West Ninety-eighth Street. Conroy's metaphysical, if somewhat dry study, *The Nature of Evil,* proved particularly illuminating. It gave me much food for thought, much insight into how sin and wickedness are manifested among the more cunning members of society.

Two more aphorisms quoted by Conroy also remain in my mind. The first, from the writings of Aristophanes: "Evil events from evil causes spring." And the second, by Cicero: "Evil in the bud is easily crushed."

So true, these aphorisms. The latter in particular. I have crushed much evil in the bud already, before it could bloom wild and beget more evil; I will continue to do so, as easily as I might flick a piece of lint from my shirt sleeve. Or as I might pluck a mosquito from the air and squeeze it to pulp between my fingers.

The helicopter flying past my building at this moment reminds me of a mosquito—delicate, tiny at a distance, spindly in its concessions to the aerodynamics of maneuverable flight. No doubt the drone of it became audible on the tape as I was quoting Cicero, and it has drawn me to the window. Outside and far below, the river stretches like a division between the heavens and the mortal world; small boats, barges, other craft I cannot identify, inch along the silvery boundary that the Eye has bridged. The helicopter, sunlight glinting off its rotary blades, flies

250

above this boundary in its aproximate center. Be it a traffic-reporting or sightseeing helicopter, do its pilot and passengers know their craft hovers in the dividing zone of life and death? That it flits as a mere shadow on an easily pierced veil?

I feel that I *can,* if I so choose, open the balcony door and extend my hand, the hand of God, and pluck it from the air. Or that from my rigid fingers will crackle the lightning of my will and obliterate the machine and its occupants.

That is illusion, of course, a flight of divine fancy; my power is not as great as that. Nor would I commit such an act even if it were. After all, I have no reason to destroy the helicopter or those in it.

I do nothing, even on a whim, which is not a part of the cosmic mosaic of my creation.

6:40 P.M. — JENNIFER CRANE

She awoke and sat up in bed, gradually remembering where she was. She stared around her at the faded blue wallpaper with its matching drapes that didn't quite meet in the center of the window, the dresser with its ornate-framed mirror, the six-bulbed chandelier that hung suspended in the middle of the room like a wary spider.

She was in the Haverton Hotel, in the bedroom of the two-room suite she had been given. She had gone to bed not long ago to try to sleep her way through some of her claustrophobic anxiety, the numbing sameness of her confinement. More tired than she knew, she'd slept almost immediately. And now, something had awakened her; she wasn't sure what, but she was shivering and covered with perspiration.

There was a knock on the connecting door. That must have been what roused her, she thought, the knocking. Her heart hammering, she got slowly out of bed and crossed the stiff-napped carpet.

251

"Officer Callahan?"

"Yes, ma'am. I didn't disturb you, did I?"

Jennifer sighed, relaxed tensed muscles. Callahan was the policeman assigned to stay with her in the suite. He was a stout and capable man nearing retirement age, the sort who combined experience with a worn but still capable physical prowess. He inspired trust and confidence, which was why, she supposed, the police department had assigned him to this kind of duty.

"No, it's all right," she said. She opened the door, looked out at Callahan's florid, concerned face. "What is it?"

"I thought you might be hungry," he said. "It's getting late; I could call room service for some supper."

"I'm not hungry. But you go ahead."

"You ought to eat something, Miss Crane."

He was right; she ought to eat something. She hadn't had any food all day. "I guess so," she said. "A sandwich, then — I don't care what kind. And a drink; I could use a drink. Is that permitted?"

"I don't see why not."

"Make it a gin and tonic. A double."

"You've got it," Callahan said. He gave her a solicitous look. "You okay, Miss Crane?"

"Yes, thanks. Just a little tired."

"Sure, I can understand that. But don't you worry. Everything's going to be fine, you just wait and see." He smiled at her, turned and went over to the telephone.

Jennifer shut the door and entered the bathroom. She was surprised at how haggard she appeared in the mirror above the sink. It wasn't food she needed, or a drink; it was sleep. She drank half a glass of water and returned to the bed.

She lay with a blanket pulled up to her chin, thinking about E.L. He had called a half hour ago, before she'd gone into the bedroom to lie down; he was at the Police Photo Lab, but he hadn't wanted to tell her what he was doing there. All he'd said was that he finally had a lead, and that if things worked out the way he hoped, the end was in sight.

Was that false reassurance? Or had he really meant it? She thought it was the truth; E.L. wasn't the sort to make meaningless statements, especially not at this stage of things. But the fact that he might be close to finding the killer worried her as much as it relieved her. When she'd dozed off those few minutes ago she'd had a bad dream about him. Its details were vague, just beyond memory; all she could recall was that it had been ugly and frightening, as if somehow in her sleep she had had a premonition that a deadly danger awaited him.

She shivered—she still felt as cold as she had that morning, even though she had long ago shut off the air conditioner—and she drew another blanket over her. *He'll be all right,* she thought. *He'll be all right.*

She remembered, then, what he'd said to her on the phone when she'd tried to tell him about Zach and her aborted pregnancy, things she had begun to wish she'd told him before. "I don't want to hear about your past, not now," he'd said. "The future is enough to worry about, the only thing that should concern us now. The past is dead; there's no point in resurrecting it and walking it through our lives. Only you and I matter. Only now, only tomorrow."

And he was right, she'd realized. The past was merely time, nothing more, nothing at all. It didn't, in the true sense of the word, exist. You couldn't see it or hear it or touch it anymore; it was gone.

Only you and I matter. Only now, only tomorrow.

Please, God, she thought, *let him be all right. . . .*

7:30 P.M. — E.L. OXMAN

The Police Photo Lab's darkroom was bathed in a reddish glow from the overhead safelight. Oxman sat impatiently on a high stool, watching Roberts and two technicians develop

253

the rolls of film taken from the patrol boat and the helicopter. He didn't speak. These were professionals at work who knew what was demanded of them; it would have been pointless for him to bother them with questions. So he sat with his impatience in check, trying to get used to the acrid chemical smell of the place. The odor made him a little light-headed and played hell with his empty stomach.

Roberts finally handed over the last batch of developed film to one of the technicians, who then went with the other technician through a door into another room. "So much for this part of it," Roberts said to Oxman.

"Good."

Roberts looked tired as he walked over and switched off the safelight, switched on the standard fluorescents. He removed his black rubber apron, folded it and placed it in a drawer. Then he motioned to Oxman, led him though the door where the two technicians had disappeared.

Oxman found himself in another dim room. The smell of chemicals wasn't nearly as strong here. The technicians were busy using enlargers to blow up the frames of film that had been developed for peak sharpness. Two of the rolls already were printed in drastic enlargement on eight-by-ten paper. Roberts led Oxman to several of these photos lying flat on what looked like an easel. They were held down and kept from curling by clips, and pieced together to form a composite—a vivid black-and-white aerial view of the Hudson shorelines taken from the helicopter. The river had been reduced to a mere few inches between the opposite banks.

"The banks are juxtaposed precisely as they line up," Roberts explained. He pointed to some angled lines penned in blurred red ink. "These were used to compute distance and angle so we could narrow down all the Jersey high rises from which it'd be possible to see into the windows of the buildings on West Ninety-eighth and Riverside Drive, just in case." He pointed to several other wet prints clipped down on a long work bench along the far wall. "Those are blowups of individual windows and balconies in the high rise where the chopper spotted the telescope. More are being printed. The ones Rudy is setting aside are those that reveal no sign of any long-range viewing device."

As Oxman watched, the long-haired technician named Rudy quickly but thoroughly studied print after print and placed each in a steadily growing pile.

"We should have all of the blowups ready within the next half hour," Roberts said. "You can wait here if you like, or you can sit out in my office and have a cup of coffee."

Oxman considered waiting in there, watching the process of blowing up and examining each photograph. But he decided a cup of coffee would do him more good. "I guess I'll wait outside."

Roberts nodded, turned and got to work.

Oxman went out through the printing room to Roberts' small, cluttered office. There was a Mr. Coffee on a table in the corner, its glass pot half full, a stack of styrofoam cups alongside. He poured himself a cup of coffee, added powdered creamer and sugar.

He remembered seeing a candy vending machine outside in the hall. He knew he should eat something while he had the chance, even if he was too keyed up to be hungry; he hadn't had any food all day, and a candy bar would provide more energy than the sugar in his coffee.

He lost a quarter in the ancient machine, then managed to wrestle out a Clark Bar; he carried it back into Roberts' office. It was cooler in there; the old window air conditioner behind the desk labored mightily, shooting out an occasional fleck of ice. Roberts had probably forgotten to turn it off this morning and it had frozen up in the heat and high humidity.

Oxman sat in a vinyl-upholstered Danish chair to one side of the desk, took a sip of his coffee. Jennifer was on his mind as he peeled off the wrapper on the Clark Bar. He was glad he'd called her after arriving at the photo lab; just hearing her voice had reassured him. Somehow, in only a few short days, she had become a pivotal factor in his life. After so many years with Beth, he'd thought he was too old to feel like this, that he'd been slowly dying cell by cell. Jennifer was both a reprieve and a new purpose.

He bit into the candy bar. And was not at all surprised to find that it was stale. He ate it anyway, washing it down with sips of the strong coffee.

He waited.

8:15 P.M. — ART TOBIN

Tobin stepped out of the elevator and crossed the lobby of 1276, toward the door that led down into the basement. He was in a foul humor, tired and royally pissed off. He hadn't been able to find Willie Lorsec. He hadn't been able to find Elliot Leroy; the policewoman, Ullman, had told him just now, when he'd gone up to see her, that she hadn't heard from Oxman and that nobody else had called to tell her where he was. And Lieutenant Smiley was still missing from the Two-four. And as if all of that wasn't enough, the cheeseburger and fries he'd eaten for supper a little while ago had given him indigestion.

Nobody tells me anything, he thought. *Keep the darkie in the dark, by God. If I was white, instead of a big old nigger cop, I'd sure as hell get better treatment than this.*

What he ought to do was go back to the Five-three, sign out, and pack it in for the day; the hell with all of 'em. That was what he was *going* to do, but first he wanted a few more words with the super, Corales. For all he knew, Corales had lied to him earlier about knowing where Lorsec lived, or where Lorsec could be found. If that was the case, God help him. Tobin just wasn't going to take any more shit today.

He opened the basement door, stepped through, and let it close silently behind him on its pneumatic stop. He paused on the landing. In the dim light from the hanging bulb at the

256

foot of the stairs, he could make out the closed door to Corales's apartment, the shadowy rows of wooden storage lockers, shelves of tools and paint cans, stacks of cardboard boxes near enough to the boiler to give a fire inspector fits. There was nothing to hear but the soft ticking buzz of an electric meter.

He wrinkled his nose at the musty smell of the basement, reached out to the switch on the landing wall. When he flicked it, three more hanging bulbs came on and chased away the shadows.

And let him see a man in a lightweight windbreaker, a big man he didn't recognize, just coming away from the boiler room toward the stairs.

Tobin blinked in surprise, stopped dead with one foot on the landing and the other on the first of the rubber-treaded risers. The big man also stopped, staring at him. They stood frozen like that for maybe an instant, and Tobin thought with sudden savage intuition: *It's him, it's the goddamn psycho!*

What happened then, crazily, was like a climactic scene in a Western movie: Tobin swept the tail of his jacket back, jerked his service revolver out of its belt holster; the big man had his hand in the pocket of his windbreaker, and the hand came out filled with a weapon of his own. The roar of the guns was almost simultaneous —

Tobin felt as if he'd been kicked in the stomach, just under the breastbone. The .38 fell out of his hand; his legs buckled, his vision blurred, a thought flashed across his mind: *Jesus no, not like this!* And then he was falling, and there was pain and noise and fear, and the next thing he knew he was crumpled sideways on the stairs near the bottom, head downward, gasping for breath, blood singing in his ears.

At the tilted angle, as if he were watching something happen underwater, he saw the big man come running toward him. Another thought: *I missed him.* He tried to move, couldn't. A part of his mind cringed, waiting for the second shot, the coup de grâce, but it didn't come; the psycho ran by him, up the stairs.

The last things Tobin heard before he lost consciousness were the lobby door being flung open and the diminishing pound of footsteps in the lobby.

8:15 P.M. — E.L. OXMAN

He was on his third cup of coffee when Roberts entered the office and told him, "We've got it, Ox."

Oxman felt his heart pump adrenaline as he jumped to his feet and followed Roberts into the printing room. But what the photographer had to show him was not one but two grainy blowups, not one but two telescopes. In one blowup, the telescope's step-tapered tubular shape was shadowed but clearly visible behind window drapes open part way; in the other blowup, equally grainy because of its enlargement, the telescope was on the balcony, mounted on a metal tripod and tilted back awkwardly to point skyward.

"Christ," Oxman said. "*Two* of them?"

"Yeah. We should have thought of that possibility. Astronomy, and just plain neighbor-watching, are common enough pastimes. But it's not as much of a problem as it might seem."

"No? Why not?"

Roberts stepped over to the table where the composite aerial view was displayed. His chemical-stained forefinger touched one of the Jersey high rises. "This is the building where the inside telescope is located," he said. "It stands roughly opposite the Seventy-ninth Street Boat Basin." His forefinger moved again. "Look at the angle from that window to West Ninety-eighth. It's possible someone watching through that scope could see into the windows of the Ninety-eighth buildings, but not very likely. The angle is too sharp. And the apartment is on the thirty-eighth floor; that's too high up."

"What about the balcony telescope?"

"That's the one the chopper spotted." Roberts pointed.

258

"And that's the high rise it's in: directly across the river from West Ninety-eighth, in Cliffside Park. That apartment is on the twentieth floor, south corner — not too high at all."

Oxman was aware of the subtle quickening of his senses, the primal elation of a hunter closing on his prey. "What's the address on the building?"

"According to the information we got from the Jersey State Police, it's the Crestview Towers." Roberts told him the address. "It shouldn't take long to get a directory check on the identity of the apartment's occupant."

"We'd better check the other one out too, just in case," Oxman said.

"Right. You want to make the calls?"

"Yeah, I'll take care of it — "

The telephone in the office began to ring. Roberts went through the open print room door, with Oxman behind him, and plucked up the receiver. He listened, said, "Yeah, he is," then handed the instrument to Oxman. "Lieutenant Manders."

Oxman cocked a hip against one corner of the desk as Roberts returned to the print room. "Oxman here."

Manders's voice said grimly, "Art Tobin's been shot, Ox."

Oxman's stomach lurched; he stood bolt upright, his hand white around the receiver. "Oh Jesus!" he said. "How bad?"

"Bad enough. He's still alive, but. . . I don't know, Ox. It's a belly wound."

"Where? Ninety-eighth again?"

"Yeah. In the basement of twelve seventy-six. The super, Corales, heard the shot and notified us."

"How'd it happen?"

"We don't know yet. Artie's still unconscious at the scene."

"The psycho again, the goddamn psycho."

"It looks that way. He got away clean, too, just like the other times. The son of a bitch's luck is incredible."

Not anymore, it isn't, Oxman thought; *his luck just ran out.*

There was a rage boiling in him, a white-hot rage that

259

threatened to deprive him or reason and judgment. But he didn't care. A man could only take so much, and the news about Artie was the final straw. The carnage was intensely personal now. That madman over in Jersey had murdered six people, one of them a cop, and put a seventh in the hospital; he had threatened Oxman's life, threatened Jennifer's life; and now he had shot Artie Tobin, a man Oxman didn't really know well but a man he respected, a man he called his friend. Enough was enough. It had become more than simply law enforcement to Oxman the book cop, Oxman the plodder; to hell with rules and regulations, to hell with the consequences. It had been his baby all along, and by God *he* was going to deliver it.

"You still there, Ox?" Manders asked.

"I'm here."

"What's happening with the photographs? Roberts and his boys come up with anything yet?"

"No," Oxman said, "not yet."

"Tell them to hurry it up. I'll call you back as soon as I hear anything on Artie's condition."

"Right," Oxman said, and hung up before Manders could say anything else.

He was staring down at the floor, his hands fisted at his sides, when Roberts reappeared in the print room doorway. "You all right, Ox? You look pale."

Oxman glanced over at him, saw the photographer catch something in that glance and unconsciously back up half a step. "I'm all right," he said. He nodded once, not to Roberts but to himself, in confirmation of what he was about to do, and then turned toward the door.

"Where're you going?" Roberts called after him. There was a vibrato of alarm in his voice; he sensed the change and purpose in Oxman. "What about the calls to Jersey?"

"Lieutenant Manders will make them," Oxman said. "I've got something else to take care of."

He left the photo lab and headed for his car. He passed people on the way, but he couldn't have said what they looked like, whether they were male or female. There was only one thing on his mind.

When he reached his car he pointed it toward the Holland Tunnel, toward New Jersey.

Toward the psycho.

8:45 P.M. — LEWIS COLLIER

There were splotches of scarlet on Collier's wide forehead, bloodless patches of white at the corners of his drawn lips, as he whipped his Toyota to the outside lane of the George Washington Bridge, blasted his horn and screamed curses at the cab that impeded his progress. He was furious, not at the cab driver but at the recent whim of fate that by rights *he* should have controlled.

He had been stalking Oxman, not the black policeman, Tobin. Oxman's partner did not deserve to die in his stead; Tobin was not a sinner in God's kingdom, the Eye had not revealed him to be one of the evil ones. But he fervently hoped that he *had* killed Tobin. The black man had seen his face in the lighted basement, could identify God if he lived.

I should have shot him again, Collier thought. But he had not been thinking clearly; the sudden appearance of Tobin, the exchange of shots, had unnerved him. He was still unnerved. It should have been Oxman who died tonight. Oxman, Oxman, Oxman!

He struck the dashboard with his fist hard enough to cause the glove compartment to fly open and its contents to drop onto the floor. The driver of a van in the next lane honked his horn and yelled something through his open window, raised his middle finger with a violent upward twist of the hand. Collier had to restrain himself from jerking the wheel to the right and smashing his car into the van, sending the blasphemous swine onto eternity's highway.

Stay calm, stay calm, he told himself, tapping the brake to slack his speed and allow the van to move ahead. This was not the time for rash action; this was a time for control, for analyzing and regrouping. Detective Oxman was still a dead sinner; his time was almost expired, the confluence of will and actuality almost at hand. At a chosen time, in a chosen place, the Angel of Death had only to twitch his right index finger on the trigger of his weapon of justice and for Oxman, Oxman, Oxman the mouth of hell would open and the fire would devour him.

There was a soothing quality in the thought. *I am God,* Collier reminded himself. *Why should God worry? I am the right and the might and the Glory.*

He relaxed somewhat as he reached the end of the bridge and took the exit for Skyline Drive and Cliffside Park. He was no longer driving erratically.

He was almost home.

9:20 P.M. — E.L. OXMAN

The Crestview Towers was an imposing stone-and-glass apartment building in Cliffside Park, some forty stories high. Beneath its canopy stood an equally imposing doorman in a medal-adorned uniform that would have made General Patton's appear shabby. The doorman touched the shiny visor of his cap in appropriately military fashion as a gaunt woman walking two small poodles strutted past in review.

Oxman parked his car a short distance away and walked back to the entrance. When he got there he drew his shield from his inside pocket and flashed it at the doorman, gambling that he wouldn't look closely and see it was an NYPD badge and not a local. There was no problem; the doorman gave the badge a cursory glance and looked away. He had already made Oxman as a cop and was busy wondering what was going on.

262

BILL PRONZINI AND JOHN LUTZ

"I'm looking for the tenant of the apartment on the south corner, twentieth floor," Oxman said. "Who would that be?"

The doorman frowned. "You don't know who you're looking for?"

"Just answer the question."

The doorman read the expression on Oxman's face correctly and it made him uneasy. He was a big man, paunchy beneath the ornate uniform, with an ex-jock's solid bulk to his neck and the slope of his shoulders. "South corner, twentieth floor," he said. "Let's see. . . that'd be Mr. Collier. Twenty-E."

"He have a first name?"

"Sure. Lewis."

"Lewis Collier," Oxman said. The name tasted bitter in his mouth. "He's got a telescope set up on his balcony, right?"

"That's right. A stargazer."

"Yeah. You know if he's home?"

"He's home," the doorman said. "He came in not five minutes ago."

There was a tightness in Oxman's groin; the palms of his hands were faintly damp. *Lewis Collier,* he thought. *He'd better be the one.* As wired up as Oxman felt right now, he didn't know what he'd do if they'd miscalculated somehow and Collier really was nothing more than a stargazer.

"I'm going up to talk to Collier," he said. "Don't get any ideas about announcing me before I get there."

"Not me, officer." The doorman still looked uneasy. "We got a lot of elderly people in the building; nothing rough is going to happen, is it?"

"I hope not," Oxman told him. It was at least half a lie.

He pushed in through the double doors, crossed the plush lobby to the elevators. They were almost invisible because their doors were walnut-paneled like the walls. When he pressed the Up button a door slid open and he stepped inside the elevator, punched the numeral twenty on a flat sheet of back-lighted plastic. The door hissed shut and the car launched itself upward.

The twentieth floor hallway was deserted. Oxman went along a thick maroon carpet to the end of the hall on the south side, to the door marked 20-E. There was no peephole in the door; that made things a little easier. He drew his service revolver, clamped his teeth together, and used the knuckles of his left hand to knock.

Several seconds passed in silence; Oxman could feel himself sweating. He was about to knock again when a voice called from inside, "Who is it?" The voice sounded vaguely familiar, but he couldn't be sure.

"Doorman, Mr. Collier," he said, disguising his own voice to approximate that of the ex-jock's downstairs. "Can I see you for a minute?"

"What about?"

"Your car, sir. There's a problem with it."

"Problem?" the voice said. Then Oxman heard the sound of the locks being thrown, the chain being slid free of its slot; the brass doorknob rotated and the door opened inward. "What sort of——"

The man inside stopped speaking when he saw Oxman; an expression of recognition, of frightened astonishment crossed his heavy features. But there was also an expression of surprise on Oxman's face, because the man wasn't a stranger to him; he knew Lewis Collier, but not by that name.

He knew him as Willie Lorsec.

9:20 P.M. — ART TOBIN

Tobin regained consciousness in the ambulance taking him to St. Luke's Hospital. He knew that was where he was because he could hear the warbling sound of the siren, see the two white-coated attendants hovering above him in the familiar jouncing confines; and he knew that was where he

264

was going because St. Luke's had been the emergency destination of the other West Ninety-eighth shooting victims, Jack Kennebank and Michele Butler.

But even though he realized those facts, his mind was still full of fuzziness; and the pain in his belly was almost unbearable. *Gut-shot,* he thought. *That motherfucker got me good. He got me good and I didn't get him at all.*

"We better pick up some time, Mel," one of the attendants yelled up to the driver. "We can't stop the bleeding; this guy's taking plasma like he figured there was a shortage."

"For him there is a shortage," the other attendant, a huge black man, said as he leaned over Tobin and applied a fresh compress. The man's white coat was stained with crimson streaks, Tobin saw. *My blood,* he thought, awed. *My blood.*

"That prick up ahead won't let me pass," the driver said. He gave the siren a series of short, urgent blasts. Seconds later, the ambulance gained speed; one of its tires bounced over something as the machine roared into a turn.

"You think we'll make it in time?" the white attendant asked the black one.

"I don't know, man. It's gonna be touch and go."

Yeah, Tobin thought, clenching his teeth against the pain, *but we'll make it, all right. I'm not going to die like this. That bastard won't kill me too. I am not going to die like this!*

Yowling like something itself wounded, the ambulance raced onward through the night.

9:35 P.M. — E.L. OXMAN

Collier, or Lorsec — whatever the hell his name was — let out a frightened bleating sound and tried to jam the door closed again. But Oxman hit it with his right shoulder, putting his full weight behind the thrust. Collier cried out a second time as the door slammed into him, sent him reeling backward into the room.

With the resistance of Collier's bulk gone, the door

crashed against the inside wall. Oxman staggered, regained his balance, and saw that the psycho had been thrown to the floor. Collier scrambled onto all fours, started to shove upward to his feet.

"Hold it right there!" Oxman snapped at him. He had his .38 leveled and his finger tight on the trigger; it took an effort of will not to squeeze off a shot. "Don't move; don't even breathe."

Collier froze in position. He was wearing dark slacks and a Navy blue pullover; behind him, on the couch, was a dark-colored windbreaker. Oxman backed up, caught hold of the door with his free hand, and threw it closed; his eyes never left Collier's face. Then he moved over to within five feet of the man, gestured with his .38.

"Down on your belly," he commanded. "Hands behind you. Do it!"

Collier obeyed. Oxman's breathing was labored and he was still sweating; his finger kept wanting to twitch on the revolver's trigger as he approached the man. He knelt with one knee in the middle of Collier's back, the muzzle of the .38 pressed tight to Collier's skull, and with his left hand he unhooked the handcuffs from his belt. It took him ten seconds to get the cuffs locked tight around the thick wrists, another five to slap at the dark clothing and verify that Collier was unarmed. The big man lay motionless through all of that, his face buried in the carpet.

Oxman straightened finally, breathing easier. He moved to where the windbreaker lay on the couch. One of the pockets bulged, and the bulge turned out to be the Smith & Wesson .38 that had no doubt killed Jack Kennebank and Marco Pollosetti, that had maybe killed Artie Tobin. He picked it up by the trigger guard, dropped it into his jacket pocket.

He stood over Collier and read him his rights in a thick voice. When he said, "Do you understand all of that?" Collier rolled over onto his back and stared up at him. The

266

man's ego, his mental equilibrium, had returned and gained dominance. Collier seemed to swell with it. The fear on his face had been replaced by a kind of defiant cunning that Oxman had seen before and knew was dangerous.

Oxman moved away a few steps; just being near Collier made him tremble with rage. He watched Collier twist himself onto all fours, then straighten up on his knees. The hatred he felt for this diseased lump of human flesh was itself like a tumor inside him.

"I feel the same for you, Detective Oxman," Collier said.

"What?"

"Hatred. I can see it in your eyes. But mine is the pure and the just, the hatred of good for evil, of God for one fallen from grace."

"Yeah," Oxman said.

"I seem to have underestimated you. The forces of evil are greater than even I anticipated. How did you find me?"

"Your goddamned telescope." Oxman could see it through the closed glass door to the balcony, like a giant finger pointing at the sky. "All those calls you made to me, all that crap about the Eye—that's where you made your mistake, Collier. Once I tumbled to the telescope, the rest was simple enough. Just a matter of police work."

"And the other policemen? Where are they?"

"They'll be along pretty soon."

"Indeed?" A faint, superior smile touched Collier's mouth. "I shot your partner tonight. Did you know that?"

"I know it, you bastard."

"Blasphemy. Evil from the mouth of evil. It should have been *you*, Detective Oxman. It was your life, your wickedness, I sought to end. An unfortunate accident that I encountered Detective Tobin instead."

Oxman had been concentrating so heavily on Collier that he hadn't really been aware of his surroundings. But now they intruded on his mind. He glanced around. The luxury apartment was filled with a mixture of expensive furniture and junk, further testimony to Collier's madness. Alongside the fancy brocade couch was a rusty old washtub turned upsidedown and supporting a shadeless, broken lamp. On the mahogany sideboard was an array of small junk items: clipless pens, a torn rubber dildo, an open ring box, dozens of other, less easily identifiable objects. Bulging burlap sacks and plastic trash bags littered the plush beige carpet. And on one wall was a crumbling corkboard with a dozen or so keys attached to it with pushpins.

"Does the room interest you, Detective Oxman?" Collier said from the floor. "All of these throwaways were collected in my kingdom by Willie Lorsec." A sound came out of his throat, more a giggle than a laugh. "A lovely joke, that name, don't you agree?"

"Joke?"

"Such a plodder you are; evil without imagination. Willie Lorsec is an anagram of Lewis Collier."

A rivulet of sweat trickled down Oxman's cheek; he wiped it away. "Why did you collect all this junk?"

"Why? As evidence, of course. To augment what the Eye observed, to uncover sin that the Eye could not see. What mortals throw away tells a great deal about them."

Now Oxman understood the method in the man's madness: In the guise of Willie Lorsec, junkman, Collier had prowled West Ninety-eighth Street learning the intimacies of the block's residents from the contents of their trash. He had also established himself as an apparent resident of the neighborhood, made everyone including Oxman think he belonged there. That was how he'd been able to come and go, to escape so readily after each of his homicides, without arousing suspicion. He had manufactured at least part of his own luck.

"Those keys on the wall," Oxman said. "What about them?"

Collier smiled again; he seemed almost to be enjoying himself now, as if he were the one holding the gun. "Keys to

268

various buildings and apartments in my universe. Duplicate keys. Willie Lorsec made friends with several building superintendents, played gin rummy with them, talked baseball with them, gained their confidence. It was a simple matter to appropriate certain keys long enough to have duplicates made, so that when the time came, God could do his work."

"Quit talking about God, damn you," Oxman said. "You're not God."

"Oh, but I am. Haven't I punished several transgressors for their sins, snuffed out their evil lives? Even Benny Hiller I led to a building where he assumed I lived and thus, through the force of my will, ended his life. I can still end *your* life too, Detective Oxman. I can still destroy you."

"You're not going to do any more destroying. It's all over for you, Collier."

"Is it? Oxman, Oxman, Oxman, you're such a fool."

Oxman took a step toward him, then stopped and shook his head. No. It *was* over; he had the psycho, had him in handcuffs, and hurting him physically was as senseless as Collier's own acts of violence. There had been enough craziness these past few days; he wasn't going to go crazy himself.

He let out a long breath that hissed like escaping steam in the quiet room. Collier was watching him with a flat unblinking stare, the faint smile still on his lips. Oxman stepped away at an angle toward a telephone that sat on a spindly three-legged table. He reached out to pick up the receiver—

And in that instant when his eyes flicked away to the phone, Collier levered up in a sudden agile motion and charged him.

The swiftness of the move caught Oxman with his body turned sideways; he tried to twist back, to bring the .38 to bear. But Collier's lowered head slammed into his arm, knocked the gun loose and sent it bouncing away, knocked Oxman into the three-legged table. He went down with

Collier on top of him, splintering the table; felt sharp teeth sink into his left ear.

The pain of the bite forced a whine from Oxman. He caught hold of Collier's head in both hands, wrenched it aside and ripped the teeth loose from his ear. He saw Collier's mouth: It was stained with blood. The man was actually snarling at him, spewing spittle and blood and hot breath. Collier's weight held him pinned for a moment, but Oxman was able to get a handhold on the pullover sweater and heave the writhing body off him.

Oxman struggled with the wreckage of the table, shoved up onto one knee with his hand clapped to his torn ear. Sweat clouded his vision; he ducked his head against his arm to clear his eyes. But because Collier's hands were cuffed behind his back, Oxman didn't pay enough attention to him. When he lifted his head he saw that Collier was twisted on his back, legs in the air; somehow, with the strength and agility of madness, he had managed to get his manacled hands over his buttocks, was sliding his arms around his shoes and up in front of him.

Oxman thought fleetingly of the Smith & Wesson .38 in his pocket, realized he didn't have enough time to get it out, and threw himself at Collier instead. They grappled, rolled. Collier's strength was enormous; he came up on top, pinning Oxman with his weight. Oxman heaved with his forearms, got his head and shoulders off the carpet, almost pulled free.

He didn't see that Collier had grabbed hold of the telephone cord until it was too late, until the cord was being wound around his neck and jerked tight.

Breath clogged in his throat; he felt his lungs constrict. Desperately, he clawed at the cord with one hand, clawed at Collier with the other. The room seemed to tilt, to soar. His left hand lost its grip on Collier's sweater, flailed out and down to the carpet — and touched hard plastic, the telephone receiver.

Oxman's fingers closed around it, lifted it, swung it

against the side of Collier's head. Did it again, and again, making dull cracking sounds against flesh and bone. The room had begun to go dim; tiny pinpoints of light seemed to explode behind his eyelids. His right arm kept moving independently, rising, falling, smashing over and over with the receiver.

The pressure on his throat lessened. And Collier fell away from him, mouth agape, blood streaming down his face. Oxman kicked at him, drove him back into the couch. Then he struggled to his knees, gasping painfully as he tore the telephone cord from around his neck.

Collier lurched to his feet, using the couch arm as a fulcrum. He hesitated for a moment, seemed about to launch himself at Oxman again; but Oxman was up too, swaying, bracing himself. Collier yelled something that sounded like "Evil!" and ran for the balcony door.

Oxman stumbled after him, saw Collier wrench the door open, go through onto the balcony, then push the door closed behind him and lean his weight back against it. Without thinking, acting on reflex, Oxman stopped two paces from the door and drove his foot against the metal frame just above the latch. There was enough force behind the kick to burst the door outward, to shatter part of the glass. And to propel Collier in an off-balance stagger across the balcony.

Collier might have caught his momentum at the railing if the Eye had not been in his way. But his foot struck the metal tripod of the telescope, spinning him half around; his arms slashed the air, wrapped around the heavy telescope and jerked it backwards with him. Eyes wide and luminous with fright, he teetered for an instant against the waist-high railing —

And then he and the Eye flipped over backwards, out into empty air twenty stories above the earth, and were gone.

Oxman ran to the railing, his shoes crunching on broken

271

glass, and looked over. Collier screamed all the way down, his arms still wrapped around the telescope. When the screaming stopped, vertigo seized Oxman and forced him to back away. He took one long look at the city across the river, the city that teemed and stifled and altered and destroyed; then he turned and went back inside the apartment.

People were milling around out in the hall; he could hear their querulous, alarmed voices. But he didn't pay any attention to them. One of his hands was bleeding, studded with slivers of broken glass, and more blood continued to leak from his bitten ear; he didn't pay any attention to those things, either. He picked up the phone, saw that it was still working, and sank wearily onto the couch.

Surrounded by the refuse of other people's lives, by the dark distorted world of Lewis Collier, he called Manders to tell him it was finally finished.

EPILOGUE

LATE OCTOBER

E.L. OXMAN

He stood at the window of Jennifer's apartment, looking down at the traffic and pedestrians on Riverside Drive. The neighborhood had returned to normal. For a while the media had reveled in the aftermath of the mass murders and in the bizarre nature of their perpetrator, making much of the fact that Lewis Collier had believed himself to be God, the fact that he had virtually lived on West Ninety-eighth Street in the guise of Willie Lorsec; they had even implied that the police should have picked up on the clue that Willie Lorsec was an anagram for Lewis Collier, that it had been some sort of subconscious desire by Collier to be caught and stopped — completely ignoring the fact, as Lieutenant Manders had pointed out in print, that no one in the Department had heard of Lewis Collier until the night of his death. But eventually the murders had become news as old and uninteresting as last season's sport's page, and the media had turned to other sensationalism to sate the appetites of their readers and viewers. And the people of West Ninety-eighth had digested their fear, had begun to breathe again and to come back into the world. They had survived; and life went on.

Art Tobin had survived too. He had spent two weeks in the hospital, in considerable pain at first, and another two weeks recuperating at home. Oxman had talked to him just that afternoon; Tobin was scheduled to return to work a week from Monday. Oxman was glad of that. Glad that Artie, his friend Artie, was alive and well. Even glad that Artie was starting to taunt him again with the same old thinly disguised insults.

Oxman himself had survived. Manders had not reported his relationship with Jennifer to Internal Affairs, but there was nothing he'd been able to do about Oxman's conduct on the night Lewis Collier died — the failure to report from the photo lab, the lone-wolf confrontation with Collier that had taken place out of his jurisdiction in another state. Oxman had been suspended from the force without pay. There had been a hearing, he had been severely reprimanded, and he was still on suspension. But his spotless prior record was in his favor, and Manders and some others in the Department were on his side; there seemed to be a pretty good chance he would be back to work soon. Maybe at about the same time Artie came back, so they could be a team again. He hoped it would work out that way; whatever else he was, he was a cop. Being a cop was all he knew. Being a cop was all he was.

Except for Jennifer, of course. Their relationship had also survived, had grown stronger now that Beth had moved in permanently with her mother and completed the mercy killing of their marriage by filing for divorce. He spent some nights here with Jennifer, and she spent other nights with him at his house in Queens — Beth had agreed to let him keep the house, because he had agreed to let her have everything else. And it had been good between them. And it kept getting better. And now he was sure.

Jennifer came up next to him at the window. "What are you thinking, E.L.?"

He turned to smile at her. "I was thinking about you."

"Good thoughts?"

"Very good. Jennifer. . . would you consider marrying me when the divorce is final?"

She cocked her head at him; her eyes were serious. "Is that a proposal?"

"Yes. I've been thinking about asking you for a week now. This seems like as good a time as any."

"I don't know," she said. "Marriage. . . I don't know. I'll have to think about it."

But her eyes said differently; he thought he saw the answer in her eyes. He put his arm around her. "All right," he said. "You think about it. We've got plenty of time."

She nodded.

"Plenty of time," he said again. Because with all that had happened to them, they had been victims only for a little while, only in a small way. In this place, in this time, it wasn't so easy not to be a victim in some way; what mattered was whether or not you survived. Maybe they could keep on surviving. Maybe the future was going to be good to them both. It was something to hope for. It was something to believe in.

Right now, it was enough.